S0-CLE-095

The Moral Tales

The Moral Tales

by Leopoldo Alas
Translated and Edited by
Kenneth A. Stackhouse

SCCCC - LIBRARY
4601 Mid Rivers Mall Drive
St. Peters, MO 63376

WITHDRAWN

ST. CHARLES COUNTY
COMMUNITY COLLEGE LIBRARY

George Mason University Press
Fairfax, Virginia

Copyright © 1988 by
George Mason University Press

4400 University Drive
Fairfax, VA 22030

All rights reserved

Printed in the United States of America

British Cataloging in Publication Information Available

Distributed by arrangement with
University Publishing Associates, Inc.

4720 Boston Way
Lanham, MD 20706

3 Henrietta Street
London WC2E 8LU England

Library of Congress Cataloging-in-Publication Data

Alas, Leopoldo, 1852–1901.
[Cuentos morales. English]
The moral tales / by Leopoldo Alas ; translated and edited by Kenneth A. Stackhouse.
p. cm.
Translation of: Cuentos morales. Bibliography: p.
I. Stackhouse, Kenneth A., 1944–   . II. Title.
PQ6503.A4C8413   1988   863'.5—dc 19   87–3555 CIP
ISBN 0–913969–12–5 (alk. paper)

All George Mason University Press books are produced on acid-free
paper which exceeds the minimum standards set by the National
Historical Publications and Records Commission.

for Marcia, Amy, and Daniel

Contents

Acknowledgments

I want to thank the members of the Department of Foreign Languages at Virginia Commonwealth University, in particular William Beck, Margaret Peischl, Alice Todd, Antonio Masullo, and Manuel Béjar, as well as the staff of various libraries, Yolanda Alfaro Maloney, Zaida R. Juan, together with Pamela Jordan for their suggestions, comments, and help in clarifying various passages of Leopoldo Alas's stories. Howard LaBrenz's care in typing the text has been an enormous contribution to the work and I am truly grateful. I want to thank my wife Marcia whose encouragement throughout has been and continues to be unwaivering. Also, I want especially to thank the eminent *clarinistas,* Noel Valis, for her interest and Fernando Ibarra for his inspiration.

Translator's Introduction

Between 1893 and 1896, Leopoldo Alas, professor of Roman law at the University of Oviedo in northern Spain, sent fourteen stories to three newspapers in Madrid: the *Madrid Cómico*, *Los Lunes del Imparcial*, and the *Ilustración Española y Americana*. These stories were distributed throughout the country and to subscribers in Latin America awaiting the next creation of the writer whom they knew as "Clarín" or the Clarion. For more than a decade, Leopoldo Alas's clear narrative voice had been gaining wide public attention with approximately eighty stories. To judge from their success, Clarín had sounded the spirit of his country as Spain bade farewell to one century on the threshold of another. In 1896, Leopoldo Alas selected several stories from among his earlier works and published them with fourteen of his latest stories as the *Moral Tales*. The author's "Introduction" suggests the criterion for his selection. These narratives represent his best efforts to portray a concept of morality as the proof of free will.

Leopoldo Alas, as a professor of law, a critic of contemporary literature, short story writer and novelist, was profoundly involved in the philosophical debates at the end of the nineteenth century, particularly on determinism, which had manifested itself in literature as naturalism. The novels of Emile Zola (1840–1902) and their Spanish counterparts in the works of Emilia Pardo Bazán (1852–1921) demonstrated the weight of time, environment, and history in determining human conduct. Following the innovations presented by the current literary trend of the period, Alas won recognition in 1884–1885 for his masterpiece, the novel *La Regenta*, which many Spaniards read as a silent protest against the stagnation of institutions and the spirit of frivolity resulting from a lack of vitality among the middle and the upper classes. This *aboulia* became the theme of two generations of novelists after Leopoldo Alas. In *La Regenta*, these social conditions contribute to the fall of the protagonist, Ana de Ozores, from the boredom of an unfulfilling marriage into adultery.

After Alas's careful exploration of the workings of naturalism in his major novel, he felt challenged to explore further the persistent conviction that characterized the stories he had been writing simultaneously with his next novel, *Su único hijo* (1890). This conviction was an irrational yet realistic optimism in which insignificant people unexpectedly triumph in the world of Vetusta, the city portrayed in

La Regenta in which traditional institutions appear less and less adequate for the challenges of the future.

In 1887, in his collection of critical articles entitled *Nueva campaña*, Alas writes about naturalism that "this doctrine, in part new and in part ancient, has given rise in Spain to a renaissance of literary foolishness over which we can never lament enough."

Alas returned to concentrate on short prose fiction, the novella and short story, because by 1890, the popularity in Spain of the fully developed novel had begun to fade, except among a leisure class of readers who, although influential, were relatively inactive. By contrast, people whose work could affect the direction of the institutions Alas described, read and discussed his short stories in the cafes, in their homes, on trains and trolleys, and often in their offices. In the 1880s and 1890s, Alas knew that the best way to convey his message of institutional atrophy and his portraits of individual struggles to readers in a position to effect necessary changes was through stories published in newspapers and magazines.

In contrast to the simplistic positivistic theses of writers such as Ernst Haeckel who, in his popular treatise *The Riddle of the Universe* (1899), stated that every action has a purely physical and material cause, and to the metaphysical pessimism of Schopenhauer who, in his tract *The World as Will and Idea* (1818), had proposed that the purpose of civilization is to dominate and extirpate evil, identified as the force of will, Clarín's observation of the people of Asturias in these stories suggests another thesis: the Cartesian notion that a free agent is one who, when all things necessary to produce an action are present, can nevertheless dissent, that there are uncaused assents, dissents and choices. Of the assents and choices opposing philosophical determinism, Clarín specifies literature itself. In his "Introduction" to the *Moral Tales*, he describes writing as a gratuitous yet necessary endeavor, gratuitous in its origin and in the creative impulse, and necessary for the collective development of the moral sensibility it reflects and fosters. His story "Lucius Varius" explores the freedom of creative impulse.

The perspective from which Alas could perceive the problems besetting his countrymen had developed during his years of study in Madrid with Giner de los Ríos (1839–1915). In the Spanish capital, he acquired the ideas of the German post–Kantian philosopher Friedrich Kraus (1781–1832) as they were disseminated in the works on ethics and pedagogy written by Sanz del Río (1814–1867). In 1878, Alas dedicated his published doctoral dissertation "El derecho y la moralidad" to Giner de los Ríos who, two years earlier, had established the first nonsectarian, independent college in Spain, the Instituto Libre de Enseñanza. The college produced the scholars, writers, and artists who brought Spain once again to the fore of European culture during the first three decades of the twentieth century.

Clarín did not see the full flowering of this new era because he died in 1901 at the age of forty-nine. But through his *paliques*, as he called his criticism of current literature, and through his fiction, he indicated the direction others would follow. Unlike most of the students of Giner de los Ríos, who abandoned the ideas of Kraus after leaving the university because of the occasional divergence of his concept of panentheism from orthodox thought, Clarín remained true to his original opinions and was unfailing in his denunciation of any departures from his conviction of the importance in Spain of the role of the serious writer. His *paliques*, "hygienic, investigative criticism," he called them, were very popular and unfailing in their ridicule of mediocrity. They won him many enemies, a few admirers, but universal respect.

The stories Alas wrote during the last three decades of the century indicated the direction prose fiction would take after Emilia Pardo Bazán (1853–1938), Blasco Ibáñez (1867–1928), and Palacio Valdés (1853–1938) had exhausted both the narrative resources of the portrait of regional customs and folklore known as *costumbrismo* and the messages of naturalism. The *Moral Tales* in particular point directly to the novel of ideas which would flourish in the work of Miguel de Unamuno (1864–1936) and Pérez de Ayala (1880–1962), both of whom acknowledged their debt to the professor from Oviedo. The naturalists' painstaking attention to the minutiae of descriptive detail, family history, and to the ambience of a particular historical moment as determining factors for character and action yield to an inquiry into the personality as understood by psychological analysis.

Clarín did not look back to a glorious past as Menéndez y Pelayo (1856–1912) did in his monumental works of scholarship on Medieval and Golden Age Spanish literature, nor ahead to a Utopian ideal which the Valencian novelist Blasco Ibáñez sought to create in his social experiments in Argentina, nor did Alas limit himself to a jovial recreation of contemporary society as his fellow Asturian and friend Armando Palacio Valdés (1853–1938) was doing. Rather, Clarín probed the depths of the individual psyche, much in the manner of a contemporary whose stories he read in serial publication in *La Revue des Deux Mondes*, Paul de Bourget (1852–1935).

The characters Clarín portrays in his stories at first appear as mediocre, insignificant people suffering from a variety of obsessions, misapprehensions, and undefinable feelings of loss. With few exceptions, they cannot perceive a future and they feel abandoned, having nothing to carry them into the rapidly approaching new era. Clarín seeks to prove through these portraits of ordinary people that despite the assault on older traditional values by newer schools of thought, positivism, Darwinism, and philosophical skepticism, these individuals continue through the exercise of the will which may manifest itself unexpectedly in resignation, renunciation, or in a spiritual triumph over adversity. His characters belong to the laboring classes, the economically insecure middle class, or a nobility unwilling or unable to fulfill its leadership role.

He portrays the poor, who throughout the century were repeatedly given hope and then disappointed by radical statements of imminent reform, *pronunciamentos*, issued by ambitious and occasionally enlightened military leaders. As soon as the desperate would translate these programs into popular uprisings, however, they were violently suppressed by opposing factions of the same military who quickly declared in favor of Spain's ancient medieval tradition of theocratic monarchy when the power of constitutionalism threatened to override their base of power. The large urban middle classes feared socialism and rallied to the cause of tradition whenever a more liberal general such as Riego in 1820 gained an advantage over the monarchy. In 1820, Spanish troops waiting in Cadiz to embark for the Americas to quell the Wars of Independence, revolted against Fernando VII, and under the leadership of General Rafael de Riego, declared for the Constitution of 1812. Joined by troops in the Galician port of La Coruña and at Aranjuez, the king was forced to surrender power to a provisional junta in the Cortes. The liberals triumphed for two years, greatly aiding the independence movement in South America, until the Holy Alliance guided by the Austrian prime minister, Metternich, decided in Vienna to send French troops under the command of the Duke d'Angoûleme to restore the absolute authority of the Spanish king.

Although Clarín was never as violently anticlerical as many of his fellow republican thinkers, he saw the role of the Church in Spanish politics as one of giving support to the middle classes' resistance to change. Clarín never seems to have doubted the sanctity of the Church's teachings but he presents an institution weakened by the challenges of the modern world. His story "Cold and the Pope" suggests that the faith of the Spanish people was sustained over the centuries more by popular tradition than doctrine and, therefore, was strongest among the uneducated. The political and economic power that the Church had acquired in Spain, though still considerable, had been diminished by the liberal revolutions of 1820 and 1868. Clarín describes an influential, educated middle class for whom the prestige of two thousand years of history had little more than sentimental appeal. "Round Trip" portrays the destructive effects of modern scientific and philosophical skepticism upon the spirit of dedication and commitment that are essential for an active faith, a destructiveness which leaves cold, unenthusiastic beliefs and opinion in its stead.

Yet the Church in Clarín's stories remains the only recourse for the poor, who find no protection in the courts, no promise in constitutionalism, socialism or commerce and no hope in learning or old friendships. "Breaker's Conversion" reveals this near total abandonment of the destitute. In "Bad Habits," those charitable institutions established to care for the poor exact a price of personal freedom and Clarín, like his contemporary Pérez Galdós (1843–1929) in his novel *Fortunata y Jacinta* (1886–87), suggests that spontaneous and unthinking acts of charity, as haphazard and counterproductive as they may be, are still the most humane way to help the poor.

The industriousness and democratic fairness of the nobility, which Clarín assumes existed during the first half of the century when Spain arose as a nation to repudiate Napoleon's invasion in 1808, give way to attitudes of aristocratic superiority. He demonstrates in his story "Torso" that this attitude in the second half of the century led to the nobility's renunciation of its responsibility to improve the economic well–being of the country, encouraging growth and productivity. In "The Trap," effective power in the provinces falls to the regional political bosses, the *caciques*, who, rather than the courts and the nobility, become the only reliable sources of justice and economic security. But this political base excluded all those who did not share their *caciques'* particular convictions. Pérez Galdós two decades earlier in *Doña Perfecta* (1876), and Emilia Pardo Bazán one decade earlier in *Los Pazos de Ulloa* (1886) attested to the duration of the same rural conditions. *Doña Perfecta* takes place in Villaviciosa in Asturias, while Pardo Bazán's novel occurs in neighboring Galicia. The northern provinces were ultraconservative and as ready to favor the reactionary Carlist faction, which sought to depose Queen Isabel II and place her uncle on the throne, as the moderate Liberal Unionists who, during the regency of Maria Christina worked to bring Spain greater prosperity through desamortization and gradual industrialization. The *caciques* formed a network of provincial political power connected with Madrid and were ready to react should the threat of change appear imminent.

An overriding concern for the poor characterizes all of Clarín's stories. This preoccupation was not limited to literary portraiture, however, because in 1891 he persuaded the University of Oviedo to establish an extension to bring learning to the working classes of the city. He established the Atheneum in Oviedo, a cultural forum which fostered study through competition and maintained a correspondence with the Athenea of Madrid, Paris, and London, and lasted until the first years of the Spanish Civil War, 1936.

The Church, the aristocracy, and the provincial political bosses were not the only institutions whose effectiveness in improving life Clarín questioned at the end of the century. Spain's military traditions also appear weakened, by parliamentarianism in "León Benavides" and by relying upon paid mercenaries in "The Substitute." The effect, defeat overseas, appears indirectly but clearly in the story "The Grand Prize in Melilla." The lack of leadership among the nobility and a weakened presence abroad presage the disaster of

1898, the Spanish–American War in which Spain lost the last out-posts of her empire, Puerto Rico, Cuba, Guam, and the Philippine Islands. Ironically, instead of weakening the prestige of the military and the government, this defeat, since it brought capital back to Spain and increased the prosperity of the middle classes, fostered the general spirit of frivolity. The Spain of musical comedy, *zarzuela*, was flourishing. Moreover, prestige was restored by the successes of Span-ish troops in putting down the uprisings of Rif tribesmen in Spain's African outposts of Melilla and Ceuta.

Since Clarín had studied in Madrid with Giner de los Ríos and had dedicated his life to teaching, Spanish education was of particu-lar interest to him. In his stories, only students strong enough to sur-vive the Spanish schools at the turn of the century succeed after-wards. The scholarly protagonist called "Número Uno" discovers that his mastery of the principles of noble emulation and successful aca-demic competition for token rewards do not help him in life.

Clarín does not spare the literary establishment of his generation either. Besides his *paliques*, which examine the works of actual writ-ers, his stories present a clear picture of the world of letters. He sees writers plagued by the vagaries of chance and the whims of taste which make it difficult for promising ones to fulfill their mission. "Lucius Varius" presents in the context of classical literature the problem of notable writers doomed to oblivion by carelessness and neglect because of the uncertain fate of manuscripts and books. The story "Queen Margaret" reveals the adverse effect of allowing the financial success of plays and opera, rather than public taste, to de-termine literary or artistic merit. "Windows" uncovers the viciously destructive competitiveness of writers, the vindictiveness of ineffec-tual literary critics, and the bitterness of victims of these abuses who, refusing to grow, gradually withdraw into bitter isolation.

As in *La Regenta*, marriage and the family appear threatened in "The Imperfect Wife" by one married woman's feelings of inferiority and inadequacy, her fear of repeated pregnancies, and her gradual disillusionment with her husband's repeated infidelities. The shallow-ness and vanity of a beautiful unmarried woman in "Snob" increase the sense of frustration that pervades Clarín's stories. "The Engrav-ing" and "Número Uno" reveal the nagging worry of parents in the nineteenth century over the health of their children and their fear that their own early demise could leave their offspring abandoned before they are grown.

Clarín's stories present a dismal picture of rural Spain prior to the Spanish–American War. Even the spirit of generosity and family af-fection which bring the emigrant Pepe Francisca in "Cornbread" back to his farm from Cuba are destroyed by the poverty of his sister and her family.

Clarín does not omit any sector of Spanish society as he observed it in his native Asturias. He does not limit his portraits to an urban society, a decadent rural aristocracy, or to the rough laboring classes as Pérez Galdós, Emilia Pardo Bazán or Blasco Ibáñez do in their novels. Rather, he integrates all these elements of nineteenth–century Spain into his collection, much as do Cervantes in his portrayal of seventeenth–century Spain in the *Exemplary Novels* (1613) or Boccaccio of Renaissance Italy in the *Decameron* (1348).

Clarín holds together the complexity, diversity and depth of his stories by a common thread: his ethical religious sense which had begun to develop while studying in Madrid with Giner de los Ríos, a moral sensibility made deeper by his reading in French literature and expressed frequently with uncommon grace and occasionally with profound humor. The stories would constitute a novel if they had the unity of a main character developed over time. But Clarín prefers not to describe the workings of one personality, such as Ana de Ozores in *La Regenta*. He explores instead the psychological intricacy of characters who would at best be secondary in a major novel, common people with ordinary problems during a century that seemed to waltz into the present, taking two steps back for each step forward. All his characters in the *Moral Tales* are minor characters whose triumphs ennoble without elevating them. The protagonist in "The Priest of Vericueto" turns his weakness for gambling into an unnecessary moral victory; the great egotist Anchoriz in "The Knight of the Round Table" through his foolish constancy gives meaning to many inconsequential lives. In "Queen Margaret," Marcela Vidal's strength in abandoning the public she fears so terribly guarantees her a life, if not of operatic fame, of lasting contentment.

The decadence of post–naturalism appears in these stories in the form of frustrated sexuality, theosophy, Satanism, and penetrating analysis of the anxieties of ordinary people who feel their century is dying and who lack a reassuring vision of the century about to begin. Clarín's compassion, however, and his rare quality of tenderness allow the reader to perceive the strength of the weak. While he occasionally tinges his stories with self–deprecating irony, Clarín's usual narrative perspective is sympathetic without becoming maudlin. Probably no short story writer in Spanish has equaled Clarín in this particular accomplishment. Certainly few writers at the turn of the century touched as many readers as he, not only awakening future authors to the responsibility of their vocation, but also opening the eyes of busy newspaper readers who could make a difference to the problems besetting the poor. At the very least, he indulged his readers' taste for commiseration and sentimentality.

Since at least half of these stories were written during the same three–year period, they do not exhibit a broad variety of narrative voices. Clarín ranges from delicate irony, gentle humor and poetic description to incisive commentary on the failure of various institutions to provide the common people of Spain with the means to face the future bravely. Although the stories appeared in 1896, and despite a fatalism tempered with humor and compassion, they are moving narratives which challenge writers not only with their definition of the responsibility of Spain's literary institutions but with the creation of memorable characters.

The precision of Leopoldo Alas's style as he explores the delicate nuances of emotion and sentiment make the translation of his stories an extremely engaging enterprise. His sentence structure, delicate use of metaphor and image and his quiet narrative voice require patient attention to detail on the part of the translator. The dark stillness of the northern cathedral city of Oviedo and of the lush rain-soaked hills of Asturias pervades them.

Bibliography

Abellán, Manuel S. "Clarín: la inversión de paradigmas ideológicos como recurso literario: a propósito de 'La conversión de Chiripá'." *Diálogos Hispánicos de Amsterdam* 4 (1984): 97–108.

Balseiro, Jose Agustín. *Novelistas españoles modernos*. New York: Macmillan, 1948.

Baquero Goyanes, Mariano. "Clarín, creador del cuento español." *Cuadernos de Literatura* January, June (1949): 145–158.

Blanquat, Josette. "Clarín et Baudelaire." *Revue de Littérature Comparée* XXIII (1959): 5–25.

_____. "La sensibilité réligieuse de Clarín. Reflêts de Goethe et de Leopardi." *Revue de Littérature Comparée* XXV (1961): 177–196.

Bull, William E. "The Liberalism of Leopoldo Alas." *Hispanic Review* X (1942): 329–339.

_____. "Clarín and his Critics." *Modern Language Forum* XXXV (1950): 103–111.

Cabezas, José A. *'Clarín', el provinciano universal*. Madrid: Espasa-Calpe, 1936.

Clocchiatti, Emilio. "Miguel de Unamuno y sus cartas a Clarín." *Modern Language Journal* XXXIV (1950): 646–649.

Conde Gargollo, Enrique. "'Clarín' universitario." *Insula* XV clxvii (1962): 12, 16.

Davis, Gifford. "The Literary Relations of Clarín and Emilia Pardo Bazan." *Hispanic Review* 39 (1971): 378–394.

Eoff, Sherman. *The Modern Spanish Novel. Comparative Essays*. New York: New York University Press, 1961.

Fishtine, Edith. "Clarín in his Early Writings." *Romantic Review* XXXIX (1938): 325–342.

García Domínguez, Elias. "Los cuentos rurales de Clarín." *Archivum*, XIX (1969): 221–242.

García Sarrí, Francisco. *'Clarín' o la herejía amorosa.* Madrid: Gredos, 1975.

Gómez Santos, Mariano. *Leopoldo Alas 'Clarín.' Ensayo biográfico.* Oviedo: Instituto de Estudios Asturianos, 1952.

Griswold, Susan C. "Rhetorical Strategies and Didacticism in Clarín's Short Fiction." *Kentucky Romance Quarterly* 29 IV (1982): 423–433.

Gullón, Ricardo. "Aspectos de Clarín." *Archivum* II (1952): 161–188.

——————. "Las novelas cortas de 'Clarín'." *Insula* 76 (1952): 3.

Ibarra, Fernando. "Clarín y la liberación de la mujer." *Hispanófila* 51 (1974): 27–33.

——————. "Clarín y el teatro político." *Romance Notes* 13 (1971): 266–71.

Kronik, John W. "The Function of Names in the Stories of Clarín." *Modern Language Notes* LXXX (1961): 260–65.

——————. "Censo de personajes en los Cuentos de Clarín." *Archivum* XI (1961): 323–406.

Lissourges, Yvan, ed. *Clarín político, I: Leopoldo Alas (Clarín) periodista, frente a la problemática política y social de la España de su tiempo (1875–1901).* Toulouse: France Iberie Recherche, 1980.

——————. "España ante la guerra colonial de 1805–1898: Leopoldo Alas (Clarín) periodista y el problema cubano." *Les Etapes d'une libération: Hommage a Juan Marinello et Noel Salomon.* Ed. Robert Jammes. Toulouse: n.p., 1979.

McBride, Charles. "Afinidades espirituales y estilísticos entre Unamuno y Clarín." *Cuadernos de la Cátedra de Unamuno* 19 (1969): 5–15.

Martínez Cachero, Jose M. ed. *Leopoldo Alas "Clarín".* Madrid: Taurus, 1978.

Meregalli, Franco. *'Clarín' y Unamuno.* Milán: La Goliárdica, 1956.

Milazzo, Elena. "Modernità ed Esemplarità de Clarín." *Cenobio* IV (1956): 461–466.

Pérez Gutiérrez, Francisco. *Leopoldo Alas "Clarín", El Problema religioso en la Generación de 1868.* Madrid: Taurus, 1975.

Proano, Franklin. "Religious and Secular Aspects of Leopoldo Alas, Clarín." *University of Dayton Review* 13 iii (1979): 97–108.

Reiss, Katherine. "Valoración artística de las narraciones breves de Leopoldo Alas." *Archivum* V (1955): 257–303.

Ríos, Laura de los. *Los cuentos de Clarín*. Madrid: Revista de Occidente, 1965.

Rodríguez Díez, Bonifacio. "Un modelo de análisis crítico para los cuentos de Clarín." *Astride the Two Cultures: Arthur Koestler at 70*, ed. Harold Harris. New York: Random House, 1976.

Thompson, Clifford R., Jr. "Cervantine Motifs in the Short Stories of Leopoldo Alas." *Revista de Estudios Hispanicos* X (1976): 392–403.

——————. "Poetic Response in the Short Stories of Leopoldo Alas." *Romance Notes* 13 (1971): 272–75.

Valis, Noel Maureen. "The Landscape of the Soul in Clarín and Baudelaire." *Revue de Littérature Comparée* 54 (1980): 97–108.

——————. "Leopoldo Alas y los Goncourt: El alma neurótico." *Hispanic Journal* I (1979): 27–45.

Valis, Noel Maureen; Mori, Francisco A., tr. "La 'Pipá' de Clarín y 'El encendio' de Ana María Matute: una infancia traicionada." *Cuadernos del Norte* 2(7) (1981): 72–77.

Varela Jacome, Benito, ed. *Leopoldo Alas "Clarín"*. Madrid: Elaf, 1980.

Villavicencio, Laura N. "Reiteración y extremismo en el estilo creativo de Clarín." *Hispania* 55 (1972): 45–54.

The Moral Tales

The Priest of Vericueto

I

The Priest of Vericueto,
Since he never sells anything cheaply,
Must have a hidden treasure
Of dusty old doubloons.

So began the little satirical poem, parodying the work of Ramon de Campoamor, written by my friend Higadillos, a compatriot of Campoamor's, a student of medicine, and a contributor to three or four newspapers of little reputation and no particular point of view. Higadillos was, of course, a good–for–nothing who at twenty years old believed himself a wise philosopher of the positivistic school because he had read Spencer in translation, was reading *Gil Blas*, some Parisian newspaper or other, and the *Revue des Revues*.

Moreover, he had lived in Paris for a while and these things, together with refusing to pay his landlady "until the end of time," made him consider himself a proven intellectual, recovering, as he would say, from all kinds of mystic and evangelical neuroses which he now laughed at with delight. It seemed to him that after all the diabolical doctrines discussed in his search for new ideals, after so many sacrilegious masses and other such barbarisms, the newest, most original and opportune style was to return to Voltaire, to pornographic and skeptical realism, to the *Kulturkampf* as he called it. War against the Church! This was the most singular novelty that had occurred to him.

"I am a primitive!" he would shout, giving his adjective a sarcastic meaning to refer to the very antithesis of what painters meant by calling the Italian mystical art of the Christian Middle Ages primitive. He was a primitive because he supposed that simplicity, sincerity and naturalness exist in sensuality, in impiety and in the frivolous philosophies of the eighteenth century.

"Gentlemen," Higadillos exclaimed in the cafe, "it is a neurotic obsession to search continually for metaphysical, ethical, and aesthetic novelties; this constant variation presupposes, in addition to an unhealthy inhibition of those mental faculties which those in power ought by right to exercise, a lack of taste and a lack of serious, solid, personal judgment. Truth is not in novelty nor in change; truth exists

in something historical, in one of those moments that human thought
has already experienced: the essential thing, the very grace of talent,
lies in verifying which of those moments, without being particularly in
style at present, is the correct one. Well then, I myself have verified
it: the fixed point is Lucretius in one sense, Rousseau in another,
Voltaire in another, Spencer in another, Zola in another, and in another, the newspaper *El Motín*. Materialism, or rather sensuality, determinism, hedonism, naturalism, ethical skepticism, these are the
quadrants of thought. The task is to go deeper at this point and not
go looking for new worlds to explore. The world has already been
discovered; now let us find the most productive mines."

One afternoon, while talking to me about his philosophies,
Higadillos asked "Since you are from that part of the country, you
must know the priest of Vericueto. What a wonderful man! He is a
living document, as people these days might say. I am going to write a
poem about him, although it might turn out completely different from
the poem about the priest from Pilar de la Horadada. I already have
three or four sections in which I imitate the unchanging verses of
Ramón de Campoamor. Listen to the beginning...." And he began to
read the poem I quoted at the head of this chapter.

Needless to say, I stopped listening to him after the fifth or sixth
verse; but what he told me afterwards in his own words about his
priest of Vericueto attracted my attention considerably, and I determined that, whenever I returned to my part of the country, I would
make the acquaintance of this character of whom that rascal of superficial, school–boy, distasteful impiety was making such fun.

II

I have my summer house on the sea where the mountains are not
very high and look like soft, gentle swells that dissolve on the beach
in graceful and more and more delicate waves until they become ribbons of lace between the sun and the sand and then disappear in a
whisper. The mountains, like groundswells of earth moving to meet
the ocean's waves, are, from the high seas of the port, giants who
raise their gray heads like curly foam through the leaden clouds; but
as they approach the beach they grow smaller and smaller until they
become hills, covered in green to their very tops, where they then
become small bluffs that are confused with the dunes in which the
mountains of the ocean also disappear.

From a hill where I have my garden, in the midst of which I have
built a small summer house, I am accustomed to gaze at the distant
horizon and at the peaks and crests of the sierras, half lost in the
mist, which form the backbone of the Pyrenees along this section of
the Cantabrian coast. When the sky is very clear at all points of the
compass, from my garden I can see the highest peaks, which look
like clusters of clouds gilded occasionally by a sun for me now absent.

One afternoon during the summer, while entertaining myself with these vaguely romantic and somewhat poetic contemplations, an image came to my mind all of a sudden, fabricated in my own way, of that country priest whom Higadillos had described to me in Madrid as a cassocked and tonsured Harpagon. In that part of the horizon, in one of those folds of white rock that stands out from among the beech, pine, oak, and chestnut trees, there in his parish lived the priest I wanted to meet. In one of the reaches of the Suaveces range sat the place called Vericueto, which gave its name to the parish belonging to my friend, the priest.

To remember him suddenly and to revive my wish to visit him was a single impulse. And since Higadillos lived nearby and had invited me several times with open hospitality, and since he really was obliged to me for the many times I had generously and without hesitation saved him from numerous, though small, financial embarrassments, I decided without a second thought to make the trip. On the following day, the train took me near the village in the sierras. From a certain train station a poor horse carried me along the worst part of the road that rose through dangerous canyons among the first hills of the Suaveces range until it dropped my weary bones in the parish of Antuna where my friend Higadillos, as happy and expansive as he was shallow and empty-headed, greeted me with open arms.

When I reminded him of his promise to take me to visit the priest and declared to him that this was the primary motive for my trip, he was somewhat disturbed, as though I had contradicted him; but he quickly regained his composure and at least pretended to congratulate me for my good memory and excellent idea.

Early in the morning of the following day, we set off on foot on our uphill journey. Vericueto can be visualized as a bell tower on the top of a pointed mountain which is rather like a steeple.

III

Vericueto consists of a flock of brown huts dispersed along with a few white shanties on the far side of the Suaveces range; it seems that these huts are assaulting the mountain from which an immense boulder threatens to fall, flattening everything in its path. At the front of the attack, that is, at the highest elevation of the village, is a group of the poorest, oldest and most humble houses surrounding the parochial church, a poor, ugly, square chapel. This church does well to hide almost completely behind the large oaks surrounding it, oaks with noisy, trembling leaves which rustle in almost no wind whatsoever. If the church were whitewashed, as the bishop had ordered repeatedly, the snow of its walls would shine between the green branches and make a beautiful contrast. But there is no such contrast because the priest abhors whitewashed sepulchres—and churches—and he does not want to allow drunken brick masons—tricksters, blasphemers and gamblers all of them, besides probably being free-thinkers like Voltaire without knowing that they are, of course—to make a profit. Moreover, labor costs a fortune, and what would people say if the priest spent money to beautify the building while not spending a cent on that other thing, the so-called peak affair?

And what is the peak affair? We shall see momentarily.

Higher than the church, higher than all the houses in the village is the priest's house, an example of humility and a protest against hypocrisy. It is not whitewashed, either, without or within. And it is falling down piece by piece and has ivy climbing up the walls, threatening to consume and bury it.

If someone were to say to that priest—and it has been a long time since anyone has dared mention his budget to him—"Why don't you put a new roof on the rectory," he answers, "Our Lord was born in a manger, in a doorway or perhaps in a cave, but surely without a roof over his head."

"But, Father, the walls are crumbling to dust."

"*Quia pulvis es....* We and the rectory walls are clay, so naturally when there is a drought we turn to dust. Besides, should one spend money on roof tiles and paint to make the rectory look like a gingerbread house and not spend a penny on the peak project to avoid the danger that threatens us all?"

Finally, the priest would conclude: "*Fiat jus et ruat coelum.* Obey the law and let the sky fall, and the rectory with it. And the law says do not let your left hand spend what your right hand earns."

But again, this kind of conversation was no longer heard. It had been years since anyone remembered to bother the priest of Vericueto about spending money, something that he would never do.

The only time the bishop even came near Vericueto, he refused to go up to the church because of the altitude and because of the threat of the peak which the priest had exaggerated to him purposely so that he would not come. The bishop was more than displeased about the peak, but it made him think: "I should hope that a bishop would not arrive the very moment the tragedy happens Vericueto.

But it is now time for us to go without fear to confront this peak affair, since we do not yet know exactly what it is.

Breathless, certainly deserving a young Veronica to wipe our sweaty brows, carrying our jackets draped over our shoulders, Higadillos and I arrived at the atrium of the ugly church. We peeked in through some chinks in the main door which let us see inside a temple that was adorned with cobwebs and cracked plaster rather than with images and paintings. But we felt a very cold draft there and the fear of catching cold made us continue our march until we reached the front steps of the rectory itself. Without stopping to greet the chickens and the growling dog who received us, we entered what should have been a main door but which opened into a kitchen.

Either there was no chimney or it was in disrepair; the smoke filled the room and after many turns escaped through the roof as best it could.

The house had a ground floor and an upstairs. The second story over the kitchen had not been used for many years. Here and there one could see from the kitchen into the attic itself and spy the roof beams where the smoke freely escaped. There was not a soul in the kitchen: only a sow, growling like a dog, came out to meet us; in fact, there were two pigs from the herd of Epicurus as the priest would have said, future Iphigenaeas to be sacrificed to the devil, not Voltairians, but rather Tevergas, the long–eared variety, which looked as though they were about to become the excellent hams which have made the reputation of that town.

On seeing that we were not about to retreat, the pigs withdrew and ran into an interior room, unwittingly serving as guides announcing our arrival.

"Who's there?" shouted a lazy but harsh voice from within.

"Friends!" answered Higadillos, disguising his voice.

"Ramona! Isn't Ramona there? What's happening? Who is it?"

"We are men of the future!" my friend sang out to the melody of the *Marseillaise*.

"Oh, come in! Come in, Grand Master of the Orient!"

Stepping cautiously, with a certain suspicion or respect, I do not know which, we entered a narrow room across a floor made of no one could say what since it was layered with years of dirt, the alluvia of laziness kneaded with dust, the remains of garbage and filth. There was no one in the living room except the two animals, looking ready to present a defense worthy of the most disobedient wild boar.

Higadillos and the author were afraid.

Then a voice from a bedroom in the back roared: "Hey! Hey! Get out of here! Ramona! Put the pigs out in the yard!"

The fabled Ramona did not appear to chase the pigs away, but hearing their master's voice, perhaps because they both had the same name, "Hey," they fled on their own through the door which we very willingly left open for them. The room apparently was dining room, library, and wine cellar. On one side, there was a great drop–leaf chestnut table; near it were pinewood shelves on which sat plates and some rudimentary kitchen utensils. In the center was a dirty, old, rough–hewn, three–sectioned stand on which several dozen books and dusty bottles lay. *The Golden Legend* was watched over by two small bottles of cider; a volume of Perrone appeared to be held prisoner by two corpulent red and gold swan–necked bottles of cognac.

"May we come in, Knight of the Levites?"

"I have already given permission to the Grand Master of the Oriental Star."

"But I am not alone."

"Let all the torch bearers of militant Freemasonry approach."

Higadillos lifted a green percale curtain and I, without crossing the threshold of the bedroom which was illuminated by a large window facing east, saw the bust of a worthy cleric sitting upright on a wide, straight, walnut bed, partially covered by a clean, white embroidered quilt. He was wearing a gentleman's shirt of fine white cloth without a collar, which looked as if it had split to allow the strong, ruddy, muscular neck to burst through, a worthy pedestal for a head which reminded me immediately of one of those engravings Gustav Doré made to illustrate Balzac's *Droll Tales*.

The general impression that face evoked was the image of the trunk of an ancient oak tree ... with folds. The face was a great mass of flesh furrowed by expressive wrinkles with two slits through which flowed pure maliciousness from its source of two small, sharp and rascally sparkling eyes which danced to the sounds of his own words. The face of the priest was not what one would expect on a miser; it was a complicated mystery in which only malice and shrewdness were apparent, revealing underneath an indefinite but certain trace of kindness and latent sense of honor ingrained in his spirit. He reminded me of one of those great satires which in the Middle Ages could wound the clergy without harming the church.

IV

Don Tomás Celorio, whom all the priests of the archdiocese called Vericueto, the name of his parish, had been the priest there for twenty years, the last two of which had not seen him leave his bed.

Little by little the spells had closed in on him and, no longer able to defend himself, he had to surrender to the weight of his enormous body and to the persuasion of the canons who demanded another priest for the parish. He therefore accepted unwillingly an assistant whom he considered an undercover enemy of his interests and with whom he refused to share any of the money he felt was by right his alone. The intruder, who actually carried out all the work in the church, had to care for all Celorio's needs and be satisfied with the miserable salary of an underling.

Celorio gave his orders and ruled from his bed like a military commander who had been wounded in the field, yet continued conducting the battle. Celorio continued to be the priest; he would not hear of a trusteeship; he wanted to have an assistant like any other priest and he would not allow even the bishop to treat him as if he were useless. "I am now an unmovable priest," he shouted, "but a priest who carries out his duties; my church is mine."

Since he could not go personally to the church, he cared for those souls entrusted to him from his bed as God and his conscience dictated. He did not baptize nor did he carry the host to the sick; he neither married nor buried anyone; but he did collect all that was due him on such occasions and, in order to keep up appearances, every afternoon or so he would gather some elderly religious women and a few saintly old men around his bed and deliver a brief sermon preaching charity and disregard for the ephemeral blessings of this world in a phlegmatic but energetic voice.

He also continued from his bed to be the spiritual father to a few privileged souls, some mystical old women who came to the walnut headboard turned confessional, and there, after kneeling next to the nightstand, they would declare their faults, which Celorio heard while patiently scratching his neck. The most amusing thing was that it did not seem proper to him to listen to sins in his shirt sleeves like a porter; he recognized the necessity of wearing vestments which allowed him to remain in bed yet which let everyone know that he was a priest. His cassock was useless because it was moth eaten and far too long. The only cassock he owned had already served him for twenty years and he had decided not to buy another. He did not need it in bed. This was the favorite of all his decisions in his campaign to cut down on expenses. But, thank God, Ramona, Celorio's housekeeper, who was rather sordid, old and deaf, had worn the black woolen habit of Dolores her entire life and the priest hit upon the outlandish idea of putting his head through the skirt which Ramona wore on Sundays. With Ramona's skirt draped over his head, Celorio absolved the daughters of his confessional who came to the foot of his bed in search of grace.

Just as the priest cured souls and collected his surplice fees from his bed, he also directed his businesses and managed his profits without getting up. Let them say what they might in the palace, the priest of Vericueto dealt in a number of goods and exercised in the village market of nearby Suaveces a form of economic dominance which, while not exactly a monopoly, certainly gave him a profitable advantage. Shamelessly and without fear of denunciation, Celorio earned honestly, but forgetful of ecclesiastical law, a very good income from the interest on several loans he had made for a variety of cottage industries and small ventures. These ranged from swine breeding and milk cows, owned in common or as a partnership, vegetables, fruit, and chickens and even silk handkerchiefs which were sold in an open–air booth or pushcart along with cheap jewelry, Indian silk ribbons, and glass beads in the form of necklaces and earrings, mixed indiscriminately with rosaries, scapularies, ribbons touched by the Holy Christ of Cueto, and medallions from Rome which had been blessed by the pope.

If the coins earned by the villagers by the sweat of their brow came running to this industrious parish priest's bait, it was due not to his evil arts nor even less to hierocratical impositions, but simply to the loyalty and honesty of his business transactions, to the cheapness of the product and to the parsimoniousness with which Celorio tried to make only a small profit on each sale. His passion was not for an excessive and fabulous profit in each transaction, but rather for a great number and variety of business deals. His motto was to admit no bribes and to pardon no debt; everything that was his would come to him, but nothing more than what was rightfully his.

"The eye of the master fattens the horse" was a popular saying which served him as a lamp and guide as long as he had been able to walk. Of course, he did not shamelessly stand behind the counter of his store, a portable bench, in the market to sell his earrings and ribbons of Christ, but he was always nearby. Besides, he would move from one stand to another, from beets, cabbages, and turnips to the fruit stand. He was sometimes even seen in the stockyard stepping gingerly among the piglets, holding up his cassock, watching, seemingly unconcerned, but always very attentive, the transactions which were in reality much more important to him than they were to the man charged with making the sale. Sometimes, he forgot all discretion when his interests were threatened by excessive demands from buyers, and he would actively play a skillful intermediary role in the transactions. He would even reveal that he was the owner of whatever it was that was for sale, whenever it was a question of the merit of his produce. This happened quite frequently when he was selling lettuce, tomatoes, or peppers, the good priest's treasures, since he was a gardener by vocation. He could tell where the vegetables came from as well as affirm their high quality since the garden of the priest of Vericueto was famous for miles around.

Sometimes, when everyone in the market was from Vericueto, that is to say, when there were no strangers, Celorio forgot all discretion and would sit on an upturned basket among his cabbages and turnips and, while eating an onion which he dipped in water, he would check the weight, collect the change and hand over the leafy cabbages which were the pride and joy of this good tonsured Columela.

The priest of Vericueto knew well that these and similar excesses reached the ears of the bishop. But experience had shown him that the latter turned a deaf ear because he felt for Celorio an affection that dated from their adolescence together in the seminary, a fondness developed at an age when friendships, once established, last a lifetime.

The idea that legitimate commerce was forbidden to priests had always repelled him. This prohibition had always seemed to him a kind of stigma that would always dishonor that industriousness so necessary in the world. "As long as the Church considers it wrong for priests to engage in fair and just trade for money, merchants will believe that they have been authorized to act a little like thieves. If only commerce were in the hands of those who receive the Lord every day, and receive him worthily, business would run more smoothly, credit would flow like silk, lawsuits and other unnecessary expenses such as the police and hundreds of other impediments would be avoided like so much expensive dead wood, a useless burden on the economic life of the country. Let pagans have the same god for thievery as for business. If Jesus expelled the merchants from the temple, it was so that He could sell there. Moreover, on ordering us to pay taxes, the price for peace and order which we owe the state, the Lord told us that there is no sin in buying and selling."

More even than his theories, it was the irresistible need for legitimate profit that kept Celorio in the irregular situation of a shepherd who converted his flock into consumers for his products, of a priest who made his parish into customers.

But it was not enough to earn money; it was necessary to save it and spend as little as possible. Celorio lived like a cenobite monk, not for penance, to mortify the flesh, which for him prospered in spite of everything because of his natural good health and his moderate and abstemious way of life, but he lived with very little in order to save a lot. The spirit of economizing became so great in him that he even sacrificed his instinct for survival. This he demonstrated by the matter we have referred to before as the peak affair, and to which we are finally going to direct our attention.

V

At the very top of that mountain, on the road and not very distant, were the church and rectory of Vericueto, far above the other houses and huts forming the parish; up there, there was, as I mentioned before, an enormous boulder, an outcropping of rock, which I do not know whether it was mentioned also, was threatening to fall upon those fragile dwellings and turn them into dust. This threat was not imaginary, but the absolute truth, because as I was able to see with my own eyes on the day that I visited Father Celorio, the huge and formidable rock seemed to be held in place by a miracle, and the principles of the laws of equilibrium that we all understand in our own way through our own observations, told me clearly that that mass of granite or whatever it was (it could not be granite, but it weighed tons) would not be able to continue for very long in a state somewhere between falling and not falling: it would fall at any minute, it simply had to fall when one least expected.

Little by little, it had begun to lean and if there were any violent storms of the kind in which the rain digs out the earth and creates landslides, that monster peak would shake loose and break some of the chain links that were still holding it in place. The fact is that, without exaggeration, water and wind were gradually undermining the centuries-old base of that mass and each day the danger was greater that it would lose its support and, since there was no other route, would fall rolling into the valley directly over the rectory of Vericueto, the church and the little village which had grown up around them. And if the boulder fell, no stone would remain standing on stone nor living thing alive in all those buildings where everyone led a precarious existence under the violent threat of sudden destruction.

The industriousness of those poor mountain people had been directed for years toward impeding or at least postponing the catastrophe, and although it may not seem so, it is true that with ropes, feeble cables, wedges and even branches and all kinds of trenches, the people of Vericueto had built something like a dike against the threatening flood of stone, and, as a time–honored obligation, they felt regularly compelled to renovate this complex mechanism of their pitiful defense.

Many strangers, upon seeing with horror that imminent danger, had suggested the idea of emigration to those good people: "How can you continue living in a place where you might suffer such a horrible fate when you least expect it?" The people of Vericueto simply shrugged their shoulders like poor villagers, and sometimes very wealthy citizens, do when someone talks to them about curing a chronic or fatal illness at an exorbitant expense.

Move? That is not a good idea. And just where would they go?

Father Celorio was the first one to consider foolish the idea of leaving the parish. That would be something like treason. Besides, the custom of living in danger had made them consider the peril so remote that the villagers born next to it were no longer afraid. In the days of their fathers and grandfathers, the "molar," as they called it for some unknown reason, was already threatening to fall, and it had not done so yet. Could not another generation get by? No one denied that there were earth slides, that the rock leaned a little more every year or so, and that their ropes, boards and trenches were a very poor defense, more useless every day. But the danger, which no one could logically deny, no longer kept them living in fear. The priest saw that the danger had become something like the threat of eternal damnation, or at least of the possibility of a very lengthy and harsh punishment in the next world, which no one there denied, but which, nevertheless, did not impress the parish very much. Everyone knew that the fires of hell or purgatory were just waiting for the evil doer, but in spite of it all, the people lived as if eternal fire, or at least centuries of it, was something like a week without a Thursday. Their attitude was the same toward the giant boulder.

Celorio was one of those who saw the danger most clearly; but he was also one who was least afraid of the catastrophe, which he felt was indefinitely postponed. "It won't happen in my lifetime," he thought hopefully, parodying without knowing it the famous phrase of a certain diplomat who likewise enjoyed orders from on high.

The neighbors had begun to fight among themselves and quarrel with the priest, principally about the cost of the poor defense that Vericueto had been building for years to keep the rock from falling. These quarrels and dissensions poisoned the life of the village much more than the fear of the common disaster. For a few skeptics, fear of the molar was merely a superstition, although they would never call it that. These exaggerated empiricists, like many men, would not admit that what had not happened in many years might happen when one least expected it. The thought of the boulder falling and destroying the town meant as much to them as metaphysics to a pharmacist. "That is a long way off!" they came to think, like Don Juan in Tirso de Molina's play.

The priest did not think like these skeptics, but rather felt that the expense of maintaining the pitiful ropes, supports, and trenches that held back the molar should be distributed according to the fear each person had of the impending disaster. Still another group felt that those who had most to lose should spend more on defense. The priest replied to this idea that it all depended. He owned more material goods than anyone else there, but he did not have a wife or children, and as far as his housekeeper Ramona was concerned ... she could go to the devil, in a manner of speaking. And above all, it was not one's material interests but his fear of danger that should be considered. Basing his arguments on this idea, he refused to waste time and money building and repairing the defense system because, after all, he was not afraid of death nor was it suitable for a minister of the Lord to put such a high price on his ephemeral earthly existence.

"If the chance of it falling determined in some way the destiny of my soul, I alone would pay for all the necessary ropes and planks. But what does my physical body matter to me?"

Afterwards, when I learned more, I understood that Celorio had other concerns; in fact, it was very important to him, as we shall later see, that his earthly life not be cut short before he reached a certain age. But he suffered the conflict between losing his life, which he needed to make money, and his horror at spending money on such an unproductive and ultimately, perhaps, useless project as buying fragile ropes for the molar.

This neighborhood war was almost always a silent one, nevertheless, and never went very far; but matters changed greatly when it became a truly political and social question, which came to be known as the peak affair.

It seems that there was one mayor of Suaveces more zealous than the others, or perhaps more of an enemy of Celorio and his party's way of thinking which, of course, was absolutist, conservative, reactionary, or whatever. The mayor held an official inspection, called a visual reconnaissance, of the peak of Vericueto and decreed that the boulder, popularly called the molar, was threatening ruin (so he said in the Town Council) and that it was necessary through a collection or extraordinary contribution that the residents of Vericueto shoulder the expense and proceed to push the rock free once and for all before it flattened half the countryside.

The people of the parish joined the priest in one miserly corporate body and raised their voices to the heavens, or at least to the boulder, and swore to die flattened like toads rather than bear such an expense because what was being asked of them was far beyond their means. Moreover, the project the mayor considered necessary was for the benefit not only of Vericueto but of the entire district. Therefore, the people of Suaveces should contribute their share.

Some said one thing, some said another; it all escapes me. But it soon became a political question of pitting one boss against another, and of elections. Finally, it was all simply swept under the rug, the Town Council or the priest, the priest or the Town Council or Pontius Pilate. Meanwhile the boulder remained as poised and twisted as ever, ready to fall at any moment.

And this was the peak affair. Between deciding whether you or I should pay, everyone forgot to deal directly with the danger that really could harm a great number of people. Of course, those most interested in the project were the most stubborn. They were ready to die like heroes rather than donate one cent to the project suggested by the mayor of Suaveces.

So the years passed and Father Celorio took to his bed. For him, the danger was now even greater. The mayor of Suaveces accordingly came to try to force his hand. He told Celorio that he should look to the danger he was in since he could no longer protect himself nor run away. Even more, remembering a statement the doctor had jotted down for him, the mayor exclaimed, "Look here, Father, this rock is hanging over you constantly, threatening you like the sword of Democritus."

"Well," replied the priest, "in spite of what Democritus might say, Mr. Mayor, I will not untie the purse strings for a laughing Democritus, a crying Heraclitus, much less for that Damocles as some people call him."

This was Celorio's position in the peak affair when I, accompanied by Higadillos, went to meet Don Tomás Celorio, the priest of Vericueto.

VI

The impression that I got from that and subsequent visits was not the one that Higadillos wanted me to have. I found in Celorio's eyes, smile and words a delicate sensibility verging on shyness which did not corroborate the grossly Epicurean, miserly and crude character whom Higadillos had described in his conversations and in his poem.

What I saw immediately during our conversations with Father Celorio was that the worthy priest delicately and without cruelty made fun of the sophomoric leaning of my host and friend who was rather weak in dogmatic and historical theology and philosophy.

Higadillos, for example, believed that Catholics were obliged to believe that Christ was in heaven seated on the right hand of God. It was something to see Celorio sputter and shake the walnut bed with his laughter when he heard this.

"But my dear friend," he exclaimed as soon as he had stopped coughing, "how can that business of the right hand of God be taken literally, if God, not being corporeal has neither right nor left?"

"But it is an article of faith!" Higadillos shouted back.

"A true article of faith, something I believe as much as if I could see it, is that you know as much of theology as I do about shoeing horseflies."

Celorio had studied a bit, although he was not too well informed about recent developments since he had begun his studies so many years ago.

I noticed sometimes, when Higadillos was not looking, that Celorio winked an eye and stuck his tongue out at him, and I understood thereby that he was preparing a great surprise for him.

Part Two

I

In the name of the Father, Son and Holy Ghost. Amen. I, Tomás Celorio, parish priest of Vericueto, want this to be my last will and testament in which I declare my final wishes, signed and written in my own hand in a form quite different from the norm in such cases, but no less valid if there is any justice left on earth. I do not leave my body to the worms because they will take it without my permission as something that belongs to them, nor do I leave my soul to God which would be to leave something to Him which was never mine but has always belonged to His Divine Majesty, and He shall prove it by sending it wherever His justice determines. The only thing that is mine is the mountain of papers among which will be found this will, tied in one bundle in a chest, unless some thief deceived by the false rumors of my wealth, which malicious gossips have spread about, finds the hiding place of the supposed treasure under my bed and, with the wrath of the disenchanted, destroys all these documents which for him have no value but which for me represent the ease of my old age, the peace of my conscience and the ransom of my outraged sense of honor. Everything that is mine to dispose of, if my inheritance is liquidated correctly and the debits and credits are justly calculated, I leave at the hour of my death to become the property of

Don Gil Higadillos y Fernández, professional philosopher and blas-
phemer and my good friend in spite of it all, who, before taking the
final step that I am about to take, will be pleased upon reading this
and will die in the arms of my Holy Mother Church, just as I ask God
in my frequent prayers.

It is also my will that this carefully folded bundle of papers not be
examined until after my will has been read (as soon as my eyes are
closed) by those persons whom I have charged with opening the chest
which I have hidden under my bed. They should verify first the contents of the first document they find, which will be this will, unless
someone else's greed has rearranged my papers.

I have said, and I hope it will be so, that Higadillos himself
should read it in a loud, clear voice; I hope and believe that he will
be present because of his curiosity; since he is my heir, his insignificant greed and great piety will oblige him to satisfy this wish which I
have so many times expressed to him. If Higadillos is not present, my
executor shall read, and if he is not present, the most respectable
person there should; I do not believe that this wish will be overlooked
because I have asked Ramona Cencillo, my housekeeper, who ex-
pects to be disappointed, and my executor Don Sancho Benítez, as
well as other parishioners who will probably surround my bed when I
expire, to see to it.

In order to explain how, having the reputation of a wealthy man,
it is that, in spite of the usury in which I have lived for more than
twenty years, I die as poor as those who expected something different
shall soon see, I am leaving the narrative of that part of my life history which is relevant to my pardon. I also am writing it so that my
heir will receive a greater benefit than merely the attached papers,
because more than them and any other material goods that pass
through my hands, the lesson Higadillos might learn, not to judge
men by appearances nor guess the depths of their hearts by the out-
ward nature of certain habits, has great value. The habit does not
make the monk.

And without further ado, I shall begin to say who I am and how
and why I became such an economical administrator of the vile interests of which for a short time I was something like a trustee.

I was born in a village not far from here in a house that displays a
coat of arms over the door, our reminder of ancient prosperity and
eternal honor, and which on my arrival enjoyed a depleted income
far short of what was necessary to maintain eight children, both boys
and girls, with the propriety required by our family name; there were
ten mouths to feed, counting my parents, and fourteen, if one included servants necessary to help us care for our land and for certain
village and cottage industries which kept us alive. I was neither the
eldest nor the youngest of five sons, neither the favorite nor the least
in the household. They loved me like the rest.

But a certain characteristic, surely my hatred of fighting and my utter dislike of my own or another's pain, and a special horror of injustice, at the unfair division of each person's share, made me always surrender my pretentions to others in order to avoid arguing, creating a disturbance or being unfair. The greatest problem was how to dispose of the competing teeth, that is, of placing those many tools which worked toward the destruction of our patrimony and cause little harm or no harm at all. The means to achieving this constant family desire consisted of marrying the girls or placing them in convents, sending one son to Havana where he would become rich, God willing; finding another one a profession, and enabling a third to take advantage of a small income which a priest in the family had left in his will to whichever one of us should embrace the ecclesiastical state. My oldest brother was weak, thin and sickly, very fond of study but not of the black skirts which our relative required as a condition for his posthumous liberality; besides, my father did not want his first-born to enter the Church; the second son demonstrated his love of travel and of the opportunities afforded by chance. It was he who embarked for America, almost without discussing it with the others. And I, though the strongest and most fond of a field laborer's life, took it upon myself, I do not know how nor why, probably because of the others' disinterest rather than my own wishes, to accept the most serious responsibility of celebrating mass and collecting the pension which, in agreement with my parents and brothers and according to their interpretation and mine of my deceased uncle's desire, I was to use to help those of my brothers who might need it and my parents also, if necessary.

I became a priest without a strong vocation, but also without great reluctance, with enough faith to take seriously the narrow discipline of my duties. The life that was waiting for me did not seem too different from the one I would have chosen anyway, and only in the vow of chastity did I see something of an uphill battle. But once I had begun to like the career and had developed an interest in theology, the celestial mathematics of Saint Thomas was really to my liking. In defense of the doctrine of celibacy, which seemed so self-evident, I would have reverted to syllogisms and even to the sword against anyone. If, at first, life in the seminary displeased me not a little, it was not because of the rigor of the ecclesiastical regime, but because I missed the freedom of the country. Finally, habit, camaraderie and the *esprit de corps* made me a raven (as they called us), enthusiastic, sincere, more determined than most and, if I was not a model of virtue, neither was I the scandal of that holy house where there were many like me who, if they dealt on occasion with the devil, redeemed their sins with due and sincere penance and who, as often as not, conquered that temptation which was not as strong nor as beautiful as certain profane writers imagine at the expense of the clergy.

I had never dreamed of marrying; even when I was free to leave
the seminary, it never occurred to me to miss marriage, with its band
of children with dozens of teeth, with their trials of hunger and finding jobs, with weddings for the daughters and so on. I had seen more
than enough of these problems in my own home; and if there were
anything which I believed a priest might miss that could be pleasing to
him, it certainly was not the state in which I had seen my own good
father, in which the water never filled the well. No, marriage was not
a temptation; but of course, marriage is one thing, a woman something else. A priest ostensibly renounces marriage and women; but he
knows that if he sins, marriage will continue to be impossible, but
love, though illicit, will not. I do not know how it is with other priests
who may not be very good; but as for me, who was average, it happened this way: almost without realizing it, the distinction which I
have presented contributed not a little to my accepting the promise of
chastity, which my state bound me to without a great deal of effort or
soul searching. Afterwards, experience showed me that the lion is not
as fierce as he is painted. If there was a fight, it was never very violent, and if virtue did not always win, the battles won for the good
were the greater in number, and the score erased my remorse for the
ones I lost. Moreover, such reversals were the common lot of most of
my young companions. Because I did not boast of my bravery in my
battles with temptation, I believe that I achieved the peace that I later
began to enjoy, because from concupiscence I distilled a derivative,
my moderate desire for profit, which could not take any other form
for me except card playing.

The financial hardships that had been the constant worrisome
theme of my family in my parents' house had yellowed all my acts
and desires; my strong and fertile actions were always directed toward
legitimate financial gain, characterized by a great desire for my own
and a great respect for others'. The temptations of love for me were
very soon child's play in comparison to my desire for money. But I
wish I could have earned it in a free and open fight against nature or
through some legal industry useful for the republic. The priestly state
forbade me all endeavor of that sort, and I had to make do with
bridge, twenty–one, and other card games that were played in the
rectories in the evening during Corpus Christi and on other less solemn occasions. There was no other way for me to slake my thirst for
legitimate gain.

II

Stuck in a village, on practically nothing, giving a sermon now
and then and dividing my inherited pension with the rest of my family, I wasted my youth without finding the Queen of Sheba in each
leafy grove, bearing up under temptation, storing up a great deal of
energy which I did not waste but spent running from place to place,

rising early, and doing my job well. But if the flesh did not make me throw myself backwards or forwards on thorns and brambles, a different impulse tormented me, the desire for gain which I could not fulfill; the prurience of greed adhered to my spirit like a rash which I perhaps caught living in the miserable penury of my family, that home so poor in its proud lineage, so aggrieved by the expense of each dinner, each pair of shoes, each roof tile that needed to be replaced, each fruit tree that died. I had nightmares about the hunger that for years I had suffered in my parents' house, and the habit of thinking about money, and yearning for money, had become a part of me.

Money seemed to me the most serious thing in the world, the realest reality, the most unyielding and most inflexible in its natural laws. "One does not play with money," I thought (if only I had not played with money!) and I believed it religiously. Everything else I doubted to a certain extent and I saw that the depth of human concerns was often illusory, mere fantasy which, if the pusillanimous failed to see it, was clearly evident to such daring, grave, and undeceived thinkers as I, who knew that anything that can be lost to chance is not very certain to begin with. This sort of half–ironic skepticism (regarding temporal things, of course) permitted me, like many others, to take great chances with a certain grace because of the scant value I had given to whatever I might lose.... But, of course, as long as it was not a question of losing money, but of only such things as self–esteem, honor, other people's opinions, fine clothes and furnishings, the constancy of friends and other worldly vanities such as the inherent value of our acts and the truth of doctrines and opinions, and so on and so on.

If someone spoke to me of miracles, I believed all that I was obliged to believe; but the many other miracles in which natural laws may be bent had nothing to do with the economic progress of the world. I did not believe in miracles with money. It seemed to me that sobriety demanded there be no exceptions made for money and that everything could be calculated beforehand without fear of unexplainable surprises. God better than anyone knows what formality is necessary in business, in exchange, in credit, and it was certain that He had disposed of everything according to His unalterable laws pertaining to this realm of endeavor. I did not consider that miracles have a spiritual end which bears fruit in the garden of religion, while gold and silver were absolutely worldly, perishable and mundane. The Lord had restored life to the dead, sight to the blind, health to the sick, but He ordered the poor to have patience and He filled their purses only with the good advice He had given the rich that they should abandon their wealth. Therefore, it was obvious that God Himself, who from the depths of his grace could extract health, sight, and life, had not wished to dispose of money since it is so vile, and knew no other way to have it move from hand to hand except to take it from others, all of which is undeniable proof of the perpetuity and certainty of the laws of trade.

Through this theology I became the most hardened player of bridge and twenty-one in the entire archdiocese. What could be done? There was no other way for a poor chaplain to obtain a little more money beyond the pitiful sums which the altar and the pulpit brought me from funerals and other petty activities. And in me the desire for legitimate profit was invincible. Besides, in my opinion, all rural clergy did nothing but gamble anyway; the good were no different than the bad; they all gambled.

We would go from rectory to rectory, from feast to feast, the same priests with the same decks of cards, some always lucky and others always folding and passing.

Of course, in each parish there were at least two major celebrations, Corpus Christi and the feast of the patron saint. Besides these, there were chapels and hermitages and other sanctuaries with their pilgrimages, high masses and corresponding banquets of honorable religious who did not offend God with their good appetites, innocent jokes and good or bad card playing. Sometimes, although I knew better, in the last hour (a very long hour that stretched from midnight until four or five o'clock in the morning), money given at mass was sometimes wagered, not without a great deal of awe and a little spicy remorse. This was done in spite of the fact that I knew how unsuitable it was to see an offering that had been earned by singing mass and reciting the sublime psalms of the poet king entrusted to the changing fortunes of a club or a spade; nor do I maintain that it is in keeping with canon law for an imitation print of Bossuet or Bourdaloue to be wagered in an all-night card game. But greater crimes are recorded in the histories of the popes; and there was no other way to kill time without creating notorious scandal.

Not only did we play in the rectories and in the homes of nonassigned priests, but we also met in the houses of friends who, though not of the regular clergy, were good comrades, faithful sons of the Church and magnificent swordsmen in the difficult art of finessing.

The count of Vegarrubia was the heart of the card parties which both regular and secular brothers attended for miles around. Reared and educated in Paris, he had wasted his health and fortune there, and now, rather than show off horses and expensive carriages in the Bois de Boulogne, he preferred to display his skill at bridge and his daring in games of chance for the benefit of half a dozen village priests and small town politicians.

He was still very wealthy in spite of his continual foolish spending, if not on the same extravagances of his days in Paris, on schemes that were no less costly. He knew nothing of the value of money, and yet he thought of nothing else, provided it was in the context of gambling; he entertained himself by watching the rage of the unfortunate losers and by defying with his own *sang-froid* their threatened serenity as they suffered repeated assaults of bad luck. For myself, at least, I can say that whenever the count, who moreover knew well how to demonstrate most delicately the superiority he attributed to his noble blood, sat opposite me, face to face in the fight for the favors of chance, making a display of his indifference toward the slights of that willful goddess of the abyss, I fairly bristled with pride, remembering the purity of my heritage, always impoverished but always worthy of respect. I now think that my valor was greater than his, since my passion for money was greater, not for the sake of the game, but for the money itself; the amounts wagered signified more to my unending penury than to his unfounded wealth. And now I know that only in melodrama are passions so exclusive that they overshadow other weaknesses; I, in addition to desiring honest gain, was very proud of my family crest, our pretensions to nobility seemed all the more worthy of defense as centuries of poverty continued testing the mettle of our true worth.

Among the neighbors and friends from afar who frequented the count's gatherings, there were a few first-born heirs and two or three barons and viscounts. One of them, the baron of Cabranes, interested me because of his truly aristocratic, somewhat melancholy and delicate bearing, and especially because I knew that he suffered similar and perhaps even greater misfortunes than I. When his father died, he became the head of a very large family consisting primarily of young women who would never marry because he had no dowry to give them since they all lived far beyond their means. They were noble and they were poor, heading for ruin as Don Quijote went to dinner at the castle, without removing his helmet. Cabranes was a very pleasant young man, but always rather sad and quiet. He gambled desperately, not at bridge, which he did not understand, but at any other game of chance played on a covered table (a strange custom).

One night very late, after a lively dinner with the count in which it had been my misfortune to drink more than usual, devilish luck persisted in placing the Baron Cabranes and myself in opposition. First he then I would win all the hands; sudden streaks of luck and strange reversals of fortune kept moving between us, leaving the other players, including the count who enviously bet his money wildly in a bid to win back everyone's attention, in the shadows. This was the preamble to the tremendous duel that was taking shape among the courteous brotherly jokes and innocent ministerial cheer offered in the spirit of the good but too copiously served wine.

A moment arrived in which I was winning a fortune from Cabranes; a few priests usually less fond than I of money and also less capable of great gestures and less concerned with the brilliance of their lineage, nudged me trying to stop me from tempting luck and suggested that I retire with my winnings which I had won honestly. However, I paid more attention to the generous impulses of the wine and to the urgings of that nobility which responds most when favored by luck and more particularly to the glances and smiles of the count who seemed to be telling me, "Come, my good fellow, withdraw if you dare. I know you want to, my noble friend. Only a gentleman like myself is capable of letting his opponent try until dawn to regain his losses like this poor trembling pale baron is doing, who, no matter how he tries to hide it, is beginning to bet, on his word alone, more perhaps than he actually owns." I did not stop; I continued winning and giving the baron the chance to recover.

III

Not only pride incited me to give the baron the time and the means to turn the wheel of fortune, sympathy also inspired me; the pity I felt for him urged me to it. The poor man feigned great serenity; he smiled, especially when the refined laughter of the count challenged him. At each new deal, Cabranes repeated:

"But my dear chaplain, this is no good at all; you are certainly going to begin losing.... Enough, enough.... I owe you...."

"Keep going," I interrupted to everyone's astonishment.

The fierce step of wagering unseen money began. But the word of a nobleman is enough! I do not know whether I believed he had the money he was betting or not, but I did take his word. A Cabranes would leave no stone unturned to find the money he needed.

The count, confronted with those two brave contenders, each one valiant in his own way, began to suggest that the game was all a joke, that the baron honestly did not believe that he owed what he was losing on the strength of his word alone. The baron, as if he needed to demonstrate his superiority, pretended for the sake of appearances to go along with the idea that it was all a jest, and said something to that effect. But he looked at the count and at me in such a manner as to let us know that what he meant was this, "Whoever believes that, that I am not going to pay, is insulting me no less than if he had struck me." No one would have struck him without risking his life.

Luck left Cabranes so far behind that my winnings reached great proportions and I knew clearly that the Cabranes family could not satisfy their debt, which did not mean that they did not consider it sacred.

I continued offering him the chance to recover his losses.

The baron did not bet everything at once, of course. Modesty would not let him double, an act which would have made the debt truly fabulous. He lost little by little. He fell from boulder to boulder down the precipice.

The moment arrived when all joking and commentary ceased; the baron kept silent in order not to swear in his desperation; I forebore out of good sense and the other because of the profound seriousness of the situation.

The first time that Cabranes's luck changed, I felt a certain joy, a relief, as if I could breathe more easily; he won again, again and again; then I began to suffer a certain superstitious apprehension; when the baron had recovered the thousands he had lost, the imaginary fortune that had just slipped through the cobwebs of my fantasy wounded me as deeply as if I had been obliged to sell my small patrimony to pay the debt.

Afterwards, there were reversals; chance flirted with us, and now more than pride, my self–esteem, self–interest, sense of rivalry and desire to fight bound me to that ill–begotten game.

Arrogance and the audacity of a lucky player continued long after I no longer owed anything to luck but a great deal to the baron; it had seemed my right to continue winning. The moment came when it was my turn to try to recover my losses.

The count began to laugh again, and now I was the one whom his noble, cold blue eyes tempted and defied.

No one dared suggest interrupting the game. A priest from a noble family was no less than a nobleman who was broke; there we stood. The chance to recover was offered to me as I had offered it to the baron. The night fled, bringing the dawn and with it the obligation for many seated at the table covered with green felt from Palencia to celebrate mass.

The count again stopped his laughing and joking when I, embarrassed in my turn, began to lose on the strength of my word. The baron, radiant with joy and with that uncertain generosity of the lucky, let it be known very discreetly that he was as ready to believe in my fictitious wealth as I had been in his.

I understood with terror that the onlookers silently gave me much less credit than they had given the baron of Cabranes. For a nobleman who had to support a large family, he was poor; but after all, he was much wealthier than a miserable chaplain who lived from church offerings and on a charitable pension.

I continued playing in spite of everything. I, too, fell from boulder to boulder into that abyss of incredible debt; the hours flew and the game had to cease, since sunlight was filtering through the balcony, filling the room with that yellow light typical of prison chapels when the hour for an execution arrives. I continued losing little by little. But I had lost thousands. The onlookers began to yawn, to become bored; their interest in the unknown was gone; the end was evident—I would not regain my losses. The count, tired of respecting my misfortune, showed his tedium and his disdain; since he had been brave enough to despise his own losses, he permitted himself the luxury of despising mine; he let it be known that the game was going to be suspended, for the sake of appearances, because it was very late, that is, very early. With a certain cruelty, he pretended to forget that the most important thing there was my situation; he took it for granted that I also gave or pretended to give more importance to the time of day than to the state in which suspension of the game would leave me.

A ray of bright sunlight entered the room like the police and shone on the deck of cards. Two or three witnesses to the duel stood up, and outside, a bell rang. It was calling people to mass, Fray Fernando's mass, which the count, the baron and the others were obliged to attend.

The cards were put away; the felt cover removed; the balcony opened, letting the daylight flow in cheerfully and drive away the shadows of the nightmare. But the reality which I alone seemed to remember remained. I owed the baron of Cabranes thousands of *duros*.

That morning, I did not say mass. When the others returned from hearing Fray Fernando, we met in the count's garden house for breakfast.

Vegarrubia either felt sorry or simply wished to dismiss me. And he repeated his theme that the game, at least that part of it played on credit, had been a joke. He took it for granted that the baron did not think that I, in all seriousness, really owed him so many thousands. Some women arrived and the count insisted on discussing how much I had lost. Then I did what the baron had done before; I pretended that I thought it was too fantastic to be real. But my way of looking at the baron must have let him understand the same thing I had understood from his glance the night before, to think that I meant what I was saying would be an insult. "I have no way to pay," my eyes declared, "but I do owe you, and a gentleman does not need the means to pay, only the obligation. I owe you, therefore I shall pay you, even though I have nothing. God works no miracles with money, a vile substance, even less for gamblers; but a gentleman such as I, even though he is a priest, pays."

The baron smiled, but I understood clearly that he would not refuse to accept everything that I would give him.

I did not even look at the count.

On the following day, I wrote a letter to Cabranes because I did not dare tell him in person that he would have to wait. In the letter, I told him essentially this: "Here is everything I have, everything which today is mine. I will continue paying as long as I can, and believe me, I will not hold back any more than the most severe law concedes to the debtor least worthy of consideration. Until I have paid everything I owe you, which is much more than I can earn in many years, bound as I am hand and foot by my vows from becoming wealthy, I accept the sentence of forced labor in this prison of sordid misery and greed until I no longer owe you anything. Please accept this manner of complying with my obligation to you, these indefinite but certain intervals for paying; moreover, I ask not as a favor to me but as my right that you do not even consider pardoning the debt, reducing it or anything of the sort. More than anything, even more than being a priest, I am a man whose obligation to pay his gambling debts has nothing to do with his ministry, because a good priest does not gamble. It is a question of human obligation only, of my sinful condition of vicious though noble manhood."

The baron answered me very politely, very correctly, as they say, allowing me as much time as I needed to pay. He did not even remotely allude to the idea of pardoning or reducing the debt. That is what I demanded of him, doubtlessly because he needed the money.

They were extremely poor.

After reading his letter, satisfied in a way but for a thousand reasons confused and angry, I instinctively took to my bed where I found my Bible opened to the New Testament.

"Light, oh Lord!" I cried and kneeling I glanced at the sacred text:

"Go and sell what thou hast and give to the poor ... and come and follow me," it said. But I read, "... and give to the baron and come and follow me."

I knew the way; everything for the baron, poverty for me. My sweat, my work, my effort, my earnings; money is unyielding and remorseless; you cannot work miracles with it, to my regret.

IV

To be indebted and to be unable to pay is a torment which Dante forgot to include in his *Inferno*. There is a good reason for calling duty an obligation: the supreme duty is to pay one's debts. My conscience told me that I would have to search seven stadia underground to find what was owed me, what was mine but which no one would give me, because one must respect the rights of others. And I respected them. My creditor was sacred to me, almost a terrible idol. I understood that particular law of the Twelve Tables which stated that the man who does not pay should be handed defenseless to his creditor: "*Ni judicatum facit ... secum ducito, vincito, aut nervo, aut compendibus....* If he does not pay, carry him to his creditor's house, and if the latter wishes, chain him and put irons on his feet...." And then, after three days in the market, if there is not one who will buy the miserable slave out of indebtedness, "*Tertiis nundinis partis secanto....* Tear him apart and divide his body among his creditors."

The baron knew this already; since I was worth nothing, and since no one would want me even if I were given away, he could cut me up for stew meat. This was the law that I believed to be just. I would have gladly sold myself across the Nalón River (since the Tiber was so distant) to pay Cabranes those thousands of *duros*. But who would buy a priest who is not for sale? Because, since I am a priest, I could not sell myself, unfortunately. I knew very well that the money I needed could never be obtained honestly. In my profession, the amount of money that can be earned legitimately is insignificant. How can a priest become wealthy? There is simony. But that was not for me. I saw that others who were perhaps less than I became bishops and amassed great fortunes; but I was neither virtuous enough nor wise enough to deserve to rise thereby to such heights; nor was I a schemer, a flatterer or a liar, a prude or a hypocrite who would usurp those honors which are due to merit alone.

Moreover, I did not feel ambitious because I lacked the imperial wings of vanity and pride; my poor barnyard flight carried me away from ambition and condemned me to a petty greed which necessitated my scratching the earth like a hen to suck up its worms. At that time, a book fell into my hands by one Mr. Bastiat in which I read a defense of saving. There the miracles of the penny were lauded. That was my road! I would follow the penny to my salvation, win my War of Reconquest and break the chains of my debt. But how could a poor chaplain who, if he buys lunch does not have enough money to buy dinner, save anything? If my profession were different, I am certain that my wit would have helped me save through my labor and watchfulness, enough money to meet my obligations but my cassock hindered me and forbade all activity; like the net thrown over Agamemnon by Clytemnestra so that Aegisthus could kill him, it kept me from defending myself.

Although I believed I was very talented, commerce was forbidden to me. No other door to the temple of wealth was open to me; a priest could not enter with dignity. How could I be a good man, a good priest and have to earn all the thousands of *duros* in order to pay a gentleman's sacred debt!

I accepted, even though I saw it meant entering a dead–end street, the humble parish they offered me; I signed the agreement with resignation and went to Vericueto like one going to a cave which was definitely not a gold mine.

I have since spent twenty years scratching the earth, caring for this poor vineyard of the Lord in which I had to circumscribe all my efforts and activities. I allowed myself to be beseiged by hunger and I treated myself like a penitent. But that is not the most painful part. It was not enough that by denying myself the necessities I was able to save something. If I wanted to get enough money together to pay little by little, I had to make others contribute, those who deserved my charity, the poor.

Charity for me was a luxury I could not afford. "I shall have charity in my heart," I told myself, but this, too, came to seem a kind

of hypocrisy to me; to want something for others and not try to obtain
it for them, to have compassion and not help them with alms repelled
me; I preferred to harden my heart and wait for better times. I would
take no bribes nor pardon any debts. Everything that I could legitimately get from the altar, I took. It was an inflexible law in the Roman way. I managed to achieve this inflexibility, this hardness by
thinking one very simple thing: that my money was not mine; it belonged to Cabranes; any generosity or liberality on my part would
have been false; a fraud because I did not have the right to be generous with money that belonged to someone else, to my creditor.

Everything I earned in my humble parish, and I earned all that I
could, all that was legal according to canon law, went to the baron,
whose poverty increased daily. He received my payments, the income
from my debt, silently, sadly and rather humbly. He never would
have claimed them from me, but at the same time, he let me understand that they were needed and that he depended upon them.

Meanwhile, my pious flock was beginning to create a legend
about my greed. "The priest has a hidden treasure!" The treasure
made many of them dream. Since they did not know that I did not
keep my savings, they took it for granted that I hid them in the chest
locked securely under my bed.

I was a cold–blooded miser; there was no help for it. At first, this
reputation bothered me a great deal; but it hurt more to be a bad
priest, stingy with the poor in my parish. And I was. Everyone paid
his due. Little by little, I grew accustomed to the role I was playing
and, as the newspapers say, I cultivated art for art's sake. I did become attached to my chains, to my torment, just as some people
become attached to an illness or to their pain; I fell in love with the
life that necessity brought me without knowing it. In saving, in stingi-
ness, in daily petty calculations and in my sordid life, I found a certain pleasure. I began to see myself as others saw me. My trickling
earnings were always directed toward paying my debt; but my miserli-
ness was my own creation; it was an attribute which grew from my
need to adapt to my environment, from exercising those instincts
which were necessary to fulfill that need. My unforgiving debt obliged
me to become an example of Darwin's laws!

My skill at business, at earning through industriousness, could
not be restrained; it broke out whenever it could, and I began certain
business dealings, which, in their own right, were legitimate, though
not particularly suitable to the dignity of my station. I began to raise
pigs and chickens with particular care. Since I could not show charity
to my fellow man, I began to show it to my animals, feeding them like
kings in order to get more from them. The money that came to me as
parish fees became bacon and fresh eggs with astonishing speed.
They, in turn, became through the world's circulation system that vile

metal, money. And the money, in turn, increased with interest in loans, went from my hands directly to Cabranes.

But my delight, my greatest consolation, was my garden, particularly the cabbages. I am not bragging when I say that there is no gardener my equal for twenty miles around.

I read Virgil's *Georgics*, I read Columela and with greater delight, I devoured Cato the Elder's *De Re Rustica*, which taught me the bucolics of greed, the eclogue of interest. To love nature, to love the country for the purpose of extracting from it my interest payments in fruits came to be the only pleasure in my life.

The gossips of the parish began to suggest that Ramona and I had come to an understanding, I know, and that my cabbages, chickens, pigs and pear trees were not my only passion.

Pure lies; when Ramona entered the rectory, my chastity was definite; I do not know whether it was a virtue or merely the habit of disuse; but my body had cast off lasciviousness. "Leave lust for a month and it will leave you for three," according to popular wisdom. Well, I had left it alone for months and it had not bothered me for years.

When, after five or six years, Ramona entered the rectory, she was still a healthy girl, that is true; but if I kept her in my home until the days of my old age and hers, it was not because of her physical charms, but because she helped me become the perfect miser. I have never met a more naturally stingy woman in all my life. She was a veritable machine for saving pennies, for not spending anything. She invented the fantastic trick which she always used of pretending she was more deaf than she was in order to escape from the house whenever anyone whom I should have invited to dinner or to tea came to visit. "Ramona! Ramona!" I would shout. From the other side of the door there was never a reply. Ramona never answered. And since the priest was not supposed to put the pot on the fire, set the table, serve the dinner and wash the dishes, the dinner was postponed until another day. Ramona Cencillo enabled me to save a lot of pennies in this fleeting existence of ours. But what she does not know is that there is no Galician peasant alive who can get the best of me, and this priest's housekeeper is from Galicia.

It is true that Ramona was the best at helping me become a miser, in marketing chickens, vegetables, fruit and so on. But does she really think that as a reward for her services I am going to leave her something? Ha! We are even. I have kept very good accounts. What she has already stolen is payment enough for her services. I have kept a careful record of her thievery; I always kept an exact balance of what I earned thanks to her and of what she stole from me one way or another; and God and my conscience know that at this moment, I do not owe her a cent. I do not owe anyone anything, not even the baron of Cabranes, who at this moment, from the sale of what remains to me and with what I have collected year after year, now has in his power all the thousands of *duros* which he won from me on that night when I perhaps won hell in a card game. Perhaps I will be damned, but I will go without obligations, as a bad priest and as a fine gentleman.

I have nothing; naked I was born and naked I die, because as far as the priest's treasure is concerned, I consider everything that I have put into it little by little to belong to my universal heir, Don Gil Higadillos y Fernández.

And it is my will that Higadillos himself, on reaching this point in the reading of my will, if this paper can be considered so, or that whoever in his absence reads this document aloud, should proceed to search the chest so that he can verify that the priest of Vericueto's treasure is, my only legacy, liquidated, which I want my friend Higadillos to keep as a souvenir and as a lesson.

V

On reaching this point in reading the document, Higadillos, who had turned green, leaned over the chest which we had taken from its hiding place under the deceased's bed, and began to take out paper after paper, all the same size and all with writing on one side: a few lines and a signature, the signature was that of the baron of Cabranes. They were the receipts for the money which Celorio, the priest of Vericueto, had given his creditor to amortize his debt, the cancer of his life. Celorio had seen the promised land, his freedom. He died when he no longer owed anything. Therefore, Ramona could tell how a few days earlier, when a poor blind man had stopped at their door to play the violin, that when she went to chase him away, as was her custom, her master cried out from within:

"Tell whomever it is to come in!"

When the blind man entered, the priest, with an expression of joy on his face, handed the man the two coins which he had held clasped in his hands while taking his afternoon nap.

Those few coins must have been the first ones that were truly his and which he could dispose of freely after so many years of serving his debt.

When Ramona saw such generosity, a mad act for the priest, she mumbled to herself:

"The priest is dying."

And, a few days later he died.

The bad thing was that Higadillos had already published in some foolish journal or other the satirical poem which he had finished that summer. And certainly, without anyone understanding why, it had become popular and sold well and the editor had given Higadillos perhaps two or three thousand *duros*.

"What shall I do with this money?" Higadillos asked me, ashamed, thinking that the humorous calumnies of his poem about the treasure of the priest of Vericueto now referred to his inheritance, a pile of useless receipts.

"What shall I do with this money?"

Finally, he did what I suggested. He spent it on masses for the soul of the priest of Vericueto, on Gregorian masses.

Cornbread

On the coastal highway almost halfway between the two flourishing towns of Gijón and Aviles, a coach stopped just after leaving the Voz forest in a small picturesque glade made pleasant by the foliage of chestnut, oak, pine and walnut trees and by the deep meadow's natural tapestry of dark green velvet which descends until it cools its fringes in a brook that hastily and noisily seeks the rushing current of the Abofio river. It was an August afternoon and very hot, even for Asturias. But a sweet breeze that slipped through the narrow valley, filtered by the restless branches of the thick oak grove of the Voz which shades much of the highway, mitigated the fever given off by the sun–drenched air.

When the wreck, suffocated under hundreds of layers of dust, came to a stop, the passengers, who were dozing and nodding their heads, did not stir. There, as best he could, on heavy feet and weak legs, a thin, dark–complected and gangly man with a scraggly beard— which the dust had turned gray—leapt out of the coupe. He wore a light colored summer jacket of good material, designed in Paris but which hung awkwardly on this emigrant to the New World who had just returned burdened down with money and a diseased liver.

Pepe Francisca—Don José Gómez y Suárez was his signature for business purposes—was returning to his hometown, Prendes, after an absence of thirty years, thirty years invested in killing himself working little by little to earn the great fortune which he could not spend on what he wanted most: to cure his liver and to bring his mother, Pepa Francisca de Francisquín, back to life.

A lad struggled to take at least four luxurious suitcases out of the trunk, together with an old, mended valise which Pepe Francisca kept as a memento because it was the only luggage he had taken with him to Mexico so long ago when he was poor in recommendations, money, shirts and hope. Pepe gave a tip to the coachman, who then signaled the run–down vehicle to continue its journey, disappearing quickly in a cloud of dust.

The returned emigrant remained alone, surrounded by trunks, in the middle of the road. That was how he wanted it. He wanted to be alone at the taxi stop he had so often dreamed about. He already had known, when he was still in Puebla, that a highway now cut through the meadow of the Suqueru where, when he was eight years old, he grazed the four cows of his father, Francisquín de Pola. He looked to the right, to the left, up and down the hills; everything was still the same. Only a few trees were missing, and his mother.

There in front, on the other side of the narrow valley, was the humble farm which his family had worked for generations. His sister now lived there, the childhood companion of his wanderings about the Suqueru, married to Ramon Llantero, a frustrated emigrant like so many who had left only to return quickly with no money. Half villagers, half gentlemen, they wasted little time losing themselves again in their natural servitude to the land, quickly acquiring the color of laborers sweating in the fields.

They had five children, and from their letters, the rich old man knew that Rita had caught Llantero's greed and it had taken the place of her affection. His nephews did not even know him. They loved him only for what he could give them. But it did not matter. They were his entire family; and whether they wanted him there or not, he wanted to, and was going to, die in his mother's bed surrounded by his people. To die! Who knows? What Vichy water could not do, what the famous doctors of New York, Paris or Berlin failed to do, what the entertainments of the wealthy and the power of money could not do, could perhaps be accomplished with the help of the air of his hometown; his "hometown," a vulgar phrase that he always repeated, meaning a variety of different things, all the deep complications of a soul lacking an adequate vocabulary to describe an abundance of feelings. What he called his hometown was his life's passion, his eternal desire, his love for that corner of green where he was born and from which he had been expelled as a child, almost kicked out by the greed of the village and the threat of hunger.

He had been a dreamy, quick-witted but weak child and had to choose between becoming a poor parish priest or emigrating; and since he felt no calling for the priesthood, he preferred the terrifying journey, leaving behind his heart on the Prendes meadows, in his mother's lap. Luck, after great struggles, finally smiled on him; but he responded with disdain, because the wealth which he had sought out of an instinct of imitation and obedience to his family's wish could not remove the sadness from his heart. His family wrote from Prendes, "Don't come back! Don't come back yet! Get more money! We don't want you here until you have earned all that you can!" And he did not return, although he dreamed of nothing else.

Finally, what he feared most happened. His mother died before he could return and he lost his health; the result of these losses was that the gold he had saved looked jaundiced. With the terrifying lucidity of a dying man, he saw the uselessness of riches, the normal goal of healthy men who are convinced of the unending, certain and constant life of solid, earthly well being.

Something else yellow attracted him and enchanted the childish dreams of this sick man who had visions of a happy and healthy life.

Abstractions tired him unless they were presented with a palpable and visible representation and his mind tended to symbolize all his heart's desires to return to his hometown with one modest ambition, which was perhaps unattainable. The yellow thing that he desired so much, that he dreamed about in Puebla, Paris and Vichy, everywhere, while listening to singers in Covent Garden or walking along Broadway in New York, the yellow substance he yearned to taste was a piece of hot cornbread, a little journeycake, the bread of his infancy which his mother broke up into his milk and which he tasted among her kisses.

"To eat cornbread once again! To eat the cornbread of Prendes, next to the fire in the kitchen of my house." What happiness those idealized mouthfuls promised him! To be able to eat cornbread symbolized recovered health and strength returning to his miserable body, the soundness of his stomach and the healing of his liver, the joy of living, of breathing the breezes from his beloved hills and from the Voz forest.

"We shall see!" Pepe said to himself, sitting in the middle of the road, covered with dust, surrounded by the trunks in which he carried the bait he needed to buy a little affection from his relatives, savages to their very hearts...if not affection, a little care and concern in exchange for the wealth which to him was no more than glass beads.

He delayed calling his relatives; he resisted calling out, "Hey, Rita!" as he had years ago, to have them come out to the highway and help him up to the house with his luggage. Because without help, he would not be able to make it up the hill. He put off calling because he was enjoying that solitude in his narrow, humble valley which received him peacefully, silently but as a friend; and he was afraid that the people would receive him less kindly, revealing their greed through the obsequious smiles with which his presumed heirs would certainly receive their wealthy relative. Finally, he made up his mind:

"Hey, Rita!" he cried out as in the past when he used to run around the brook and called from the meadow for his lunch to his sister who was in the house.

A few minutes later, surrounded by Rita, her husband Llantero and the five nieces and nephews, Pepe Francisca rested in the hallway of the old house on an old leather easy chair which was a legacy from his forefathers.

But the air of his hometown did him no good. After one feverish night, filled with memories and the strange discomfort that comes from finding the home of one's dreams is cold and silent, Pepe Francisca felt he was tied to his bed, held there by pain and fatigue. Instead of eating cornbread, as he had wanted, he had to go on a diet. Nevertheless, although he could no longer eat the food of his dreams, he wanted to see it, and he asked for a piece of poor yellow cornbread to keep on the bedspread where he could look at it and touch it.

"But of course!" All the cornbread he wanted. Llantero, the greedy brother–in–law, the unsuccessful emigrant, was ready to turn his whole harvest into cornbread in exchange for the treasures in the trunk and the wealth that still remained in America.

Rita, as her brother had feared, was a different person than he remembered. The affection from their childhood had died; she was village woman, faithful to her husband to the point of obeying him even in his faults. She was now like him, greedy and totally vicious. His nephews saw him as the uncle with untold fabulous riches who was taking too long to share them because he was not as close to dying as they had hoped.

Attention, solicitude, care, and demonstrations of affection were not lacking. But Pepe understood that in reality he was alone in his parents' house.

Llantero, even though he was the craftiest fox in the district, could not hide his greedy impatience.

When he was able, Pepe got out of bed to try, by holding on to the furniture and leaning against the walls, to go down to the corral to smell the odor of the stable, which, for him, was exquisite, since it reminded him of his earliest childhood. The cow stalls smelled like the lap of Pepa Francisca, his mother. While almost dragging himself along, he searched around the beloved corners of the house to sniff his sweet memories, the invisible relics of his childhood at his mother's side, his brother–in–law and nephews nosed around the trunks, insinuating at every moment their desire to sack their prey. Pepe finally gave them the keys. Greed stuck its hand in up to the elbow and filled the house with rare and precious objects whose use those greedy savages were not even certain of; and meanwhile, the emigrant sentenced to death tried to look out into the garden and with useless efforts to extract a few crumbs of affection from his sister Rita, the one who had loved him so much.

His last fever caught him on his feet, and with it came a soft, melancholy delirium, an anxious obsession with his heart's whim, to eat a little cornbread. He asked for it between clenched teeth; he wanted to taste it; he carried it to his lips, but his sickened sense of taste repelled it in spite of his deepest desire. That heavy, yellow, viscous mass of dough that symbolized a healthy village life to him, the joy of living at home in his beloved town, made him retch. Llantero, who had reached the bottom of the trunk and was getting ready to claim his fat inheritance, coddled the dying man, humored his mania; and every morning he placed before his eyes the best toasted loaf of cornbread, prepared just the way he liked it.

And one day, the last one, Pepe Francisca, in his delirium believed he tasted the yellow bread, the bread of the villagers who spend year after year breathing the air of their hometown surrounded by their loved ones, his fingers, grasping anxiously the edges of the sheet and thus signaling his death, found pieces of cornbread which he broke into crumbs.

"Mama, more cornbread," sighed the dying man without anyone understanding him. Rita sobbed occasionally at the foot of the bed; but Llantero and his children searched the depths of the trunks in the next room fighting over the last spoils, cursing one another quietly so as not to revive the dying man.

Breaker's Conversion

It was raining torrents, and a furious wind, which Breaker did not know was called the auster, swept implacably across the earth; like a cavalry charge, it cleared the streets of pedestrians, twisting the streams of water falling from the clouds into obliquely striking whips. It was impossible to find shelter on the porches or in the doorways because the wind and water invaded them, too; every creature sought shelter; doors closed with a crash; little by little the noisy city grew quiet, and the unleashed elements took the field like an army which had won an assault on the town.

Breaker, whom the storm caught stretched out on a wooden park bench, first took shelter under the leafy branches of an Indian chestnut tree and was, as the saying goes, soaked to the bone, before climbing onto the bandstand in the gazebo. But he was quickly chased from there by a whiplash of faithless clear water which had lain in wait to attack him from the side with the cold fangs of a crystal serpent, which seemed to lick lasciviously the pale flesh appearing here and there through the holes in his clothes, which were falling from him in rags.

His old, stiff, cheese-shaped hat, which made one wonder whether hats could suffer liver ailments, since it had turned from black to yellow as if it had jaundice, looked like the Alcachofa fountain with its circle of spouts. When he lifted his feet, shod in straw shoes that looked like terra cotta, the mud gave them the appearance of the root system of an ambulating bush. Still, Breaker looked just like a miserable little tree or bush on whose dry leafless branches someone had hung dirty rags out to soak, or perhaps to convert the dead bush into a scarecrow that walked and ran about fleeing the storm.

Breaker was forty years old and had made so little progress in his job as delivery boy that he had almost given it up without having acquired any benefits from the guild. Therefore, he was always broke, and for this very reason they had thrown him out of the miserable hovel where he had been sleeping. They had become tired of this scandalous all-night drinker who had not paid his rent for years and years.

"Well, too bad for them," Breaker said to himself without knowing what he meant, and stretched out on the public bench to toughen

his hide, he thought, until the fury of the heavens showed him otherwise.

Economy states the law of work as satisfying one's needs with a
minimum of effort. Breaker vaguely thought that the important part
of the rule was the minimum effort and that his needs had to go along
with him and be minimum also. He was often very disoriented and
usually drunk; he slept a lot, and since his stomach was ruined, he
lived on illusions, flatulence and the bad taste in his mouth, on old
and frequently spoiled food, a lot of red liquid and sometimes white,
if it was brandy. He wore what other people threw away, and with
pride in his parsimoniousness believed it was his right to refuse to
carry packages except, perhaps, on Palm Sundays or whenever a little
money was an absolute necessity.

One day, seeing a labor union demonstration at which someone
was carrying a sign asking for "Eight Hours of Work," Breaker
thought trembling, "Christ! Eight hours of work! And they throw
bombs around for that! With eight hours of work, I'd have enough to
live all summer, which is the most difficult time because of all the
tourists."

If he had fifty cents in his pocket, Breaker was unable to handle
a suitcase or even stand up straight.

But he did have a certain kind of passive bravery verging on the
heroic in the face of hunger and cold.

Usually, he walked around sadly and quietly, and he believed
with a certain degree of vanity in his bad luck, which he called not
merely bad but beaten beyond recognition.

His nickname Breaker (he could not remember his last name; his
first name must have been Bernardo, although he would not swear to
it) had been his since childhood, without his knowing why, just as
dogs do not know why they are called Spot, Boy or Ruff. If he had
known what sarcasm is, he would have considered his nickname sarcastic since he had probably enjoyed fewer breaks than anyone anywhere. The fact was that approximately thirty years before (all cold
and hungry years), there had been three street heroes, a kind of
Three Musketeers of the back alleys, called Smoker, Breaker, and
Cord. The tragic story of Smoker, Breaker knew, had already made
the papers, but his own story never would because he had outlived his
glory. No one remembered any longer his boyish pranks; his reputation, which had almost become a justification for his delinquency,
had died and disappeared, as if the neighborhood as it grew older
had lost its sense of humor and was no longer in the mood for jokes.
He himself now avoided excusing his laziness and destructiveness as
the feats of that famous street hero, Breaker.

"So? The world is cruel; no one remembers the good times." He
saw the young men of years ago walk by with graying hair, men who
used to laugh at his tricks and give him money to see him buy his

cigarettes and wine. But he would not approach them to ask them for anything now, because they would pretend not to know him.

He knew very well that he was alone in the world. Sometimes he thought that a newspaper or an old broken book, which he heard a laborer slowly trying to read aloud, might have been company for him; but he did not know how to read. He did not know anything. He would sidle up to a group of workers standing on a corner in the square, wasting their time pretending to look for work, and he would listen quietly to their more or less incoherent conversations about politics or social questions. He never ventured his opinion, although he did have one. His main idea was that it was foolish to ask for eight hours of work. But, rather than listen to their foolishness, he wanted them to read the newspaper to him. He paid more attention to what the newspapers said, the ideas were better put together.

But even the newspapers never got to the point. They all said that no one earned enough money, that a daily wage would not buy the necessities. What exaggerations! If more people were like him, they would be able to live on practically nothing! Oh, if he could work the eight hours that they asked for as a minimum (he did not think the word "minimum" of course) he would consider himself rich with what he would earn. "It was all about asking for tools, land, machinery and capital, just to work! Christ! What madness!"

There was something else the poor required, which no one remembered: consideration, respect, what Breaker had come to call, in his messenger–boy philosophy, "give and take." What was give and take? Well, nothing; just what Christ had preached, as Breaker had sometimes heard, the Christ whom he alone knew, not to serve Him but to heap insults upon, with no particular malevolence, of course, just because he wanted to talk like the others and swear like the rest. Give and take meant common courtesy, the freedom to go where you like, to live on an equal basis with gentlemen and to know how to read; to go to a theater without money, which had nothing to do with the desire to show off or have a good time. Give and take was not keeping a ragged man out of all the warm, comfortable places because of his dirty clothes. Since it was apparently impossible for everyone to be equal as far as the wherewithal, that is, money, is concerned, for everyone to have decent clothes and even new clothes occasionally, since there was not enough money for everyone to have a share, why could not equality and brotherhood be established in everything else? Things which could be done without any expense, such as having the rich and the poor treat one another with the same courtesy, as inviting a friend for a drink, as having everyone teach whatever they know to the poor, as greeting them in a friendly manner, letting them sit next to the fire, walk across carpets, be senators or bishops, have a good time without bothering anyone and even take a bath once in a while if people felt a person needed to. This was give and take; this is what Breaker felt Christian democracy was all about and what socialism should be, like the world itself, "socialism," something that is social, interactive, together: give and take.

He left the bandstand and ran out of the gazebo, soaking wet, cursing under his breath the Founder of give and take, and the Founder's Father, and he ran into the town looking for better shelter. But everything was closed, at least to him. He walked over to a cafe, but did not enter. It was a public place, but the waiters would throw Breaker out when they saw how dirty and shamefully ragged he was and that he was not about to spend anything. A working messenger boy would have been allowed in, but he was little more than a beggar, not even a beggar because he did not beg, he just wore the uniform and they would probably literally kick him out. He knew it from experience. He walked past the provincial government building where the lockup was. "They would let me in if I were drunk, but not sober and without having done anything." Breaker had no idea what else might be in that great building; in his opinion the building was a jail, a place to hold people against their will, to fine them or draft young men for the war. He walked past the university in whose cloisters a few magistrates, who were not needed in court, walked about while the storm continued. It never occurred to him to enter there, since he did not even know how to read, and everyone there was learned. The guards would throw him out of there, too. He walked past the courthouse, but there was no need for witnesses that day, the only proper business Breaker could have there since he was not accused of anything. As a perjuring witness, unaware that he was committing a crime, on many occasions he had sworn to tell the truth, and in effect he had, about whatever they ordered him to say. He vaguely realized that it was wrong, but the reasons were so complicated! Besides, when fine young gentlemen like the lawyer, the clerk, the bailiff or some rich citizen asked for his testimony, it could not be too bad because those who ordered him to declare as true whatever they had told him to say were considered respectable by the entire town.

He went next to the library, which, though public, was not for people who, as he appeared to be, were poor beyond hope. Instinct told him that they would throw him out of that large room heated by two giant fireplaces which he could see from the street. They would be afraid that he would steal their books.

He passed by the bank, the barracks, the theater and the hospital, all closed to him. At every one of these places there were men in caps whose only purpose was to keep Breaker out.

He actually could go into the stores, providing he left immediately as soon as it was obvious that he who had nothing was not going to buy anything. In the bars, he always found a little give and take!

In the meantime, the skies poured buckets and he trembled with the cold, soaked to the skin. Breaker ran alone through the street as if pursued by the water and the wind.

He came up to a church. It was open. He went in and walked to the main altar without anyone saying anything to him. A sexton or a beadle walked across the nave next to him and looked at him without wondering why he was there, without suspicion, as if he were just one of the faithful. Nearby, next to the epistle pulpit, Breaker saw another beggar, kneeling, deep in prayer; he was an old man with a white beard, who sighed and coughed a lot. The temple echoed with the hacking of his cough; it was a sad, annoying sound which must have bothered the other devout people scattered through the naves and chapels; but no one protested, no one paid any heed.

In comparison to the street, the church was warm. Breaker began to feel less uncomfortable. He went into a chapel and sat down on a pew. It smelled pleasant. "It was incense or candle wax or both and more; it smelled like his childhood." The flickering of the candles was homey; he liked the tranquil saints who looked at him sweetly. A bishop with a shepherd's cap in his hand seemed to greet him saying, "Welcome, Breaker!" And he felt it was only fair that he should reply with the sign of the cross, but he did not know how.

He did not know anything. When his eyes became accustomed to the darkness of the chapel, he perceived a group of women kneeling in a corner opposite a confessional. Now and then, a figure left the group and approached the large, dark box from which another similar figure withdrew.

"There is probably a Carlist in there!" thought Breaker, with no desire to offend the clergy because he honestly believed that Carlist meant the same thing as priest.

He began to enjoy what he saw. "But what a lot of patience that gentleman must have to stay in that closet for so long. I wonder how much they charge? Evidently nothing. Those women are leaving without paying."

And nothing happened. They did not throw him out of there. When there were fewer people in the chapel, since the women, once dismissed, left soon after, Breaker saw that those who remained noticed his presence. "What if I am doing something wrong?" he thought; and just to be safe, he knelt. The noise he made on the rail attracted the attention of the confessor who looked out through the door in front of him and watched Breaker with interest.

"Was he going to throw him out?" Nothing like that. As soon as the priest dismissed the penitent who was on the other side of the small grating, he looked out the door again and signaled to Breaker with his hand.

"Are you calling me?" thought the ex–messenger boy.

He was indeed calling him. He blushed, something he did not remember ever doing.

"That's funny," he said to himself, but he was very pleased and sat up straighter in his place. They were calling him, thinking he was going to make his confession. They made him go ahead of those young men who were waiting in line. What a great honor for Breaker! No one had ever treated him like that in his life.

The priest insisted, signaling with his hand, thinking that Breaker had not seen him.

"Why not?" the derelict asked himself. "Try everything. It is not like the Town Hall, here. When I wanted them to let me vote, just to see what democracy was all about, it turned out that, although it was for everyone, it was not for me because of some business or other with the tax records."

And he stood up and went to kneel in the place that the penitent had left vacant.

"Not over there, over here," said the priest, making Breaker kneel before his knees.

The poor devil felt something strange in his breast and warmth on his cheeks, somewhere between embarrassment and an unknown feeling of tenderness.

"My son, pray the act of contrition."

"I do not know how," answered Breaker humbly, understanding that there one must tell the truth honestly, not like in the courtroom. Besides, the words "my son" had touched his soul and one had to take this very seriously.

The priest led him through the prayer.

"How long has it been since your last confession?"

"Well, my whole life."

"What!"

"Never."

He was a virgin mount of unconscious impiety. He had only been baptized; he had not even been confirmed. No one had been concerned with his salvation, and he had only taken care, and badly at that, to keep from dying from hunger.

The priest was a pious and prudent man who guided him and taught him what he could in a brief period of time. Breaker was only a great sinner from the point of view of sins of omission; aside from that, his worst faults were his unrestricted drinking bouts and his rascally cursing, which was as harsh as it was free of unholy intent. But while he may never have gone to confession, his penances had been considerable. He had fasted often, and the cold, the wet and the hardness of the holy earth had mortified his flesh more than a little. In this respect, he was a worthy recruit for the desert; he had the body of an anchorite.

Little by little, Breaker's heart began to participate in the conversion that the priest so seriously and in all good faith was trying to realize. His heart was easier to convert than his head, which was hard and did not understand.

The priest had him repeat the articles of the faith and his loyalty to the Church, and Breaker did so very willingly. But the priest wanted something else; he wanted him to express spontaneously in his own way what he felt: his love and faith in the religion in whose breast he was being sheltered. Then Breaker, after thinking it over, cried out as if inspired:

"Long live Charles VII!"

"No, no; that is not it at all! It is not necessary..." said the priest smiling.

"But they call all Carlists clerophobic..."

"That is not it, either, man!"

"Well, priests..."

Finally, putting off purely formal and linguistic questions, it was agreed that Breaker would continue the lessons his new friend was giving him in that temple which had been open to him when all other doors were closed, there where he had escaped the sharp lashings of wind and water.

"So you have got religion, Breaker," the other derelicts said to him, joking at the seriousness with which day after day the poor devil kept working at his conversion.

And Breaker replied, "Yes, and I am not ashamed of it; I have gone over to the Church because at least there, there is give and take."

Numero Uno

Primitivo Protocolo's good parents raised him like a hothouse plant. The child certainly needed care because he was very sickly; every draft gave him a cold and he was always first victim, the nominative case, of all the epidemics that Herod's agents, the microbes, sent against the tiny troops of the city. The boy was skinny, stoop-shouldered, dusky and parched; he was a living example of chicken pox, measles, scarlet fever, jaundice, colds, bronchitis and diarrhea, kept alive only with great quantities of sulphurated castor oil and Scott's Emulsion. His body was like the fourth section of the newspaper: a living advertisement for the best-known patented medicines.

In spite of everything, it was evident that this tadpole would not let go of life; his earnest desire to bury his roots in this evil world gave him a strange energy in the midst of his debilities; and the proof of the value of this nervous tenacity was evident in that, although he was always on the brink of dying, he never did. He always more or less recovered as soon as one illness left him and before he fell victim to another. With one-tenth of his suffering, any other person would have died ten times and even if he could have survived somehow, he would have gladly turned in his resignation from an existence fought for at such a price.

But Primitivo, as well as his parents, was determined that this frail stalk would resist every storm, and resist he did, at the cost of sweat, worry, fright and money.

Don Remigio, his father, could not conceive of a world which would outlast his little boy. Since there were so many good, healthy and flourishing things on earth, he felt that the divine plan would be fulfilled only with a protracted age for that miserable bag of sparrow skin and bones in which a few molecules had unwillingly joined together to form pathetic tissues which were fighting to break apart and take the music of their oxygen, nitrogen, carbon and other elements elsewhere.

Even in the most violent attacks of illness, Primitivo maintained an expression of firm resolve not to die, in those bright black eyes which stared at everything as if wanting to possess, use, capture and corner it.

If this excessive desire to live at any cost was a kind of concupiscence, there was no runt alive more desiring than this miserable weed who was a diamond to Mr. Protocolo.

For this very reason, the spectacle of continued danger, of the constant threat that that entire diminutive and weak structure might fall apart and be carried away by a diabolic draft of air, was all the more regrettable.

His flesh would not prosper with even the best morsels, the most reputable tonics and after the most complete convalescences, and the boy would not grow, even to stretch out in his bed. What grew in him, in an extraordinary manner with each fever and each upset, with each attack of bronchitis, was what his father called his talent: a sharp intelligence for understanding and remembering whatever discursive subject matter that had managed to survive in that moral atmosphere of commonplaces in which his risky existence was transpiring.

But Don Remigio, instead of being frightened by that alarming precociousness, sought food and exercise for it. Instead of having to go through on his own all that portion of sordid mathematics discovered by Pascal, that other prodigy whose father had hidden every book that could teach him mathematics, Primitivo could save himself the effort because his father surrounded the bed—in which his son was more evidently dying than living—with as many technical books, maps and scientific instruments as necessary for him to learn what no one else his age knew.

So it was that when Primitivo abandoned his bed and was first able to attend school, the institute and prep school, he numbered his classes by his triumphs and by his colds. He always returned home sick but laden with honors.

In school, he was at the head of the class and every little while he brought back a basket of medals and honor certificates. Neither he nor his father ever tired of all these prizes, of so much ostensive testimony to his overwhelming superiority above the rest of mankind.

Father and son enjoyed such prizes with the gluttony of all–consuming, sugar–loving gastronomes. They lived in a perpetual surfeit of vaingloriousness.

Unfortunately, the current system of instruction was not lacking in elements to satisfy this rascally vanity, because the norm was to convert "noble emulation" into a brutal fight to feed pride and egoism. Intellectual worth was measured by the devilish rod of odious comparison, destructive to all humility and charity. When the child entered a particular school, he saw the heavens open before him, because there those chicken fights of application and merit acquired heroic proportions: those who knew the most were major generals, military chiefs, Achilles, the Cid.... Primitivo, who was knocked over by the breeze if a bird flew too close to him, was always the Napoleon in those campaigns in which, if there were no actual bullets, there was something no less dangerous, no less mortal an attack on the health of those children: their self-respect, their hatred of others' merit forced them to work fifteen or more hours per day.

This illustrious little runny-nosed boy left well prepared to undertake the more serious studies at the academy which would grant him a license, the immediate objective of his career.

Of course, Primitivo, just as in grade school and in high school, was always first in the academy: if there were grades, he received outstanding marks with honors; if there were class ratings, he was *número uno*.

In the Protocolo household, no one could imagine a greater misfortune than the one that would strike them if for once Primitivo had fallen to second place. Horrors! One dare not even think it!

And that rascal, as he began to grow a little sturdier, as if square roots and logarithms fortified him better than tonic and cod liver oil, was developing...well, let us say, a little meat on his bones which could pass for healthy flesh. He was still parched looking and yellowish green. But he had improved somewhat and many months had gone by since he had caught a bad case of pneumonia.

Among all the youthful victims of the polytechnical principle of noble emulation, Primitivo earned a reputation for learning that was equal to the fame of the seven learned men of Ancient Greece.

Of course, Protocolo-Lepijo's knowledge was limited, by choice, to textbooks and their contents; the boy simply despised anything he did not know; and so, for example, he considered all literary men and lawyers imbeciles and ignoramuses because the first group did not require a profession and the other usually enjoyed its financial rewards without too much effort. Simply because the examinations were not rigorously scientific, he considered law so much frivolity; and so it was with everything. He was so totally ignorant of anything that he had not studied according to his own perfect system that he did not even suspect its existence. From these premises he deduced that he knew everything worth knowing.

It became second nature for him to see himself as *número uno*. Even when physical weakness made him dream that strange plurality of selves in that alarming anarchy of consciousness in which it seems that each mysterious center of one's life shakes off the yoke of its particular cerebral dominance, even in those mad visions in which he became many different Primitivos, he continued being the first among them all; yes, all those inner Primitivos were the first ones in line. Of course, Primitivo left the academy as *número uno* in his graduating class and he transferred this advantage to the Primitivo corps' muster.

But the sad part was that he believed the world was another class roll or muster in which the first place belonged to the boy who knew and could explain in a wink the most mathematics, whether or not in agreement with Euclid.

His idea was that no one would get ahead of him; he was *número uno* in the academy, which was also first in demanding more than any other.

He began to notice to his great astonishment and displeasure that society did not overly admire him.

His office supervisor was already condescending toward him in a way that mortified him and seemed unfair; in his supervisor's class, his supervisor had graduated in one of the last places.

The second person who had treated him with less consideration than he felt he deserved was a very pretty blonde whom he approached at a dance only to be soundly rejected with the frivolous excuse that she had already said yes to a government official who had no more than a high school diploma but who was taller and better looking than Protocolo and who weighed at least thirty pounds more than he.

He began suffering many such unpleasant experiences. He went to the theater and saw that the audience overwhelmed with applause musicians, dancers and tenors, poets and even orators; but it never occurred to anyone to ask to see the *número uno* of Primitivo's graduating class. He was the type of wonderful mathematician to whom it would never occur to make simple calculations with the following data.

Each year in his school there was another *número uno* who graduated with the same great honor. The academy could document, excluding those who were deceased, at least thirty or forty *número unos* who were no more nor less than he. Considered in this manner, Primitivo came to form part of a general chorus.

In the entire nation (not to mention other countries), there were many *número unos* in each graduating class. Therefore, it was necessary to multiply twenty times forty at least.

There were many other schools which, without calling themselves academies and designating students' merit by numbers like so many hotel rooms, also had their little geniuses; that is, their own *número unos*. At this point, no one knows what the multiplying factor might be.

Besides schools, in industry, in the liberal professions, in the school of life, there were a multitude of activities in which many young people engaged their "noble emulation" and in which the smarter and more fortunate were correspondingly *número unos*.

Therefore, Primitivo began to get lost in a veritable multitude. Moreover, everything in life is not intelligence, diligence, in learning or in art. There were those infinite *número unos* whom chance had moved ahead; first in energy, bravery, favor, grace, maliciousness, shamelessness, physical beauty, hard work, opportunity, pure luck...so many different kinds! And this entire considerable portion of humanity was worth as much as poor Primitivo. They were all first in something, all sadly underrated *número unos* in each one's own particular kind of human misery.

But the Protocolo boy did not figure things in this way because, while he did improve his health somewhat when he finished school and he did stop looking so much like a chicken, his constitution did not improve because all the disappointments in his life turned into bitterness.

He wanted life, mysterious, complex and varied as it is, to be a kind of race for the first place, a race of *número unos* governed by the rule of rewards analogous to those employed in such contests by the Jesuits or by the academies. And since life was not that way, his pride, his bitterness and his constitutional weakness turned Protocolo's character into a moral substance that was a yellow, viscous, nauseating poison. Envy, the inspiration of his wit, allowed him to create for himself a certain reputation for satire which only earned him quite a number of slaps in the face, snubbings, frights and more serious setbacks.

He could find no consolation in his spirit for so many disappointments because there was nothing vague, poetic, mysterious, ideal, or religious about him. Everything in him was positive to the second degree, numbered, orderly, and squared. Everything for number one and let everyone else in line bray like a jackass.

And since the uncertain good health he enjoyed was fictitious, when he reached the age when others began to grow a stomach, to put on that healthy corpulence that would carry them into old age, Primitivo, consumed with spite, disappointment, and his own bile, began to fall apart, to shrivel up and double over, to become the square root of his own little person.

Then he simply disappeared from the world. The newspapers said he died from consumption; the truth was that on one very hot afternoon, *número uno* evaporated into stinking rottenness. Since his father had already died, Primitivo left this planet with no one to mourn for him. Why should those in second, third, fourth or last place have cried for someone who had despised them so much?

And there was still the worst part.

The life hereafter!

When they asked him for his title to glory, the prize which he wanted, his academic graduation certificate listing him as *número uno* was just so much old paper.

When Primitivo began to lose patience, they said to him, "Just look at all those people who have to go first ahead of you."

And they went in front of him to occupy their place in glory on God's own class roll, a better place than Protocolo's was reserved for these infinite sheep and lambs from the human flock who had never been *número uno* in anything during their fight for existence. The humble lambs who patiently allowed themselves to be fleeced in life went passing by: the poor, the humble, the saints, the martyrs, the plain and common people. Many of those blessed ones did not know how to read. Not one knew how to count. There they were the aristocracy.

Next came the middle class virtues, and sweating with gloom, Protocolo began to figure out that the kind of merits he presented there were the last in the esteem of the one who gave out the rewards. Christ! In glory, the academy's *número uno* was coarsely vulgar.

Anonymous, nondescript people without tickets, wandering shapes on the train of life's dangerous journeys, kept getting on ahead of him.

And Primitivo Protocolo, with his ticket in order, his *número uno* printed clearly for everyone to see, waited in vain, forgotten on the platform, for a charitable hand to load him on among the stacks of bundles in the last baggage car.

And he is still waiting his turn there; waiting as one must in Sancho Panza's story of the goats.

He will eventually board, because God's mercy is infinite. But God only knows when *número uno* will be actually called to the charity ball.

Bad Habits

Doña Indalecia was a sixty–one–year–old widow who was born to be the chief administrator of a government office or an investigator with the Internal Revenue or perhaps even better, a police chief. But her beliefs, preferences and misfortunes led her to the path of religious piety. She was a zealous church woman, not of the kind who gaze at the saints, but of the kind who rush madly about performing acts of charity in a corporate manner, whether collective, joint–mandatory or anonymous. She was very religious and very charitable, but only within an organization; she believed more in the Church than in God; she thought that Jesus had let himself be crucified so that one day there would be a shining College of Cardinals and a Congregation of the Index.

She was consoled by that sad prophecy, "The poor ye shall have with you always," because this meant that there would always be the Saint Vincent de Paul Society, the Little Sisters of the Poor, and so on. She loved charitable organizations more than she loved charity; one could say that human suffering did not evoke her pity until the unfortunate were gathered under the protection of some grand fraternal order. In her opinion, the poor were only those who were officially registered with some organization or other; to these she dedicated her life. But, the poor souls! Her methods were horrendous! She had an Inquisition at the tips of her fingers; she was an Argos for uncovering petty vices and discerning true from false need; she would not give away a crust of bread unless she had a written requisition. Her glory was to see luxurious, clean, orderly, well–disciplined progressive and modern institutions in which those who sought refuge could not breathe except according to the regulations. And to speak more truthfully, Doña Indalecia would have preferred that an institution, which had been created so clean, so immaculate, so completely brand new, never be used, never be spoiled by the wretches for whom it was intended. She came to see the institutionalized poor as an abstraction—a passive, cold idea. And so, when some unfortunate man who required help revealed that he had the same weaknesses as everyone else, Doña Indalecia rebelled. Bad habits among the destitute seemed monstrous to her.

Her convictions about the form charity should properly take, with reasons and accounts, became more firm after her conversations with

progressive thinking priests, professors, and after reading certain
books.

When she read that spontaneous and gratuitous alms, given in the
street by chance, was blind charity like blind faith, counter–productive and something akin to a crime, she was overjoyed. "Of course!
That is what I have always said!" She saw a criminal in each beggar
and an anarchist in each pedestrian who gave away a quarter.

Her vigilance not only pursued false beggars with their petty
vices, but also the wealthy who did not know the proper way to be
charitable, who gave money away blindly, sometimes wildly.

She had been watching, without his knowing it, Don Pantaleón
Bonilla, the director of the provincial library, a little old man whom
gossips considered very absent–minded, when in effect his mind
never wandered since it was always on one thing or another. Bonilla
had an obsession—his books, his philosophical theories and ideas
about scientific bibliophilia. He did nothing but go from his house to
the library and from the library home, always hurrying in order not to
waste time, bumping into pedestrians, lamp posts and tripping over
curbs. When one of his collisions gave him a bruise, he sighed and
instead of coming to his senses, straightened his glasses, which he
thought were to blame for everything.

He was extremely courteous to Doña Indalecia; he always ad-
dressed her, that is, tipped his hat, without really seeing her; but the
poor man did not realize that she was following him and that she was
scandalized by his conduct.

"And he is supposed to be a learned man!" Doña Indalecia
would say to herself when she followed him from corner to corner
until she dropped him off at the library. "There is no charity to be
gotten from that man; there is no organization strong enough; he is
ruining everything we do! This is outrageous! The governor should
take a stand on this as he has done on abusive language!"

But Bonilla never noticed anything; he thought he was innocent.
The fact was that as soon as he left his house, beggars surrounded
him; the lame, the crippled and ragged women with three or four
small children grasping onto their skirts, their blouses or their coat-
tails, ambushed him; barefoot street urchins like little curs grabbed at
his sleeves. And what was Bonilla's crime? Nothing to it! He threw
away coins like a hot air balloon throwing off ballast to stay aloft.

As could be expected, excessive demand overwhelmed his comings and goings. The chorus of beggars became a crowd, an uprising,
a wave cutting off the spendthrift's path. Don Pantaleón came to realize one day that they would not let him pass by.

"But what is this!" he exclaimed looking all around him as if
asking for help. "Where have all these poor people come from?
Aren't there any policemen?"

"If there were, you would be under arrest," answered the voice of Doña Indalecia who was following him and who, when she saw him turn around, stood directly in front of him.

And after the widow scared the poor and the beggars away, doling out blows with her parasol, her fan and even her rosary, just as Jesus threw the merchants out of the temple (this comparison is Doña Indalecia's), when Bonilla saw himself free of the pests, the good woman, to collect her reward for her services, delivered him a proper sermon in a bittersweet voice.

"I cannot believe," she managed to say to him with many more words, "that a learned man like you does not know that to practice charity as you do is an offense to God and to society! You are corrupting these poor people, encouraging their laziness and subsidizing their bad habits. All this money you throw right and left is spent on alcohol and other such nasty things. When you die and ask the poor whom you have helped to carry you flying into heaven, you will find that it cannot be, because your wards will be in hell; and those who are not going there will be so drunk that they will not be able to stand up to help you," she began.

Smiling with great interest, Don Pantaleón listened to the old woman. When she ended her sermon, he realized that he had no valid argument to answer her with.

"And so, Madam, for years and years, without wanting to, I have been corrupting society and subsidizing vice? And completely without intending to! I have so many things on my mind! No, as far as reading goes, I have read what you just said about orderly and organized charity. Famous philanthropists and very classic saints have convinced me that lazy, disorderly, casual and empirical alms giving is harmful. But, since I never have the time to even turn around! However, I will mend my ways; I will. From this moment forward, I will not involve myself in other people's business; everyone should mind his own; you take care of charity and I will take care of my books; everyone has his calling."

For a while, Doña Indalecia could see that Bonilla was improving; beggars no longer approached him on the street. They allowed him to walk by freely knowing that he was no longer tossing away coins. The widow sighed with satisfaction. It was a conversion.

But after a journey she had to make to establish some charitable organization or other in another province, she returned and found, to her great disappointment, that her good Don Pantaleón was casting grain to the right and left like the mill of Saint Isidore the Laborer. The swarm of beggars followed him again, like bees whose hive is being moved from one place to another.

After several days of spying, the implacable widow summoned the demagogue of handouts once again.

ST. CHARLES COUNTY COMMUNITY COLLEGE LIBRARY
WITHDRAWN

But this time it was he who spoke at great length. "What do you expect, my dear? Apparently, it is a bad habit, a vice. I do not have any others. I have tried to follow your advice. I have not given away any money for a long time, and it has not set too well with me. Not giving away money has been worrying me. I felt a strong urge, a kind of remorse, and a thousand doubts began to bother me. Perhaps you and your organizations were wrong. And I am not able to handle doubts or new problems. I have enough to do with my own! Imagine, Madam, me trying to establish a criterion for morality. Why should we be good, moral people, anyway? To tell the truth, I am not yet certain why. But just in case, I do try not to act like Cain.

"So, do you think that because of the few miserable pennies I throw away, I am going to burden myself with such complicated questions? Besides, I do not have the time or strength to exercise any kind of methodical, wise and orderly charity. And there are many people like me. Should those of us who occupy this inferior position be denied the right to exercise charity? Let us be the petty cash of philanthropy and give away some small change. I honestly do not know what to do with my spending money unless I give it away. I do not smoke, gamble, or go out with women, and I do not drink. I have to have some bad habits! Let me have this one. I assume you do not want me to start drinking! Excuse me Madame, but I do not have the time or the inclination to stop giving handouts. If I do not do it, I feel something is missing and the energy I spend trying to restrain myself is energy I need for other things, and I become distracted from my more important thoughts and duties. It is terrible! I am going to start giving money away again like clockwork. I ask you not to worry yourself about it and make it worse. And do not come preaching to be about heaven. I do not expect such a great reward for the money I give out. Nothing of the sort. It is enough for me to believe that I am not condemning myself by giving this handful of change to that woman who has a baby hanging on each arm.

"And just look at that pale, sickly and shivering fellow over there. Do you think he is going to seduce some lovely young girl from a good family with the money I am giving him? And after all, Madam, if they are anything like me, if they, too, have their bad habits, well, you religious people have no faults; but that is not the case with learned men nor with the poor; if they have bad habits, they have to be cheap ones, small stuff. And so, this one is for you, and this one for you, and this one for you...."

And Bonilla, carried away with his speech, began to throw small change away by the handful, like the laborer who throws seed without thinking, just hoping, about the plants which will grow. And as he gave away large and small coins, Pantaleón would say, "Here, take this, for your bad habits and vices."

The Duet

The grand hotel Eagle stretches its enormous shadow over the quiet water out to the floating pier. It is an immense square building, graceless, five stories high, a chance stopover, a travelers' hospice, an anonymous cooperative of indifference, the shareholders' enterprise, a contractual directorship which changes often, twenty servants who leave and are replaced every week, dozens and dozens of guests who do not know one another and who look without seeing one another, who are always "the others" and whom everyone assumes are the same people who were there the night before.

"One feels lonelier here than in the street, almost as alone as in the desert," thought the shapeless form of a man drawing on a cigarette, wrapped in a summer coat and leaning his arms on the cold steel railing of the balcony on the third floor. In the darkness of the cloudy night, the glow from his cigarette shines like a firefly. The sad spark moves, fades, disappears and glows again.

"That is another traveler, smoking," another figure two balconies to the right on the same floor thinks. And the woman breathes a weak sigh of vague consolation for the indefinable pleasure she gathers from having unexpected company in her sadness and loneliness.

"If I should become suddenly ill and if I called out in order not to die alone, that man smoking over there would hear me," the woman continues thinking, clasping a fragrant, heavy woolen shawl to her fragile, delicate chest.

"There is a balcony between us; his room must be number thirty-six. When I had to get up and call the maid this morning because she did not hear the bell, I saw some very elegant men's boots left in the hall."

Suddenly a distant light went out and created the effect of lightning seen after it has passed.

"The light on the point has gone out," the figure in room thirty-six thinks with some sorrow because he now feels more lonely in the night. "One less person awake, one more person asleep."

The ships at the pier, the cumbersome barges tied to the docks in front of the hotel looked like shadows in the darkness. The water acquired a voice and shone a little, like a visual apprehension, like the remembered trace of a light that has passed, like the phosphorescence that is caused by illusory stimuli in the retina. In those shadows which were sadder because they were not complete, it seems that the idea of light and the imagination composing vague forms require help so that one can perceive, even though only confusedly, what can be seen below. The barges move little more than the minute hand of a great watch. But now and again they strike against one another with a tenuous, sad, monotonous noise accompanied by the tide which is heard in the distance, imposing silence with a voice like an owl's.

The town of businessmen and tourists sleeps; the houses sleep.

The figure in room thirty–six suffers anguish in the silent dark loneliness.

Suddenly, as if it were an explosion, a dry, repeated cough makes him tremble, a cough like the sweet song of a mourning dove coming from the right, two balconies away. The man in room thirty–six looks and perceives a figure darker than the night, the color of the barges below. "The cough of a sick person, a woman's cough." And thirty–six trembles, remembering himself; he has forgotten that he was doing something foolish, verging on the dangerous. That cigarette! That sad nocturnal vigil in the night air! A deadly orgy! That cigarette was forbidden; opening the balcony at such an hour, in spite of the fact that it was August and there was not a breath of air, was forbidden. "Back inside, back to your tomb, to your horrible jail, cell number thirty–six, back to bed, to your niche."

And thirty–six, without another thought for the woman in room thirty–two, disappeared, closed his balcony door which made a sad metallic complaint and gave the same sad feeling to the figure in thirty–two that number thirty–six, while smoking, had felt when the spotlight on the point was extinguished.

"Completely and totally alone," the woman thought. Although she was still coughing, she remained there as long as there was company, the kind of company that stars must share as we see them from here below, stars which, though they appear to be similar and together there in the infinite, do not know of one another's existence.

After a few minutes when all hope that thirty–six might return to the balcony was gone, the coughing woman withdrew also; like a soul that takes the form of a will–o'–the–wisp, breathes the perfume of the night, and then returns to the earth.

One or two hours passed. Inside, one could occasionally hear the footsteps on the stairs and through the halls of an unidentified guest suffering from insomnia. Rays of light entered through the gratings of the doors into the luxurious cells, which were horrible in their vulgar uniformity of elegant furnishings, turned about the room and then disappeared.

Two or three clocks in the city struck the hour with a solemn tolling which had been preceded by the light ringing of the less ominous and less significant quarter hours. A clock somewhere within repeated the alert.

Another half hour passed. The clocks announced it.

"Agreed, agreed," thought number thirty-six in his bed and imagined that an hour so solemnly struck was like the signature on a promissory note which the creditor, death, was presenting to his life. Guests were no longer coming in. Shortly, everyone should be sleeping. There were no longer witnesses; the beast was free to stalk its prey.

In fact, in room thirty-six, a rapid, strong cough which carried an inherent hoarse protest began to sound as if from under the slab of a crypt.

"It was the clock of death," though victim number thirty-six, a man thirty years old who knew desperation alone in the world with no companions except for the memories of his parents' home now lost in the distance by errors and misfortunes, a man with a death sentence stuck to his chest like a shipping label on a package at a railroad station.

Like lost cargo, he traveled everywhere, from town to town, looking for healthy air for his sickly chest, going from inn to inn, a pilgrim on his way to his tomb; each hotel he chanced upon looked like a hospital to him. His life was very sad and no one cared. There was nothing about his particular fate written anywhere, even in the Sunday supplements to the newspapers. Romanticism, which had had a certain compassion for consumptives, was out of style. No one was pleased with sentimentality, or perhaps maudlin feeling had gone elsewhere. Number thirty-six did feel a certain silent anger and envy for the proletariat, who was winning the sympathy of the entire public. "The poor workers!" everyone repeated, but no one remembered the poor consumptives, people like himself waiting to die, whom not even the newspapers mentioned. The death of one's fellow man, unless it attracted the attention of the Fabra Agency, did not matter to anyone.

And he continued coughing in the dismal silence of the sleeping inn, which was as indifferent as the desert. Suddenly, he thought he heard a soft distant echo to his own cough, an echo in a minor key. It was the woman in room thirty-two. There was no guest in room thirty-four. It was a vacant crypt.

The woman in thirty-two was coughing, in effect; but her cough was, how should one say, more poetic, sweeter, more resigned. Thirty-six's cough protested, sometimes roared. Thirty-two's cough almost seemed like the response to a prayer, to a *miserere*; it was a timid, discreet complaint which did not wish to wake anyone. Thirty-six, strictly speaking, had not yet learned how to cough, since most men suffer and die without ever learning how. Thirty-two coughed with control, with the art of an ancient, resigned and wise suffering which usually manifests itself only in women.

Thirty-six came to notice that thirty-two accompanied him like a sister keeping watch; she seemed to cough to keep him company.

Little by little, half awake and half asleep, in his feverish dreams, thirty–six transformed the cough in room thirty–two into a voice, into music, and he seemed to understand what it was saying as one vaguely understands the meaning of a melody.

Thirty–two was a woman, twenty–five years old, and a foreigner. Because of her poverty she had come to Spain to be the governess in a nobleman's household. Her sickness had forced her to leave their protection, however. They had given her enough money to get along on her own for a while, moving from inn to inn; but they had separated her from the children, of course. They were afraid of contagion. She did not complain. She thought first of returning to her own country. But why? There was no one there waiting for her; besides, the climate in Spain was better. It was naturally benign. This place seemed very cold to her, desolate with a very sad, blue sky. She had moved north because it reminded her of her own country. She did nothing else except move from one town to another and cough. She hoped madly to find a city or town where people cared about sick strangers.

The cough from room thirty–six evoked her concern and sympathy. She knew immediately that it was a tragic cough also. "This is a duet," she thought; and she even felt a kind of embarrassment as if it were an indiscretion, a kind of prearranged meeting in the dark. She coughed because she could not help herself; she tried very hard not to.

This woman in room thirty–two was half alseep, also, and suffering from a low fever; she, too, was almost delirious. She also transported the cough of room thirty–six to the land of dreams where all sounds are words. Her own cough seemed less tragic when it leaned on that manly cough which protected her from the shadows, from loneliness and from silence. "This is how souls keep one another company in purgatory," she thought. By an association of ideas, which was natural in the governess, she moved from purgatory to hell, to Dante's hell and saw Paolo and Francesca embraced in the air, blown by the infernal winds.

The idea of a couple, of love, of a duet, occurred to room thirty–two rather than to room thirty–six.

The fever inspired in the governess a certain erotic mysticism. Erotic is not the correct word. Eros, healthy pagan love, has nothing to do with it. But after all, it was love, the love of an old marriage, some peaceful company in the midst of the pain and loneliness of the world. And so what the cough in room thirty–two wanted to say to thirty–six was not too different from what thirty–six in his delirium began to imagine.

"Are you young? So am I. Are you alone in the world? I am, too. Does a solitary death terrify you? It does me. If only we knew one another! If only we loved one another! I could be your help, your consolation. Can you not tell from my cough that I am a good person, discreet, delicate, home–loving, one who would make this precarious life a nest of soft feathers, one in which we could approach death together while thinking of something else, of our affection? How lonely you are! How lonely I am! How well I would take care of you! How you would protect me! We are two stones falling into the abyss who strike one another on the way down and say nothing, who do not see or sympathize with one another. Why must it be this way? Why should we not get up right now and join our pain and cry together? Perhaps from the union of our weeping a smile would be born. My soul asks nothing more, nor does yours. And yet, you see how neither you nor I move from where we lie."

And the sick woman in room thirty–two heard in the cough of room thirty–six something very similar to what thirty–six desired and thought.

"Yes, I am coming! It is time and it is natural. I am ill, but I am a gentleman; I know my duty; I am coming. You will see how delightful the love that you know only from books, and can only imagine, actually is among tears while contemplating death. I am coming, if this cough would only allow me to. This cough! Help me, console me! Your hand on my chest, your voice in my ear, your gaze in my eyes...."

Dawn broke. These days, not even the consumptives are as romantic as they should be. Number thirty–six woke up, having forgotten the dream of the duet of the cough.

Perhaps thirty–two did not forget; but, what was she going to do? The poor invalid was sentimental, but she was not crazy, nor was she a fool. She did not think for a minute to look for the reality corresponding to her night's dream, the vague consolation of the company of a nocturnal cough. It is true that she would have offered herself in good faith; and even awake in the light of day she reaffirmed her intentions; she could have dedicated the rest of her miserable life to taking care of that man's cough. Who could he be? What kind of man was he? Bah! Just like all the other Russian princes of one's dreams. Why even try to see what he looks like?

Night returned. The woman in room thirty–two did not hear anyone coughing. Several things told her that there was no longer anyone in room thirty–six. It was as empty as room thirty–four.

In fact, the sick man of room thirty–six, without remembering that changing one's position is just changing one's pain, had fled from that inn where he had suffered as much as in every other inn. A few days later, he left the town. He did not stop until he reached Panticosa where he found his last inn. No one knows if he ever remembered the duet of the cough.

The woman lived longer, two or three more years. She died in a hospital, which she preferred to an inn; she died among the Sisters of

Charity who were able to console her somewhat in that terrible hour. Psychology would have us imagine that one night during her sad insomnia, she remembered and longed for the duet; but probably not during her last moments which were so solemn. Or maybe she did.

Lucius Varius

Scriberis Vario fortis, et
hostium Victor, Maeonii carminis aliti...

The poet Lucius Varius was striding down the Clivus Capitolinus as if carried forward by his own weight. Whoever saw him walking by in such a hurry would probably have thought that he was just another businessman leaving the Temple of Juno Moneto, which he had just passed on his left.

Without stopping to pay homage or even to look at the solemn gold statues of the twelve major gods, the *Dii consentes* high on the pedestals he was walking past, he went directly to the Temple of Saturn which appeared to him as an impressive mass on his right hand side. But the poet ignored the temple just as he had ignored the gods and continued on his way; neither the Olympic powers nor the daily business of the treasury had anything to do with the concern that was pulling him along in distraction down the hill.

In front of him, beyond the prison walls of the Tullianum, the sun was setting and that is what Varius watched as he descended. The sun was dying and he was remembering that other sun that had set in Brundisium that would never leave the tomb at Pausillipus, the poet Virgil. He did not notice the Concordia, which he passed on his left although he looked in that direction; he directed his attention to something higher and more distant, the Tabularium, which stood on the side of the Capitolinus measuring itself against the mountain.

He gazed at the Tabularium because it reflected his thoughts. A bitter, ironic smile came to his lips. He stopped. "The sun is in the western sky, Virgil, the tomb, glory, the Tabularium, eternity and nothingness!" All these thoughts passed over his brow. The Tabularium was the archives, a useless precaution of Roman pride to immortalize what is most fleeting and perishable. The archives were used to save manuscripts. For what purpose? Where were the archives for souls? Papyri, diptycha, multiplices were all saved there; *tabullae* and *pugillares* filled the compartments of chests, but the poet is sent to the grave. Ah! The entire funeral ceremony with its *libitinarius*, *pollinctores*, *dissignatores*, *tibicines* and *praeficae*, the entire apparatus of the *funus publicum* was folly because it all ended in the *capulus* or in the *cestrinus*, the sarcophagus or funeral urn, in oblivion. And after *"Molliter cubent ossa,"* fine words, nothing.

Oblivion. Will the poet be forgotten also? Had Tucca and he done wrong by disobeying the deceased's wish to have his poem thrown on the fire and keeping the work safe for immortality?

September was almost gone, the month in which they had buried Virgil a few years ago. And Rome, the Rome of the Forum, the Comitium, the Rome bustling at the foot of Janus Bifrons, the Rome of bankers and merchants who forgot the three neighboring Fates and committed themselves to commerce with a fervor worthy of eternity, certainly did not think of Aeneas's poet.

The bees interested in business buzzed around the doors *qui sunt in regiona Basilicae Pauli* brushing into Varius without seeing him. He was still alive but they no longer saw him! He continued on his way, bringing himself to the *vicus* gate, walking automatically, impelled by habit, and found to his surprise that he was among his own kind, surrounded by the movement of literary life among the bookstalls where, seated or standing, readers chatted, the literati came and went with their copy slaves carrying their beginners' notes, triptycha and poliptycha, some with hands still stained from the printer's ink in which they had soaked the calamus. Varius, standing among these men, felt a sudden irrepressible repugnance. The passionate ephemeral life of literature at that moment horrified him. Erroneous criticism, new taste, envy, and wrath were in the air forming part of the feverish anxiety which is typical of things which are impermanent and fleeting. To him, it all seemed a mortal, cruel fight occurring in a flash of lightning.

Life was a flash whose light was used by passion to wound, satisfying a desire to destroy others' well–being. Among the many horn cases and polished wooden handles of rolled manuscripts illuminated by the last rays of the sun, he saw the titles of his departed friend's work: the *Bucolica*, the *Georgics* and the *Aeneid* as well as his own sons, the offspring of his wit, his *Panegyirc to Augustus* and his famous tragedy *Thyestes*.

But there on the shelves, in the *nidi*, it was as if these works had been buried alive. He trembled; it seemed to him that his writings there, on the book dealers' shelves, were a part of him that had died, something of his own soul that had been buried. The parchment, the papyrus, the waxed tables would die, too. In the bookstalls, the body was in state; in the libraries, it would lie in the sarcophagus. What else was the Tabularium but a pantheon?

Without speaking to anyone, ignoring the chatter of sycophants and neophytes who smiled and greeted him, he set off towards the *Via Sacra* on his right. He left behind the Portia Basilica and, stopping with his back to the Curia Hostilia, he looked silently and disdainfully at the Forum in front of him, the Forum which was silent at that hour; but in his imagination it was still teeming with the noise of frothing calumny and lies. There, rhetoric was used for evil and harm, more openly than in books. The deserted Rostra resembled the remains of shipwrecks on the sea of political and religious passion. So much wrath and so many deceptions had been spawned there; and blood had been spilled there, most recently the blood of Caesar! Caesar, the hero of his poem. As if he wanted to protect his image of Caesar so that they would not kill it, too, in that place, so that they would not drown his fantasy and heart in those emanations of bloodshed and hatred which he felt rising up from the Forum, Varius fled in search of cleaner air and climbed the Palatine, passing on his left the temple where the vestals lived.

However, not only was it difficult for him to breathe in the Forum; all Rome was suffocating him. Breezes coming from the east passed over his soul, those breezes which we sometimes feel like a gentle wind among the wheat, like the verses of Virgil, gusts of spiritual desire and a pious contemplation of the future. The poet of terrific feasts and the complacent courtly singer of Augustus, Varius felt his Roman life had become a form of slavery and, without knowing for what, he began to search for something more, something new, something pure and free, more noble, which must be there toward the east. His sweet friend the Mantuan Swan felt upon approaching death a desire to turn his eyes to the east, to cross the sea and touch the soil of that Greece which is the master of men's souls.

"The sea, to the eastern sea!" Varius thought. And in a moment, he traced in his mind the itinerary of the imaginary voyage. First, to Naples to bid farewell to the Pausillipus tomb; then to Brundisium, and from there to the sea, to plow the waves aboard the Liburnia across seas immortalized by Homer and Virgil.

At dawn on the following day, Varius left Rome, leaving the Esquiline in the distance on his left side, and nearer, on his right, the Palatine and Caelian hills. He then began to travel across Latium, the land of the hidden god, along the Campanian highway. He reached Naples, visited Virgil's tomb and meditated there a while; a few days later, he headed toward Brundisium; he passed Venusia, famous also in the history of poetry, and crossed the ancient mysterious land of the Iapyxygis, sons of the Orient, perhaps, and entered a town where the poet had last seen the light of day.

A narrow, heavily laden ship took him on board in the port of Brundisium, and with no little melancholy, he left Italy, which seemed to come bid him farewell on artificial islands in the port, islands crowned with temples and statues, guarded by high walls which thrust into the sea a dike of arches under whose roofs the light played with the sparkling waves.

Standing on the bridge, a solitary Varius contemplated the foggy line on the horizon which meant land. To the north was the Illyrian coast; farther south were Caonia and Epirus. Across the Molossan heights he could see the Pindus range.

Afternoon was descending when, leaving behind the coasts of Corcyra, the ship reached the Chimerium promontory. Varius was writing in the light of the sunset with a flying stylus, noiselessly scratching the thin wax coating on the polished spruce wood. The proximity of this land which is so sacred to the muses infused him with a feverish inspiration; he wished to enjoy the breeze, to open the sails of his fantasy to the breath of poetic dreams. But he was working on a poem which he had entitled "Death." With a symbolic fatality, the ship flew, pointing its bow toward the estuary of the Acheron which poured its tribute of water into the sea. Very nearby, directly off the bow, was the Acheron, the river of the dead; on the port side was the Chimerium.

Varius did not believe in the mythology that filled his verses with names and images; but if as a philosopher he did not believe, as an artist he was pagan in his heart and in his fantasy. Besides, he was vaguely superstitious after a fashion. At first, he ridiculed superstition, but he was as weak confronting it as he was when facing the vice of his own intelligence.

He had attended that feast at which Augustus had parodied the celebrations of the twelve major Olympic gods in spite of his official zeal to try to restore the cold Roman cult as the official religion. He had smiled when he heard Horace declare, "It is fine for the Jew Apella to believe all of this, but I know what is important with respect to the gods." He, like all Rome, followed a tendency which is often noted in the west when one's own religion begins to decline and when skepticism and negation reign; there is an oriental reaction; Theosophic mysticism, the strange beliefs of Oriental magic and mystery fill the spirit of those who abandon to oblivion the lares and penates and the cult of Vesta which could no longer find priestesses.

Varius did not believe positively in anything; but anything prestigious—a hallucination, a trick—would find its weak, docile reason to be included in his love of enchantment. Augustus himself pursued Mithra, Cybele, Isis, and Serapis, and yet he was afraid of lightning, of the flight of eagles, and always put on the right shoe before the left, just as a precaution. And Augustus was a god. Why should Varius, his poet and priest, differ?

The Chimerium was straight ahead, Greece was the nearest coast, the Acheron mixed its own melancholy waters, which in turn had received the waters of the Cocytus, into the waves through which the Liburnian galley was plowing. What more could one expect? Everything was a symbol of death, of shades beyond the tomb, of the underworld. Varius came from Naples and had passed close by the Avernus, that mournful lake untraversed by birds and on whose banks the Sibyl of Cumas spoke from her cavern. Everything was illusion, sinister, a sign of death. And Varius recalled the start of his journey, that bad humor which had overcome him descending the

Clivus Capitolinus and had made him despise the noisy, ephemeral, and insubstantial life in Rome which he had fled. And, still, he maintained his desire for immortality, his yearning for eternal ideality.

His verses, which also spoke of death, were plowing the wax at the measured pace of his silent and subtle stylus. Suddenly, as if feeling in his brain the magnetic weight of intense staring, he lifted his head and saw before him the sirens of Ulysses, the winged women, the sad nymphs with soft voices, the divinities of pillage with souls of vultures clearly apparent in their sinister beauty, thin faces with a plastic perfection about their features. The sirens surrounded the ship and, dragging their wings on the waves, followed its course; the crew was sleeping; Varius, alone with the enchantment, his ears open, his hands untied, heard the song of the sirens calling him to death.

The chorus sang, "Lucius Varius, why do you work in vain? You are working for death and oblivion. Abandon art, abandon life and die. Behold your destiny, the fate of your soul and your verses. You will be forgotten, your books will be lost, your fate will be that of so many other sublime minds whom, very soon, the world will call antiquity. Very soon, a wise pedant will pretend to know all that classical antiquity knew, thought and dreamed. They will call classic everything chosen by chance to survive, for a while, universal destruction. You will not be considered great by posterity because your works will be lost; rats, moisture, centuries of ignorance and a hundred other similar elements will be your critics, your Zoilus; they will destroy you and the world's indolence will have a fine pretext for not admiring you, for not even knowing that you existed. In vain your fame reaches the clouds; Virgil admires you in vain and has said as much; his words will be attributed to friendship and sweetness; Horace will speak in vain of your aquiline flight through the realms of epic poetry; pedants of the future will claim that by praising you, Virgil and Horace were praising Augustus, whose courtly singer you were. The arrival soon of a severe, loyal and noble man called Tacitus whose praise of your tragedy Thyestes will be in vain; posterity will not believe in you and will know nothing of you. You belong to the shipwreck. Like you, hundreds upon hundreds of illustrious minds in this Greece which you are seeking, in this Italy which you are leaving, will perish from fire, dispersion, dust, blood, barbarism and ruin, and because of the simple decomposition of matter. Egyptian papyrus will be scarce; parchment will be expensive; there will be no lasting surfaces on which to write; and upon the very same pages on which your wisdom, ideas and dreams are written, other men will write other sciences and other errors, other dreams, superstitions, hopes and laments. Along with your tragedy Thyestes, the tragedies of three hundred and fifty tragic poets will disappear, and humanity will say that there were only three great tragedians in Greece, those whose works survived. And, of the six hundred Helenic historians, very few will remain. The same thing will happen in your land. With you, Cornelius Gallus, Asinius Pollio, Calvus and the venerable Ennius, Mevius, Cinna and Varro as well as the chorus of Latin tragedy will perish. Just yesterday you contemplated in Rome the Tabularium with envy. The archives! They will be no more. They will be dust, then air, then nothing. You visited the Vicus Sandalius, the refuge of new and old books. The Vicus and the books will be ruins, dust and wind. Pomponius Atticus's desire to collect copies and editions will have been in vain. This passion to store volumes will grow in vain. Sanmonicos Serenus will be so proud of his library of sixty–two thousand volumes! Rome will one day have twenty–nine public libraries, a little dust from the desert which will stop moving for a moment to deceive the vanity and curiosity of mankind with capricious forms. The winds of oblivion will continue to blow and the dust once again will cross the desert. Varius, move ahead toward death, be oblivion. Do not write. Die."

"Die, die, to not write any more," repeated the chorus.

Varius trembled. He passed his hands over his eyes; he shook off the delirium and drank deeply the breath of the cool afternoon air, and by the last light of the sun, he continued tracing his stanzas, plowing the wax with the silent subtle stylus that moved with even measure.

He believed the prophecy. He felt his verses had sunk already into the nothingness of oblivion, but his inspiration continued burning in his brain, stronger and more free. Varius breathed deeply; his soul shook off a chain which fell broken at the feet of the traveler, the chain of time, glory, and his vile self–interest.

"Ah, everything is dust," Varius's hexameters said to death, "everything was nothing, everything passed, everything fell into oblivion." But the breeze was pleasant; and gracefully rocking his spirit, the rhythmic meters refreshed his soul. The western sun was sublime in its orange, pink and gold sadness; the colors of the sea charmed his eyes; the peace of the waves was like silent music, and Varius, whom the world would never know, as long as he lived, was a poet.

The Imperfect Wife

Mariquita Varela, faithful wife of Fernando Osorio, noticed that for some time now she was becoming an intellectual without intending to, without expecting to squeeze any benefit from learning. The situation was simply that since her oldest children, Fernandito and Mariano, had become little gentlemen, could put themselves to bed, and spent most of the day at school, she had more than enough time on her hands, after taking care of all her responsibilities, to bore herself silly. And in order not to be idle, in a fantasy world concerned only with first accusing and then completely forgiving her husband, spending her time thinking badly of him, she had discovered a passion for more and more reading, something so unusual in her that at first she thought it was funny simply because it was so strange.

She would read anything. At first, since her husband was a doctor, she began to deal with his book dealer; but she tired very quickly of her repeated shocks over the horrors which human suffering permits and even more over learning about those scandalous medical techniques, many of which were presented in living color in those large, glossy prints of which Osorio's library was a veritable museum.

She took a different direction and read moral treatises, philosophy, and literature and came to understand conclusively that all that one derives from extensive reading is a vague sadness that exists somewhere between voluptuousness and resignation. But it was less horrible than the shock of contemplating human physical suffering in medical books.

She succeeded in finding numerous examples of edifying Christian literature. At this point, she came to an abrupt stop and started taking reading seriously because she began seeing something useful in it, something that would help her in her station to understand her status as a beautiful woman who was happy, well cared for, loved, content and who was beginning to see in the distance the unhappiness of old age, wrinkles, and gray hair and the melancholy death of good sex. This horror was still quite far off, but it was a bad symptom to be thinking about it so much.

At any rate, her moral and religious readings helped her more than a little to accept her life. But what often happens in such cases happened to her also; she was happiest as long as she was a neophyte and kept her childish illusions of considering herself a good person simply because she had good thoughts, excellent intentions, and preferred those honorable meditations and readings. She became less happy when she began to glimpse the true nature of perfection without deception or vanity, without that insane confidence in one's own personal merit.

Then, upon seeing the remoteness (much farther off than old age and its discomforts) of true virtue and real merit without pretensions, she felt her soul fill with bitterness, with icy loneliness. "Without me, without you, and without God," as Lope de Vega had said, without me, that is to say, without herself because she did not respect or know herself and thus distrusted her vanity and egoism; without you, that is to say, without her husband because, well, that best kind of love had flown away a long time ago; and without God, because God exists only where true virtue lies, and there was no positive virtue in her. She had to be brave to continue sounding the depths of her soul where, after so many efforts to be humble, pardoning injuries and loving the cross of matrimony which she bore alone, she discoverd that it was all presumption, romanticism disguised as piety, hysteria, and psychological suggestion derived from loneliness, something merely to help her bear her husband's absences as he followed his worldly distractions. True merit and certain virtue were further beyond, much further beyond these.

And the bitterness of having to despise herself, if not because she was bad but because she was not very good, was the only solace which she could permit herself, to which she could always appeal without ever being disappointed when, having completed all her daily responsibilities, which she now thought were ordinary and easy—even though she felt that they were difficult—she remained alone and awake by the lamp, waiting for her good husband Osorio who usually returned, sometimes very late, with his shining and vaguely dreamy eyes, flushed cheeks and in a friendly and jovial humor, generously covering his eternal companion's neck and forehead with kisses, which, according to her instinct and apprehension, came there from his lips but were given by his soul somewhere else far away.

One night, Mariquita was reading *The Perfect Wife* by the sublime Fray Luis de León. She read, blushing with shame while her heart froze, "And, for the same reason, God does not state here that a wife should be pure and faithful, because He does not even want her to imagine that it is possible to be otherwise. Because, truthfully speaking, it is a form of impurity for the chaste wife to think she can be otherwise or to think that she is doing something for which she should be thanked."

And as if Fray Luis had written for her alone, at that very moment, and was not writing but speaking into her ear, Mariquita felt so ashamed that she hid her head in her hands and felt on the back of her neck, not a parting kiss from her husband, but the breath of the

Augustinian friar who, with the words of the Holy Spirit, scorched her brain through her cranium.

She tried to be brave in her penance and continued reading, and even reached the passage a little farther on which read, "And certainly, just as he who sets off for Santiago, although he never arrives, is considered a pilgrim, so without a doubt, the woman who permits herself to think of these things, which are the road, is already on the way to whoredom."

And with her hands always pressed to her head, Señora Osorio remained thinking, "Me, on the road to perdition and because of the very thing which, if it now makes my conscience feel sorrow, pain and remorse, I had always taken before as the harsh proof of the merit of my sacrifice, my bitter draught!"

In a series of sad, ashen pictures, Mariquita's history passed through her memory, her most recent history of respected wife who, though loved, had no illusions and who was in effect alone and constantly alienated from the rest of society.

She was almost always alone, because every now and then she returned for a few days or for a few hours. First the alienation had been complete; the battle of motherhood: pregnancy, birth, nursing, toilet training, scares and sleepless nights next to the crib; then back to the beginning: pregnancy, each time more frightening; with less strength and more presentiments of terror; birth, the fight with the wet nurse who always wins because weakness overcomes the mother; more sleepless nights, more concerns, more fear, and a husband who begins to desert, in whom something which seems to be nothing begins to disappear, only that most wonderful kind of love, the wife's dream of a lifetime, her only love affair, the only sensuality permitted to her but always only in moderation.

Like a ray of springtime sunlight, with some respite from motherhood, the woman is reborn and continues to be the object of others' admiration as expressed in quick, subtle flirtations: a pantheistic phenomenon so subtle and universal that it brings joy and pleasure without appearing sinful. What one desires is to see oneself in the eyes of others as in a mirror.

Her husband himself offers her the opportunity to return to the theaters, to dances, banquets, and promenades because he feels remorse and does not want to carry things too far. He insists, he actually insists, that his little wife, why not, circulate and return to society and entertain herself modestly. And Mariquita returned; but society was now different. To begin with, she no longer knew how to dress, to dress really well. Without knowing why, as if it was shameful, she refused to wear her jewelry; she did not dare wear dresses too tight nor remove the numerous foundations which she wears now to stave off the attack brought on by her pregnancies, the attack which carries threats of more serious illnesses. Besides, she understands that she has lost her sense of style. A secret instinct tells her that she should try to appear modest and to look like just another one of the many women who fill the theaters and go to dances without anyone really seeing them.

Very late, at a certain hour of the night, without even trying to prevent it, she yawns; and if the gathering has something to do with music or with a sentimental drama, when they reach the sad part, she remembers her children, their blonde heads resting on the pillow alone by the light of a small night lamp, without their mother. What a terrible sin! What remorse! And for what? Just to allow herself the rather unpleasant satisfaction of sniffing out other people's love affairs, of trying to catch wayward glances, of contemplating the triumphs of those beautiful women who today enjoy their brilliance as she had enjoyed hers once upon a time. Such yawns! Such remorse!

With the memory of her impressions of these unpleasant evenings out still fresh in her mind, Mariquita resolved not to return to society, and for a long time she kept her word. Her husband's cajoling her to make the sacrifice was all in vain; she would not leave the house.

But the years passed. The children grew up and the last birth was a long time ago. Age brought a certain corpulence, a certain physiological equilibrium which comes with health and good, rich blood, and an inner springtime begins to bloom, coming to the surface as the reminiscence of certain flirtations, as a longing for old dreams, for innocent foolishness and for the serious, triumphant though dead love of her husband.

Mariquita remembers now, reading Fray Luis, the nights she had spent at that time.

She was always late for the show because her children detained her, because she tarried over her hair since she was out of practice setting it, and in spite of her daring cosmetic experiments, because of the difficulty she was having finding in her mirror the Mariquita of other days, the one who had had so many admirers.

Her admirers of other days! Here, she truly felt a remorse that had not become anything else and which before, when she was going through it, had been the icy disillusionment of a shameful and intimate bitterness. Here and there, in various chairs in the balconies and boxes of the theater were some of those former admirers. Time had been kinder to them because they did not take care of children and stay locked up in their houses for years and years. For those illustrious and elegant men, the years stood still! They were still apparently impressed by beauty, but by other women's beauty, the more recent ones, the younger ones; those rogues were faithful only in their admiration and love of youth. Long dead jealousies, the fight for the continuation of a dream and of sexual instinct had made her attempt all kinds of foolish acts, in an effort to try to exercise on those former Platonic lovers the powerful influence which her glances and smiles had had. She looked at them in the same manner of years ago; some did not fail to notice the provocation and participated in this melancholy sweet reminiscence.

Then Mariquita (she was unable to see this) became more animated and younger looking; her eyes, extinguished by sleepless nights at the side of the crib, recovered the brilliance of her passion, of satisfied vanity and inspired coquettishness. Brief flourishes! Quickly those former admirers let her know unwillingly through their distraction that there was no need to carry this love any further. What is over is done. They returned to the object of their present admiration, to the contemplation of a constantly renewed youth; and at this point, Mariquita, the former mistress of those hearts, did manage to catch now and then a glance that had gone astray, guided perhaps by compassion, perhaps carrying a lie in its expression. How horrible! How shameful! To coax such a petty demonstration of an ideal love, she suffered these sordid disillusionments. And so, frozen and confused, she had stopped presuming, stopped seeking glances, because of her pride and dignity, of course. But that pain, the pain of that disillusionment, she now thought after reading Fray Luis de León, was the pain of adultery!

So great a sin with no pleasure! Disillusionment which was criminal to experience! It entailed humiliation, a loss of self-esteem and remorse. And she, who had offered to God as redemption for other ordinary faults and venial sins the defeat her vanity suffered—more than her vanity—the defeat of the pure feeling of pleasure derived from the burnt sacrifice of affection!

Yes, she had walked, barely able to conceal her delight, those first steps toward the shrine of Santiago, therefore she worshipped whoredom—certainly not! That was too much to accept. The angelic Augustinian poet would have to forgive her. But while she was not totally despicable, neither could she consider herself good: neither good nor bad, and still suffering greatly. She suffered immensely and she was not perfect. God could not love her, nor would her husband. Her husband because he was weary, God because He was offended.

And the unhappy woman thought, while waiting up for her husband who was probably with other women, "Dear Lord! True virtue is so lofty and heaven so high that sometimes they seem mere dreams and illusory because they are beyond our grasp!"

The Engraving

I used to attend the lectures of that philosophy professor with a profound interest that the classes of many other illustrious faculty in the same university did not inspire in me, others in that scientific Babylon, some of whom expressed with enthusiasm and the fire of conviction, many with self-assured pride, a multitude of philosophical systems, the entire corpus of varying modern theories which today seek to rule the realm of thought. The great wave of positivism, Taine's science of *petits faits*, predominated; for each course in pure metaphysics there were four or five in the critical history of philosophy, and twenty in physiological psychology under this or some other usual course title.

Dr. Glauben lectured on metaphysics, and with the entire methodological apparatus of the most recent developments, he used his course to prepare his students to understand that there was a heavenly father. This idea, which the majority of professors and students would admit as readily in an elegant salon as in the intimacy of their home, was in the lecture halls of one of the most prestigious universities of the country an occurrence which could have cost Dr. Glauben his reputation as a deep thinker and competent man of science, had his arguments supporting his unembarrassed and daring affirmation been clearly drawn from among the decidedly outmoded ideas of any of the classical schools of deist thought.

But far from considering Dr. Glauben antiquated, students and professors attended his lectures or read his articles with attention and profound interest. At first, they succumbed to the temptation of accusing him of mannerisms, of being too innovative and revolutionary in philosophy, too fond of exploring uncharted areas of inquiry. This was the general opinion initially, but after a few sessions, one noted that Dr. Glauben was absolutely sincere, that he sought for truth with genuine feeling and that he was searching for the idea of celestial paternity along the paths of rigorous logic as the only rational explanation of the world in which he expounded the history of his love, the supreme longing of his existence.

His weapons were of the most modern manufacture; he fought with the most recent discoveries of a discreetly attenuated positivism, with the same discourse and auxiliary sources used in the sciences. Everyone knew that there was no intellectual in the country who could surpass Dr. Glauben in the fields of contemporary science; he was a sociologist, physiologist, psychologist, naturalist, mathematician, logician and linguist. He was up to date on the latest discoveries; he handled the facts as well as anyone and had gone through all the grand illusions of ingenious idealism which had dominated his country. He presented the question as a Wundt or Spencer would have done, and he concluded like Saint Francis, Bossuet or Chrysostom. "There really is a God, God the Father; to deny our Father in Heaven, that is in the infinite and the absolute, is utter madness which will seem impossible in future ages.

"Rather than conceiving of a humanity which had passed from the theological to the philosophical age and from there to science, humanity as far as knowledge is concerned was in a period of embryonic struggle, very similar to the life of savages in their extrascientific interactions, a period which is a kind of intellectual chaos, from which, no one knew exactly when, one would escape to approach gradually a definitive theological age.

"That science looks for knowable truths, ones that are not merely believed, does not mean that less progress and less accomplished work will have been done when the final solution turns out to be something already obvious to the common, simple faith of the great majority of people. It is irrelevant, for the world of scientific progress, for the purpose of indicating the strength of the scientific method, that the conclusions of science regarding the mystery of the world be these or any other conclusions in particular; the quality of an affirmation is extrascientific; what matters is the mode of the affirmation; that the truth be either A or B does not matter to science; what is important is to know that the statement is true and that it is demonstrable. There may or may not be a God. No matter how much science may progress, in this matter it cannot conclude more than one or the other of these two statements. Therefore, there is nothing unusual in thinking that in some distant period of scientific understanding, so remote that one cannot even glimpse it yet, what may be affirmed as certain will not be any newer than this: Our Father is in Heaven."

Whoever may have maintained as a usual presupposition that the assumptions of contemporary thought are superior to those of classical thought, after attending Glauben's lectures for a few days would forget the habit of favoring any historically determined style of thinking whatsoever. Glauben analyzed with cold impartiality the most recent hypotheses which other professors expounded as astonishing novelties. He compared them and mixed them with older theories and they often acquired thereby the appearance of weak and transitory ideas. He had a rare, though not at all malicious, ability to erase the prestige which the polish of newness gave those doctrines which he submitted to his examination. And yet, he did not offend anyone; often, the very inventors of the theories that he subjected to that "historical bath" listened to him and could not really feel mortified because he did not disdain any idea; whether ancient or modern, thought was the nobility of the soul.

Glauben was tall, thin and pale. He was about fifty years old and had wavy black hair that was not turning gray; it was silky hair which obediently followed his fine, aristocratic hand. He touched his hair often as if feeling the movement of his ideas. At the same time, he placed his elbow on the desk, resting his chin on his palm, while his fingers still moved through his silky, black hair. He smiled almost constantly through a pained and melancholy expression. His gaze wandered distractedly in quick glances that were searching for nothing beyond himself; sometimes, at the slightest noise from the other side of the lecture hall door, his eyes looked frightened. If a student came in late, Glauben interrupted his talk and looked at him restlessly without breathing; after the student had walked in front of him and found his seat, Glauben breathed easier, smiled again and continued his interrupted chain of thought. When the hall clock struck the hour to end the lecture and the students showed their impatience to leave—there was no need for the beadle to call them—the professor considered the class terminated, whether he had concluded or not. On rare occasions, because he might not be able to overcome the distraction of his own lecture and thus would forget the time, he always had prearranged for a clerk to announce the hour. But whenever this ceremony took place, Glauben looked at the uniformed and restless usher in silence as if afraid that he had some particular message for him. "It's time," the good man would say with a slight bow. And Glauben, with a forced breath and smiling, would say to his students, "We will continue tomorrow."

After having heard his lectures over a long period of time, when I was taking a second course in philosophy with him, I became something of a personal friend. I was invited to his house. He was a widower; he had three children, two girls and a boy; the oldest girl was nine, the boy five and the youngest three. Glauben did not go out very much. When he took walks with his children, he returned early because he saw the evening coolness and setting sun as the lurking enemy of the health of his offspring. The cold, darkness, and dampness frightened him. If he went out alone, he would also return home quickly; he would hurry upstairs to the fifth floor, knock loudly at the door, and pale, with restless eyes, hasten to ask while they opened it for him, "How is everybody?" "Fine, fine," they answered. And Glauben would smile again and regain his normal color; and he would enter his home as peacefully as if it were paradise.

If they detained him too long after a lecture, at his club or at a university meeting, he began to grow restless and was finally unable to resist the temptation to go running home.

He did not travel. He was a great believer in the principle that a man of learning should see much of the world, meet many people and become acquainted with different customs and ideas, and so on; but he would not budge. While he envied those representatives who attended professional conferences, he never accepted such assignments.

One day, after we had come to trust one another, I dared to ask him why he never left the town and why he spent so little time away from his house. He liked me and believed that my respect for him and his ideas was sincere. He looked at me with a certain malicious sweetness and smiled in a way new to me, and after passing his hand over his forehead, I saw a new expression there, one less happy—something like grief—but still openly disposed to sharing personal confidences.

"I have," he said, "a kind of illness. You must promise not to tell our friends in psychological pathology anything about it, now! I do not want them to classify and present me in their clinical literature as an unwilling fine specimen to prove one of their hypotheses. But the truth is that I am something of a case. My sickness has a history whose origin is very clear, very definite. It appeared, or rather broke out, suddenly, during a crisis."

Glauben was silent for a moment. It seemed that he was doubting whether he should continue along that path of personal revelations.

With a calmer, more sober voice, he continued. "The thing is more serious than it seems because the secret of my illness is in part the secret of my philosophy."

He turned toward me to see the effect his words were having. He knew very well that, regardless of how much his apprehension as an unhealthy person might matter to me, if indeed he had any, his philosophy was much more important to me because I was incorporating it into my own thinking. It was becoming a part of me and beginning to guide my conduct somewhat.

"Have you noticed," he continued more worried at every moment that he might be speaking indiscreetly, "haven't you noticed that when we talk here privately about the ideas we discuss in lecture about my method, direction and above all, my conclusions, that I do not become as enthusiastic and I do not encourage you to adhere to my ideas and that it even appears that I am not grateful enough to you for your heated defense of my ideas in which you present them for me so faithfully, adding, besides, the charm of your own youthful spirit and a certain poetic flair?"

He was silent and smiled again as if asking my forgiveness for the harm which his words might cause me.

"Yes," I dared to reply, "I have felt on occasion a relative coolness, something like a wish on your part not to insist, as if you were presenting something which might offend your dignity."

"It is not a question of personal dignity but of something which might cause me a certain remorse and a twinge of conscience."

"Nevertheless," I exclaimed somewhat frightened, "your straightforwardness, your trust in your own ideas, I could never doubt them, even if you yourself..."

"That is very kind of you. But that is not the point. I try to speak truthfully; I firmly believe that what I express is true and reflects my feelings. I also believe my method is rigorous and leaves nothing to be desired; it seeks to impose no gratuitous presuppositions. That is not it."

After another brief pause, he continued. "It is this other thing." And with his hand forming a fist, he quickly gestured up and down in the air. "Since my wife died, I have held onto my children, just as if we had been shipwrecked. As if the entire world were the depths of a treacherous sea and my lap were the only safe place for them. My children without a mother—this idea had been a constant, unrelinquishing torment—an undeniable fact with no possible consolation. Because of its vast indifference, the world was their enemy because there was no mother. Even I, in spite of my love, seemed a stranger to that most intimate affection which the little ones needed; my clumsy male caresses and angularity were not the soft warm nest which their mother had provided. I know the meaning of anguish and suffering, my friend. I saw threats against the lives of my children in everything; the cold was their mortal enemy: a draft could take them away from me, and the cold indifference of strangers could take them from me, also. I could conceive of nothing more horrible, of no greater loneliness than their life without a mother. But there was an even more profound loneliness and a more complete abandonment.

"One night at the club, I opened a British journal and saw an engraving. It was a copy of a painting by Gregory or Hopkins or someone, titled *Orphans*. A dark-haired girl about ten years old, leaning against a carpenter's bench, was supporting with her other arm another little girl about three years old who was sitting on the same bench, but pressing her head very close against her older sister on the opposite side of a five- or six-year-old boy who was standing pressed very close to the big sister, as if seeking protection under the poor girl's ragged apron. They were alone; there was no mother or father. They were orphans, absolutely alone.

"At first, I was overcome by the objective impression caused by the artistry and was able to look at the engraving. But this disinterested observation merely allowed me to see more clearly. The three orphans looked alike, but the little ones, between themselves, looked into the distance at the future that was being imposed upon them, a mysterious and threatening one, with only a vague awareness of the cruel fate that was waiting for them, of approaching danger. In the thin, intelligent face of the older sister, there was a certain premature wisdom together with a certain resignation derived from her effort to be brave by force of will alone; this wisdom and resignation were inappropriate for her age, but there by the difficulties of their misfortune. She, so tender, so weak and so innocent, put her arms around her little ones, sheltering them. It did not matter, she seemed to say with a humble melancholy that was peaceful and resigned, defying the battle against hunger, cold and indifference, the chaos of existence into which they were falling. The little boy wore the most painful expression of the least calm; but he also seemed to be the least attentive to the cause of his sorrow; he was suffering greatly, but at the same time in an incoherent way he was darkly distracted by the spectacle of everything going on around him.

"But the supreme art of pathetic expression was in the face of the little three–year–old as she pressed her curly head against the frail body of her sister, seeking there the support of the mother who would forever be absent. The expression! What horrifying melancholy tranquility is found in the pain which is unaware of its own existence! What cruel, sublime brush stroke could portray thus the unjustifiable and meaningless suffering, the sacredness of innocent life, helpless, weak, abandoned and alone in an illogical and chaotic universe. Forgive me, but neither then nor now do I have the words to express that angelic expression in those eyes of the three–year–old who has neither father nor mother and who was searching for protection in the fragile embrace of another orphan.

"This contemplation dominated me. I felt I was becoming ill, very ill, deep within me; and nevertheless, I continued looking, suffering, understanding and imagining the suffering that is possible in life if one allows the imagination to expand and go deeper. My children could suffer the same fate; their father could leave them; I could be gone. Who knows? Perhaps that infinite suffering was the very beginning of death? Complete abandonment! My children alone in the world in which I know—I am a philosopher for a good reason— that no one loves as truly as a parent. This idea implies infinitely imminent suffering; I do not know what would have happened to my mind if my eyes had continued drinking in the bitter wine of that image, continued reading that bible of possible pain in that sublimely cruel engraving. Fortunately, I began to feel ill outwardly; I was dizzy and my stomach began to complain. I fell back in my chair and was confused for a moment; soon after, I left the club without anyone having noticed how much one man had just suffered there.

"I never looked at the engraving again. But ever since that evening, everything has become a series of symbols representing my misfortune to me—my children's loss of their parents. When I watch them playing, when I see them kiss one another with tender, angelic affection, I see the engraving; I see them alone, sad, orphaned, surrounded by the nothingness of a universe without paternity. Their bowed heads, their hair blown by the wind, their sad, sometimes dreamy, eyes, the thoughtful air of one, the solitary dove–like babblings of the little ones...all these scenes turn into portraits, prophetic sketches for the posthumous drawing. That is what they will look like when I am gone. Without a mother and then without a father!

"My spiritual life became impossible. I had to hide my feelings, of course; suicide, besides being immoral, was absurd because it was the very end which I feared: my children's abandonment. It was necessary to continue living, just as I had been. I found refuge in my work, in philosophy and in reflection, and I found there the remedy for my suffering. The idea of reality, of a universe without paternal affection, was too horribly miserable not to be false.

"The world could not be so evil a place. Creation, like my children, needed a father. And through old and new doctrines, oriental and western systems of philosophy both immanent and transcendental, I went searching for paternity as the categorical imperative of suffering. The infiniteness of evil, the absolute existence of desperation which the nonexistence of God the Father presupposes was too perfect a form of evil not to be something artful, a mere hypothesis, a polished theory, a geometric, regular and abstract figure which did not occur in reality but only in the sick mind of man. It could not be that the universe had no Father, our Father, into whose bosom I shall leave my children should my madness kill me before my time.

"By thinking that there is a God, a Heavenly Father; by thinking that in spite of all appearances to the contrary, the universe is a loving nest, a lap, I can live without a shield of strength. If my children should have no other father than I! But they do have one, don't they? Isn't it true that I prove it every day in my classes? That there is no valid positivism, no intellectual schools without the traditional, classical, serious, aesthetic and harmonious idea of an Eternal Father in Heaven, that is, omnipresent?"

Dr. Glauben had stood up, and so had I; he was trembling, I do not know if from fear; he probably was very pale. He told me as much. And he extended his hand to me, adding more calmly, "Do not worry yourself, I am not mad yet, completely raving at least. Sincere? Absolutely. I firmly believe everything I say in class. And it seems to me that I prove my statements."

He paused. "All in all, my integrity as a thinker, as a man of science, obliges me to declare these things to you; you now know my illness; you already knows its consequences, which are the subjective reasons behind my system. Do not be taken in completely, however. I can be, could be, mistaken. But when you have children, believe in God the Father."

The Torso

The Duke of Candelario claimed as his half the province, and he was not far off the mark because his pasture lands seemed endless and armies of tenants paid him rent. He had inherited a great deal from his illustrious ancestors but he had also acquired no inconsiderable portion by certain means which no one could call ill–conceived or beyond the service of his country.

He was advanced in years, one might say advanced in his golden years, first, because of the skill with which he had invested his time in things that would bear fruit, second, because of his usually healthy, happy nature, and third, because of the constancy of his strength and energy. He was a worthy farmer on a grand scale, intelligent, active, impartial with the poor, but he was attentive to legitimate gain. In this manner he increased his wealth continually and helped those around him earn a livelihood; he benefited only from the land.

If at this stage in his existence he served his country by making his estate productive, in years past he had served it by risking something worth more—his blood and at times his life. He had been a valiant soldier who became a general, and at all stages of his career he had had the opportunity to prove his worth in true tests of valor. But he was respected in his part of the country more for his open, cheerful and straightforward character than for his military accomplishments.

One should not assume that he thought the less of his family tradition because of his democratic leanings; this was the capital trait of his character and his blood. He had won the epithet of the Duque de los Abrazos for a very good reason. He often threw his arms—he called them his "oars" and they were not strangers to farm implements—around the shoulders of a humble field hand in a sincere gesture of friendship. The farmers worshipped him and accompanied him in his healthy, active life as hunter, laborer, and comrade at country celebrations.

He had almost always lived on his estates in a great palace that looked like a feudal castle in which the most aristocratic seigneury was evident in every detail.

This manorial lord inspired confidence in everyone who met him; his regal mansion, located in the midst of his lands, surrounded by forests, evoked dispassionate respect.

As long as Don Juan Candelario, the Duke of Candelario, lived, he surpassed everyone in the traditional reserve and formality imparted by noble lineage, in the imposing and aristocratic air of his house; even more impressive was the arduous conquest of his worthy spouse's silent opposition. She was as noble as he and no less worthy, but had less democratic tastes and was less expansive in her dealings with her social inferiors. The Duke, though he would often joke playfully, had an iron will and no one could command in his presence. Therefore, his great palace was open to everyone—because he wanted it that way—and he insisted on being treated as a wealthier farmer than the others, but not as a different sort.

He had only one son. As soon as it was possible, the boy's mother hastened to send him to England where he would study at Eton, then at Oxford and then in the worldly school of British society. The Duke did not object because it seemed reasonable to him that his heir receive a solid education and lessons in the life of a grand gentleman which he knew he would acquire at such a great distance. But this did not keep him from sighing occasionally when he noticed that Diego had surrendered to ideas, habits and manners that were quite different from that Castillian plainness which for Don Juan was natural and indicative of a correct upbringing.

His son looked more like his mother than his father, and the education that the latter called correct, cold and extreme, sealed these differences, which he lamented. But he did not complain. Everyone would be what they were intended to be. As far as the Duke was concerned, neither his son Diego nor anyone else would change him; therefore, as for the successor, let him be what God willed. He allowed everyone else to live with the same freedom he had claimed for himself, the freedom to live as he chose. But for the present, as long as the old Duke was alive, his household, regardless of the young gentleman's reaction, would continue functioning as it always had.

Diego, in fact, had an irresistibly strong dislike for his father's way of life. He, who had had students as servants and had learned in college to measure the distances that reality established by necessity between different social classes, saw a certain hypocrisy, or at least a ridiculous illusion in very bad taste, in that pretension to equality which could never be more than superficial and extend beyond appearances. These democratic pretensions, he thought, are a grotesque comedy which annoys us and would humiliate the poor villagers, too, if they had any sensibility.

What he could bear least, what nearly drove him to kill, were the happy confidences shared by the master of the house and the servants. Here the grotesque and unseemly verged on torture.

"It would be preferable," Diego told his mother secretly, "to do for one's self rather than be served by others in this manner. A servant who is not a respectful machine, a perfect automaton, is the greatest impertinence that could ever exist in the home. I have always distinguished true noblemen from the *nouveaux riches* by their servants. The servants of the *petite bourgeoisie* are usually careless in their dress, incorrect in the proprieties of service and all without the master of the house, who is probably a tyrant, ever noticing anything amiss which could broadcast his humble origins. A servant instinctively recognizes a true gentleman, and although he may have to suffer under a more severe discipline, he is happier and takes his post more seriously."

Don Diego almost felt hatred for his father when he saw how the Duke was treated by Ramón, a former companion of his military glory and trials and a hero from the ranks who had become the gardener, something of a manager and clearly the favorite in the Duke's household. Ramón worshipped Diego. Before the boy went to England, the veteran had fought his nurses and tutors to win the child's affection and the right to take care of him. So, when the boy was not sitting on his healthy knee, he was sitting on his wooden leg, if he was not riding on his shoulders grabbing his ears like the flanks of a horse.

When the boy was away, the gardener's affection did not wane; it became idealized when the formal little gentleman, who was now cold and polished, returned with the airs of a great lord whose slightest gesture revealed the true nobility of his blood. Ramón quickly changed half of his affection to respect; if once he had loved him like a household idol, now he feared him like a god, with a loving fear, recognizing the supreme justice of that superiority that was so evident in him. If with the old master of the house Ramón was personal, it was to follow orders; he had been implicitly commanded to act in that manner. About this there were no conflicts because he respected in the depth of his conscience the blood from which the young man derived his nobility. The Duke would have reacted violently had Ramón come to him with the formality dictated by protocol.

It is true that little by little, the veteran had come to assume that that equality and camaraderie were natural; and since everything Ramón said and did was acceptable to the Duke, and since his zeal for the prosperity of the manor was heartfelt and passionate, Candelario valued him more than a treasure. Ramón allowed himself to be guided along that peaceful route. Even in the presence of the young duke, he continued treating the older one with the same egalitarian frankness as always; he and everyone else would have been reprimanded severely if the Duke of Candelario had noticed that some new will was being obeyed and new customs were being introduced.

"When I die," Don Juan once said, "they can hang you from a tree or dress you in a green waistcoat if they want; but as long as I am alive, things will go on as usual!"

The years passed. Diego lived as a great gentleman in society far from his father. He married a duchess and did not return to the Candelario palace until his mother died. He did not remain very long. Just long enough to be convinced that the Duke would fill as much as was humanly possible the emptiness caused by his mother's death with the influence exercised by Ramón. Without deception, without duplicity, without ambition, and by virtue of his intelligence, energy and zeal, the gardener invaded every area of command. The Duke would say helplessly, "He is my very arms and legs, even though he does not have both of either."

This was true, because the veteran had lost one leg in the war, and afterwards not long ago, had lost an arm on the roof of the palace during a fire. It did not matter; Ramón directed and supervised everything with what he had left.

Diego, when he saw him so badly maimed, gave him a nickname which made the Duchess laugh, for she did not approve of servants becoming friends with their masters either; he called him the Torso because he was practically nothing but his trunk, and that, though old and wrinkled, was still as strong as an oak.

A little before he died, the Duke called his son to his side. The poor old man lay helpless on his death bed no longer able to feel the energy that had made him the absolute master of his household in other days. A few days after Diego arrived, Ramón, also very old now, had to relinquish his position. The dear young gentleman who would not cease caring about him, either, but at a distance, let him understand in no uncertain terms that he was seriously mistaken if he felt that that familiarity between gentlemen and servants, which his father Don Juan Candelario had imposed, was a natural law of society. True respect and true loyalty to one's employer consists of something else—in knowing how to maintain that proper distance that exists between the classes.

From then on, since Don Juan unfortunately no longer directed the business of the household, everything would change. Everyone would occupy their proper places; he, Ramon, since he was the gardener, would return to his gardens and live in the Pabellón de la Glorieta, on the hill at the end of the park.

It was not necessary to tell Ramón twice. "New bosses, new days." He was faithful as a dog, when what was demanded was friendship and shared confidences. He had been affectionate and personable; he would have slept at the feet of the Duke to show him the warmth of his loyalty. Now they were ordering him to the gate to keep watch outside like a good mastiff, so, outside he went to the Pabellón de la Glorieta, into exile.

And he took himself there, somewhat ashamed of having taken so seriously his role as favorite and administrator.

Don Juan noticed the change, but no longer had the spirit or strength to protest. Besides, he, too, was abdicating and willingly; it was natural that his son should want to begin his reign, he encouraged him to do so just to have the pleasure of seeing his heir in command, his own pride and joy. "Diego is a great gentleman," Don Juan said to himself, "I, at best, have probably been a great country farmer."

Don Juan died and the changes that had begun were accentuated and became definite. Those domains in the heart of Spain had acquired the appearance of British manor houses which are described and depicted occasionally in *The Graphic*. Everything was English; everything, as Don Juan would have said, was cold, correct, and proper. There was a manager, but not Ramon. The servants were automatons wearing the green waistcoats which the deceased had often joked about; there were always guests in the palace, but they were not the neighboring farmers, but rather stern and formal gentlemen.

Ramón hardly ever left his house at the high end of the park. He considered himself confined, especially since he was told that his responsibilities as a gardener would henceforth be honorary. Of course, he would continue receiving his salary, but without having to exercise the functions of his office. Don Diego would take care of him in his old age with all due consideration. The only thing he would be missing was the personal trust and confidence of years past. He did not complain, he changed his life. He was the most respectful, the most proper and the least communicative of the servants. He accepted his fate and without shame gratefully took his rewards for a lifetime of service. Nevertheless, in a corner of the garden, he worked as best he could almost always by himself.

The Duke and the Duchess came and went. They lived in the Candelario part of the summer and the entire autumn. Ramón saw his beloved Don Diego only two or three times during the entire season. Distant rumblings, echoes of domestic squabbles, reached him as gossip carried by those servants wearing their green livery, servants as proper, refined and respectful as one could ever expect. Ramón felt tears come to his eyes when he heard the servants' rumors in which they gave the domestic tragedy the air of a comic opera to avenge themselves for their constant humiliation. "The young gentleman is not happy!" he thought in his loneliness in the garden house. But God forbid he should speak a word of consolation to him!

One afternoon, Ramón saw Diego approach the gardens alone, in silence and with a terrible frown knitting his brow. Ramón was seated on a wooden bench, resting from his job of watering the vegetables, a task which was becoming more tiresome every day. The Duke walked past him, staring at the ground; Ramón stood up on his one remaining leg and lifted his only hand to his forehead in a gesture of removing the hat that was not there. The Duke saw him and looked at him with a sudden tenderness in his glance. He put a hand on his shoulder; but when he noticed that his servant's eyes had filled with tears and questions, fearing that the Torso might start speaking out of place, instead of permitting him to ask about his suffering, with a sudden gesture he cut him off and said, "How is the rheumatism?"

"The doctor says that I will end up losing the use of my other arm," and with the stump of his missing arm he tried to point to the remaining one. "I think he is right because it is as heavy as lead. But the worst of it is not that, but that my leg insists on asking to go on leave and I do not have another one in reserve."

"You know that you will always be taken care of."

And the young gentleman, the very one who once upon a time playfully bounced on that leg that was dying because it was tired of working alone, continued on his way, his heart sunken again in worry, his gaze directed toward the earth of his estate, which could not answer his infamous doubts about his outraged jealousy, the suspicions he had regarding his honor.

After a hundred stormy episodes, the Duke was alone—separated from the Duchess whose infidelities were proven true—alone, without children, with no love for anything in the world and like the greater number of men, with no true friends. He retired to his estate, seeking shelter on the Candelario as in the bay of a desert island. It was not a familiar port where his people were waiting for him, it was shelter in an inhospitable land. The world for him was now a desert island; in the Candelario, he starved for affection, for faith and for dreams, but he did not fight against the sea. He lived in the terrible calm of a cemetery. But even in cemeteries, affection makes its choices. In the palace, there was the usual formality. The servants, always dressed in green, always greeted him and bowed almost to the floor; their service was solicitous and polished. The Duke lacked for nothing, his body was tended to as by flying hands in an enchanted castle.

But he had too much of one thing—absolute propriety. The servants, according to their old customs, instilled by a lengthy disciplined tradition, considered the Duke a happy superior being who, by divine right, by the privilege of his blood and greatness, had no weaknesses. To suppose that the Duke needed consoling or help, that he was asking or even begging with his glance for protection, for the warmth of affection, was absurd and totally irreverent. None of those servants, not even the most truly faithful ones, believed that compassion for that gentleman, that to consider how sad he might be in that frightening solitude, was one of their responsibilities.

As far as the neighboring farmers who were dependent upon the household were concerned, many years had passed since any of them remembered the way to the palace, at least the way to the Duke's living quarters. The new Duke was an abstraction to them; his seigneury was a legal concept, not a power represented in recognizable form.

Don Diego was aging from sorrow, boredom and loneliness. Alone with his greatness, he felt like one of the nobility of King Midas's lineage; everything he touched turned into cold respect.

Weakness from the attacks that had begun suddenly made him nervous; he began to hate his voluntary servants because they did not guess what he needed most now, affection, human kindness, anything but humble or servile consideration. He began to court his palace staff, to try, indirectly by flattering them as best he could without abdicating his authority, to coax something more than their perfectly officious and meticulous service. It was useless. No one could suspect what he wanted. He lived among the furniture and the half-living, not among men. The trees in the park leaned in the breeze as he walked by and greeted him, they greeted his suffering without understanding it; the servants did exactly the same; their lord would walk by and they would bow like the trees.

One day, near evening, the Duke reached the end of the park and lifted his head upon finding himself next to the isolated garden house. There within, as if buried alive, was Ramón, who simply refused to die. He had been forgotten by everyone except for the young boy charged with taking care of him. The veteran had been losing ground, but he had not wanted to abandon the house where he had been a faithful watchman; he did not want to die. The young gentleman never visited him. Ramón spent the day sitting on a wicker sofa playing solitaire with a deck of old cards on a marble table, using his only remaining hand which he now could hardly move. He was so weak that each oily, creased card seemed as heavy as a stone slab to him. His other leg had become wooden also; it would not move. His eyes were bright, but he was as deaf as a post; everything sounded like the noise of rustling trees behind his back. Since he could not hear, he scarcely wanted to speak, particularly since he did not want to talk to himself. Besides, there was hardly ever anyone to talk to.

One idea constantly concerned him: "I wonder how the young gentleman is getting along down there?"

Don Diego hesitated, but could not restrain himself. His heart made him take a few more steps and enter the sad house of the exile, of the confined man, of the one buried alive, of the trunk propped up in a corner like an old piece of antique furniture—the Torso of flesh and bone.

The Torso, when he saw the Duke in front of him, tried but could not stand up. He lifted his hand a little, but could not touch his forehead. He saluted by blushing, from joy and respect. What a wonderful honor! The young gentleman had come to see him in his tomb!

The Duke put his hand on his shoulder and sat next to him on the wicker sofa.

"What kind of solitaire is that?" he asked with signs.

"King's solitaire."

"Did my father teach it to you?" Don Diego asked again with gestures, pointing twice with his hand at the clouds in the sky....

"Yes, my lord the Duke," answered Ramon, lifting the stump of his missing arm. "The Duke, who rests in peace," the Torso repeated, unable to hold back two small tears.

Nor could the present Duke; perhaps he did not want to contain himself, letting his head fall on Ramón's shoulder, he wept copiously in silence, like an idolater reconciling himself with an image, with a god of the lares, and he tells the motionless Torso his most intimate sorrows, which no one else cares about.

Windows

My so-called friend Cristóbal was always sad, no, that is not the word; he was aloof, disinterested and he abstained from all strong emotions that demonstrate trust and enthusiasm. I do not know how to explain it. Life was painful next to him. His clear blue eyes with pupils that burned and questioned from the depths of a mysterious darkness were the Pedro Recio of all expansiveness, wonder or optimism. It was impossible to love, to admire or to trust in the presence of those eyes; they vetoed everything with their *a priori* disillusionment. The worst part of it was that they made their statement modestly, almost timidly; Cristóbal's glance was shy and never held for very long. One might say he distilled his ice and ran away.

Why was Cristóbal like that? Why did he look at people in that way? One day I happened to find out.

"The best friend one can have is money," someone I do not remember said in front of us. As soon as we were alone, I said to Cristóbal, "Those empty skeptical statements of popular wisdom are superficial and plebeian; they always annoy me. I think society owes its sad moral state to a great extent to that coarse popular positivism which, even though it is so short-sighted, can kill an ideal with an old popular saying."

"Nevertheless," Cristóbal's eyes were saying in their way until his smile finally gave way to speech. "Money may not be a great friend, but perhaps there is no better."

Other people lament the faithlessness of a woman. I had fallen in love with the idea of friendship; I felt it was the reason I was born. I had a friend in my youth; we shared our enthusiasm like the manna of our faith in the future. Together we set out to conquer our dreams. When the infernal winds of disillusionment struck us in the face, we did not loosen but rather grasped more tightly the bonds of friendship. Like Paolo and Francesca, the infernal winds swept us away together. The two of us lived for art, poetry, and thought; but I was a playwright and he was not. Except for a talent for theater, which Zola denies even exists—probably because he does not have it—Fernando and I shared everything. Our success and our money were common property.

Everyone, with the usual authoritarian opinions, sanctioned our friendship; we were considered united by unbreakable bonds. So be it, we said. And in our spirit was born one of those hermetic false dogmas with which humanity persists in deceiving itself.

I had noticed that Fernando was an extreme egoist; it was as natural for him as for a ruminant to chew its cud. But I had noticed that I, too, although a more refined and complicated type of person, was another one. "How can our friendship survive two such personalities? It is in the air," I thought, noticing that my friend was vain because of me; he worried, hated and disliked because of me. I, too, felt personally offended when someone criticized Fernando. I was the only one who had the right to find fault with him, but I saw no maliciousness in criticizing since I examined with a certain pleasure my own faults and deficiencies, thinking that this made me humble. One of the masks that Satan most willingly dons to tempt us is that of a saint.

One night, a play of mine had its debut. It was one of those works that breaks convention and tries the patience of the common audience, which is never as antagonistic as the author supposes. To make a long story short, based on the loud reactions it evoked, its success was a disaster. A minority as select as it was small defended me with untenable paradoxes, with hyperboles that raised me to the heights just to see me fall. During the small reception afterwards, there was a veritable storm of critical contention. The tendency was to congratulate me, but with a deadly intent. As I moved from group to group, the people discussed the direction of the theater and tore me apart. Then my friends appeared. They praised me highly and lent a protective hand to the play and the direction it was pointing in. I accepted their congratulations with an innocent smile, knowing quite well that I was the sacrificial lamb.

What no one said, but what everyone was thinking, was, "It is not a question of the genre; it is not a question of new forms; the problem is with this dim–witted journeyman. He has attempted more than he can handle. He was wrong. That is the whole point. He was simply wrong."

That is how my enemies thought; they intimated as much through insinuation, always attacking me indirectly. That is how my friends thought, too, defending me openly but insinuating their true opinion even more, through their defense of me and the play.

And Fernando? Fernando was almost physically violent in his defense. He almost came to blows over it two or three times. I only heard him at a distance; I did not see him.

He was unaware that I had heard him. His furiously passionate defense was loyal and sincere. He was inspired. He was usually measured and almost cold in his statements, but that night he became very emotional.

"He is blinded by his friendship," people everywhere were saying.

I wish I had not been blind myself on that evening!

Just as one rescues the glorious remains of a flag after a defeat, Fernando got me out of the theater and went with me to an elegant restaurant where we had reserved a dining room to discuss the evening's events.

When we entered, I noticed my friend's face for the first time that night, reflected in a mirror. I felt a chill. I dared to look at him directly. And in effect, he looked just like his reflection. There was even a hint more passion there than I had noticed in the mirror. He was radiant. In his eyes shone a supreme happiness that comes only from joy, which cannot be confused with any other emotion. Fernando was very different from me in this respect. He loved strongly and had good luck; women for him meant as much as friendship did to me; his success in love affairs made him happy. His face, generally dull, expressionless and cold, came alive with a diabolical animation whenever he increased the love he felt for himself by winning the love of another. But I had never—not even on that solemn evening when he asked me to leave him alone with his most prized conquest, the wife of a friend—seen him as beautifully transfigured by strong, pleasant emotions as I saw him that night in the caf dining room.

While we were having dinner, I stared at Fernando's eyes. That is where the great mystery declared itself. "Look at the happiness there! The greatest happiness which the body and soul of an artist is capable of! This cynical egoist has no regard for duty or sacrifice!"

If the soul a window had... Ah, but it does. I read Fernando's soul through his eyes as in a book of modern psychology by Bourget.

Fernando was brutally happy that evening, to speak frankly, like a beast. He knew well from personal experience that the quintessence of an artist's feelings in what he believes to be his heart, perhaps because he does not have a better one than that delicate and thin bubble, is a coagulation of sick pride. I was suffering unspeakable pain; he knew that false friends and the public had tortured me to the depths of my artificial soul of a poet. But he did not realize that his own vanity, egoism and envy were like jackals feeding on the remains of my fallen, wounded pride.

What mystic light, the infernal mysticism of strong, worldly passion, burned in his eyes. How ecstatic he was without even realizing it! And how talkative, how generous, how expansive! He was in love with everything that night. He would have carried charity to heroic proportions. The egoist's joy inspired this mirage of self-denial. Doubtless he still believed that the world was his! He heard the music of the spheres. And what concern and attentiveness he showed me. What a brother he was to me. I can swear that he would have fought for my reputation. And the poor man did not even know that he was enjoying the highest pleasure of a civilized savage, of a spiritual cannibal, and that his joy was being fed on the blood of my soul, on the marrow of my hardened bones of incurable vanity, the flesh and blood of a professional writer.

That spectacle, which irritated me at first because it was extremely painful, was becoming little by little a melancholy kind of sensuality. The bitter exploration of Fernando's soul through his eyes was becoming an interesting process of continually more laborious refinement. My wounded pride did not take long in recovering with the intimate and secret pleasure that comes from analyzing another's misery. I learned much philosophy in a very brief time. At the end of this supper where the only apostle was a Judas, without my realizing it, during dessert, my little play became a very distant cause for sadness; the mishap had taken on its proper poetic perspective. My failure, the hidden martyrdom of my self-esteem, the faithlessness of false friends and companions were left behind, confused with the common misery of the human condition, lost among the many necessary fatal hurts that come with life. In my mind, like the sun of justice, my resignation shone, my cold analysis of another person's soul, my profound philosophy which was neither pessimistic nor optimistic because it never gives to historical data more value than they actually have. And what comforted me most was an intimate feeling that the intense pain Fernando's unconscious betrayal was giving me did not make me hate or even despise him, but rather made me feel affectionate pity for him. I forgave him because he did not know what he was doing.

My belief in friendship, I said to myself, will not fail tonight like my pitiful little play did; Fernando does not really care about me; he is not my friend. And so? I will be his; I will care about him. His friendship does not exist, mine does.

In such a state of mind, I arrived home. I entered my room and began to undress, thinking about Fernando radiating his joy and passion. My spirit swam in the austere happiness of a satisfied conscience, in the sea of that rational, mystical superiority of a humble and resigned soul. What did my play, my self-esteem, such worldly things, really matter? What did it matter that the person I considered my friend was satisfying his ferocious envy with my failure? The most serious thing, the important thing, noble, great and eternal, was my own satisfaction, to be pleased with myself, to rise above the common man, above the petty emotions I saw in Fernando. What a horrible expression I now saw in my own eyes! Through those windows I saw infinite pride and satanic joy. I was pale, but my eyes were aflame with satisfied pride and self-love. I saw Fernando burning in them, reduced to ashes, the unfortunate victim on the altar of my pride, a miniature hell. And looking for the friendship I thought I had, through the windows of my eyes, I did not see the angel which friendship would be if it existed; I only saw demons, and I, the author of the drama was the worst, perhaps because of the perspective...

Cold and the Pope

The newspaper said, "It is not absolutely certain that His Holiness Leo XIII is ill. His health remains good; but one must not forget that his is the constitution of a very old man, a man whose spirit has worked and continues to work very hard. He is weak beyond a doubt; but one must not judge from appearances what his constitution may be able to withstand. Behind that frailty, pallor and those delicate muscles there is strength, a lively resistance that someone seeing him, unaware of his mettle, would never suspect. He frequently had colds; his greatest battle is with the cold. Fires are not lit in his rooms. After he retires for the evening, he needs many covers over his thin body. It seems impossible that his weak limbs can withstand the weight of so many blankets."

Aurelio Marco, ex-philosopher, interrupted the article which had brought tears to his eyes with its ideas and images.

It was the evening of January 5, the night before Epiphany. In the village where Aurelio had taken refuge, after having traveled over the greater part of the world, the innocent mystery play—the traditional act of going to wait for the Three Wise Men—was still a tradition, no less than when he was a child and had followed the poor musicians of the municipal band who were disguised with pieces of ribbon and cheap paste jewelry as melancholy kings with hungry faces who marched through the streets, plazas and highways by the light of smoking torches.

In the distance, there in the street, the strident elegy of a badly tuned clarinet moved away slowly.

"The pope is suffering from the cold!" thought Aurelio. And a tenderness derived from that symbol of ineffable and sad mystery darkened his soul with visions shot through with sharp, luminous ideas.

His memories of other Epiphany feasts, the fading sound of the clarinet, and the news story he had just read returned him to his feelings, to the faith of his poetic youth and tormented adolescence. The aesthetic truth of the sublime legend touched him deeply and he experienced something which Goethe's Faust felt on listening to the bells tolling the Gloria and popular Easter songs.

"Errin'rung halt mich nun, mit kindlichem Gefuhle..."

"Such memories revive in my heart the feelings of childhood and return me to life. Oh, let me hear you again, celestial songs; a tear has fallen from my eye and the earth conquers me again."

Aurelio Marco was growing old and his spirit required a shield. His pure manner of thinking was graying as was his hair. He was leaving behind his pretensions to positivistic thinking, which denies everything it cannot explain, and he had returned, not to the dogmatic faith of his elders, but instead to a love and respect for the Christian tradition. He did not go into the cathedral because he did not want to profane it. He remained frozen at the door. He attended the celebration from outside, contemplating the sweet austerity of the Gothic architecture, seeing in the towers a musical hymn of sincere piety. But such sentiments, such ideas, which he called religious common sense, did not warm his heart as they had during his inwardly stormy youth, setting him afire with flashes of a poetic faith that was expectant, personal, and original and which shone at times through the shadows of his doubts and denials.

Now, he thought, his feelings were freer, more sincere and more prudent and tolerant of contrary ideas; he doubtlessly approached the golden mean of wise measure. But how cold it was!

The pope also feels the cold. He is cold to his very bones.

Aurelio Marco stood up suddenly, as if to escape from his thoughts. He remained looking at the light of his lantern which shone red behind a translucent shade. He made a singular strong and noisy sound with his lips as if he were kissing adversity and his resignation at the same time. Lifting both hands to his forehead as if looking for some mechanical or artificial means to think the thoughts he wanted to, he spoke almost like someone turning to face a divinity seen close at hand directly overhead.

"Oh, if I could only, even in my dreams, believe again what I now feel but do not believe! Why are poetry and love in me believers while my mind is not? If the Church could see my feelings, would I be considered an enemy? In the eyes of the Church, I must be like so many others, a sick branch but still one of its own. What do I have to do with the pope? And, nevertheless, what chills I suffer from the same cold that assaults him! It all seems a tender and melancholy symbol of something."

He sat down again in his leather easy chair, believing that he could hear the complaints of Balthazar's clarinet in the distance. Leaning his head on his chest, he fell asleep.

He had returned after seven years. A strapping village girl took him by the hand and running along made him almost fly over the fine dust of the road. Her hair flowed out and bounced on her shoulders like wings, letting her feel the breeze on the back of her neck.

It was night, a clear, icy cold night with stars that looked as if they had just been washed. The highway, he well knew, was the Castillian highway to Madrid, to the great world of his ambitious dreams. It led to a mysterious joy that was vague and indefinite though sure. Nevertheless, looking more carefully to both sides, he did not recognize the road. To the left and to the right were countless buildings, every one of them sad, solemn, and made of stone. They were tombs. That huge mass looked like the funeral monument of Cecilia Metela. It was the Castillian highway, yet it reminded him of the Appian Way.

"Where are we going? Where are all these people going? To wait for the Wise Men!"

In his heart and mind, Aurelio experienced the excitement of childhood with the knowledge and experience of adulthood.

What did it mean to wait for the Wise Men? Nothing, just a game, and illusion. And yet, what joy and exultation! That deception which did not deceive anyone deceived everyone. It was an image, a symbol of life, to run through the freezing night up the Appian Way. Hardly aware, hardly able to distinguish oneself from the crowd, just as in life where we hardly know ourselves, everyone pressed forward, struggling for position, tripping over one another to be among the first to arrive at the goal, to reach their dream. They went out onto the roads to meet the Wise Men whom they knew they would never meet.

"Here they come! There they are! That light!" everyone shouted jokingly.

And Aurelio almost believed them and began the race in earnest. The light came from an inn. There were no wise men there, only drunks and their women who were also asking about the Three Kings.

"Farther down the road! A little farther on! There is another light! Another inn! Keep moving! Farther up!" Tombs and shadows on all sides, cold, brilliant stars in the sky, darkness and hope confronting the distances. "Keep moving."

The crowd begins to thin out. The illusion is beginning to tire them. The inns begin swallowing them up as they return to reality, only to fall into the illusion of drunkenness, which has no ideal, to wake up to bitterness. Aurelio and the strapping young girl, who pulls him along almost carrying him, discover that they are alone. It does not matter. They continue anyway. The road bends at the top of the hill. The horizon widens and is broken only by the symmetrical shadow of a huge church crowned with an immense cupola. Aurelio finds himself alone in the nave whose vaults disappear into the high shadows. The apse of the great church is in ruins and opens onto the countryside, to the mountains and stars. On the main altar there is a humble cradle in a crche. On the Evangelical side there is a hospital bed which is clean though poor. In the cradle, a rosy–cheeked child moans and trembles with the cold. In the humble bed, a tiny old man with transparent skin as pale as wax shivers to his very bones.

The stars seem to spill waves of cold onto the crib and onto the bed. It is so cold! They are so unprotected! A mule and an ox are standing next to the crib. The ox breathes clouds of steam onto the child. The old man dying of cold from time to time lifts his trembling head and looks in the direction of the crib and smiles gratefully at the ox warming the child with his breath. The cold makes the old man delirious as he thinks about the consolations of the nightmare that frees him of pain. "If he does not freeze, neither will I."

Aurelio sees three people dressed in purple and gold, wearing crowns, suddenly enter the nave of the church. They, like the mule and the ox, are life–sized figures from the crche. He recognizes them. They are Balthazar, shoemaker and clarinetist in the municipal band; Melchior, sacristan and trumpet player, Gaspar, baker and cornet player. The Three Wise Men stand around the old man's bed. "He is dying of cold," says Melchior.

"He is freezing to death in this eternal night of a world without faith, without hope, without charity!" said Gaspar.

And Balthazar, sighing, said, "Let's cover him with our cloaks."

Balthazar threw his heavy purple cloak over His Holiness Leo XIII, the little old man in the humble bed; Gaspar threw his; Melchior, his.

The ox saw them and left the child for a moment and came to warm the pope with his breath because he was dying of cold.

Aurelio Marco, kneeling, felt the ineffable emotion of religious sorrow, of pious submission to the pitiless lessons of the impenetrable and holy mystery. "The child in the crib is dying of cold at the moment of his birth! The old man, the pontiff, Peter's successor, vicar of the child on earth, is dying of cold in his extreme old age!"

The ox, Aurelio recognized, was Saint Thomas Aquinas, the mute ox who with the breath of his doctrine sought to warm the freezing pope. The blankets of the Wise Men were revered tradition, the grandeur of a world that adheres to the Church in order to save the capital of Christian civilization and the power of inherited faith and mystic beauty.

All of this was to no avail. The old man was still shivering.

The Wise Men no longer knew what to do to give warmth to the weak and trembling old man.

They looked at the heavens. Through the destroyed apse they saw the starry vaults. There, peaceful like a fleck of gold, was their faithful guide, the Eastern Star, but as cold and indifferent as everything else.

"If the sun would only rise! If the sun would come out!" the Wise Men said.

And they covered him up well, tucking the blankets around the pope's frail body as he lay there dying from the cold.

The pope, from time to time, smiling and shivering, lifted his head and looked at the crib on the main altar. In his delirium one thought stayed in his mind. "If He does not freeze, neither shall I."

And Melchior, Gaspar, and Balthazar as a chorus repeated, "If only the sun would rise!"

Leon Benavides

"A Lion I bear on my shield,
And his name is Benavides."
Tirso de Molina, *La prudencia en la mujer*

I wager anything that the majority of readers do not know the
history or the name of the lion in front of Congress, the first one you
meet as you come down the Carrera de San Jeronimo. Well, his
name, of course, is Leon. Naturally. But his last name? What is his
surname? His last name is Benavides.

But it would be better to let him speak for himself, to hear his
story as he himself had the kindness to tell it to me one moonlit night,
when I was looking at him more closely and discovered something
different about him that I did not notice about his companion on his
left.

"What makes this lion interesting, more solemn, noble and melancholy than the other one? At first glance, they look identical."

Toward the center of his forehead was the answer to the mystery,
in the wrinkle between his brows. I do not know how, but there was
an idea there that the other one did not have, and for that difference
alone, the one was a great symbolic work of art, almost religious in
nature, while the other was common and rather ordinary. The one
recalled patriotism, the other jingoism. The one was anointed with a
sacred idea, the other was not. But where was the sculptural difference? What fold did one have on his forehead that the other did not?

Determined with profound interest to discover his secret, I contemplated the higher lion. How often, I thought, we see things like
this, two beings so different that they represent totally different
worlds. Names and formalities often conceal under appearances of
similarity and even of identity the most distinct qualities, sometimes
even antagonistic elements.

Lost in these thoughts, I was surprised by a metallic voice. It
vibrated in the moonlight just as the famous voice of the Egyptian
statue resonates in the rays of the sun. The voice, sweet, hushed, and
trembling, came from the lion's iron throat. "It's a scar. The difference you seek between my companion and me is only that. I have a
scar on my forehead. The scar reveals a soul and for that reason you
find me interesting. Thank you. Since you have noticed I have a spirit

and the other one does not, hear my story and the history of my scar."

"I was born in the mountains in the province of Leon many centuries ago in the highest reaches that divide with peaks of eternal snow the Leonese counties from the Asturias. I was made of hard, polished white stone. From my mountain top I could see in the distance, toward the northeast, other mountains which were also white, and as a result of contemplating how they, like I, were thrust upward into the splendor of the blue sky, I came to love them as the most worthy object of my lofty thoughts. The sun illuminated us. From me to them and from them to me there came and went brilliant flashes of light. They are the Covadonga range.

"One day, the irons of a noble mountaineer made me leap from my place and pulled me from my mother's womb, the mountain top, and below in the canyon the harsh instrument of a stonemason worked me so that, from the depths of my granite nature, he little by little brought into relief a figure, and from that day I had a soul. I was a lion, an idea. I was a lion rampant on the plain of a shield. From that day to this, I have passed through a hundred avatars, through numberless metempsychoses, but without ever losing the unity of my idea, my being a lion.

"My idea was born, strictly speaking, from a mistake. My name should not be Leon, but Legion. My etymology is *legio*, not *leo*. The city of Leon to whom I owe my being is called Leon, as everyone knows, for having been the seat of a certain Roman legion. But there is something greater than grammatical logic, and the transformation of Legion to Leon has been justified by history. The Leonese were lions during the reconquest. From my mountain origin, where the pure, cold north wind from the canyons darkened me with the patina of noble time, I descended with the Benavides, whose pride I was and whose deeds I inspired, to the plains of Castille and I raced through Extremadura and Portugal and even placed my claw on the lands of Andalusia. Through marriages for love and marriages of state, I was often entangled on the plains with eagles, castles, helmets, bars and pennants. Sometimes, I was made of stone, other times of iron, and often I was made of gold and silver. Sometimes I ran through fields of battle floating in the air on the embroidered relief of an ensign, leaping across the breast plate of a noble knight or noble lady in the hunt, the image itself of war.

"But one day, I wanted to try my luck in life, to cease being a mere symbol and to have blood, and I became a true lion with claws and teeth and had the honor of being defeated by the Cid, Rodrigo Díaz de Vivar, the one who won Valencia.

"Century after century passed, and from one transformation to another I became a man without losing my true lion nature.

"In my incarnation, I wanted to be born where I had been born in stone, and I was a Leonese from the mountains. When they baptized me, they named me Leon. My parents were the Benavides. But the Benavides were poor, forgotten noblemen who worked their land as their servants had done before.

"In my village, like Pizarro in his, I terrified my neighbors because from a very young age I began to show who I was through my mad deeds which always were true to my lion nature. I must tell the truth. From the time I was a child, I spilled blood, but always in defense of my dignity or of the defenseless, fighting always like the Cid my conqueror against fifteen or more enemies.

"They called me Wildhair because my beard was like a tangled jungle, and my hair grew so curly, abundant and coarse that my head would not tolerate hats. They seemed to suffocate me like a harness.

"On holiday outings, I was destructive and committed my greatest deeds. I had no ill feelings toward anyone, not even against the mountain people on the other side of the range, whom my townsmen usually fought on such journeys. I did not hate anyone. But love, wine or anything else turned me to fight. The eyes of dreamy, dusky girls from the Leonese mountains expected feats of bravery from me and the blood of the defeated. Sensuality for me had its musical accompaniment in acts of heroic strength and brute fearlessness. Afterwards, since the devil ruins everything, I only got my hands on fragile bones and weak muscles. They could not beat me. They knew how to irritate me but not how to win. No one considered me bad, although everyone was afraid of me. And between blessings and tears from the girls, the old folks and children, I found myself forced to leave the town for prison. I was twenty years old.

"By means of heroic deeds and unheard-of victories, and saving an entire town by spilling my blood, which was abundant and almost black, I won my freedon and became a soldier. I like war, but peace was horrible! There is this thing called discipline. During war, it is a whip that enlivens and brings comfort. In peace, it is like a trainer's burning prod that horrifies, humiliates, and makes cowards of men, embitters them and belittles the character even of a lion, who everyone knows is, by nature, noble.

"The things a petty lieutenant made me suffer, a little man who smelled like a brothel and who constantly was preening his moustache! He was very proud of himself because he could read and write. He made me suffer because of the damned buttons that kept popping off my shirt. My chest kept expanding, unexplainably, and when I breathed hard, like a bellows, pop, a button flew off. And the lieutenant was there in front of me, under my chin, insulting me and trying to shake me. 'Stupid, lazy, good-for-nothing recruit!' And the regimental cap? It would not stay on my head. Everytime we were under fire, the cap, or whatever it was, leapt from my head because my hair suddenly started growing and going into tangles. I do not know why, but I could not stand anything on my head. And did I get into trouble! What humiliation I had to suffer because of this. In action, I was the bravest, but in the barracks, I was always on report for some infraction or other. I spent my life confined to quarters.

"Finally, during one terrible campaign in which our men were dying like flies, without compassion, drawn and quartered, I became what I am, a wild beast. I do not know that I did, but it must have been tremendous. On the battlefield, alone, surrounded by enemies, I became what I had been during the time of the Cid. But this time, I was the Cid. I overpowered, crushed, clawed, tore everything apart. I bathed in blood and even sank my teeth. I was a lion, after all. Afterwards, everyone commented on my heroism, on the victory that was my doing. But the flood flowing from my mouth gave me away. It was not a wound. The blood was not mine. It seems that in my teeth they found flesh. It was evident: a case of cannibalism. What could anyone say? There was no precedent. But by reason of analogy, honor, discipline and the cause of civilization were also bleeding. The firing squad was made up of the very same comrades I had saved. They fired and I fell dead. Only one bullet struck me. But it was enough because it hit me between the eyes. They buried me like a deserter and I revived in the form of a bronze lion, never to return to a life in flesh and blood again. The bullet killed me forever. And I will never leave this figure of an angry sphinx whom the mystery of fate lends no peace but only fires my anger crystallized in silence. This scar is as much a scar as it is an obsession."

The lion stopped talking and with supreme disdain, turned his head a little to look at his companion a few steps down, the lion without a scar, arrogant in a common sort of way, rather comic, plebeian and insignificant.

"I," concluded Benavides, "am a lion of war and of history, a lion with a scar. I am noble, but I am a beast. The other lion is a parliamentarian, a lion of words and rhetoric."

Keen

I feel sorry for people who, in matters of taste, have no other criterion except style and therefore will not find this true story to their liking because it is a study of the spirit of a dog, and everyone knows that psychological fiction, very much the rage many years ago and back in style about ten years ago, now seems childish, arbitrary and foolish to the stylists of Parisian letters who are the tyrants of the latest fashion. The classical Greeks did not have a word for the concept we express today with the word "style." Among the Greeks, according to Egger, beauty apparently did not depend upon whim or the effects of boredom. Oh! The Greeks would have understood my hero whose story reaches the world rather late, now that the young people of Paris and even Guatemala write ephemeral reviews in which they make light of Stendhal and of Paul Bourget himself.

At any rate, Keen was a white French poodle. He did not know why they called him Keen, but he was convinced that this was his name and he answered to it, satisfied with this relative knowledge, just as positivists are satisfied with the relative knowledge that Clay considers knowledge without assurance, without a firm base. If Keen had known how to write his name, and I think he came close to it because there was never a smarter, or more high–spirited, dog in the world, he would have signed his name, without knowing that he was writing in very bad script, "I, the King." Because his true name was King. It was just that people who pronounced English badly said Keen in Spanish. So we must spell it Keen.

There has never been a greater irony by antiphrasis because there had never been a less imposing animal in the world. Everyone, men, dogs and even cats, ordered him around because it seemed to Keen a national weakness, unworthy of a true thinker, to be carried along by that inveterate instinct of dislike which makes enemies of cats and dogs without any rational explanation.

Keen was born with a silver spoon in his mouth. He was the son of a purebred French poodle and the property of a very wealthy, sensitive young woman who spent her days eating bonbons and reading novels by Braddon, Oliphant, and other British writers. He was born along with four or five brothers and sisters in a cute little basket which could be considered his golden cradle. A few days afterwards, the more or less violent death of his litter mates left him alone with his mother. The young lady novel reader took care of him as if he were a crown prince.

But as Keen grew, and very quickly, his mistress's dream began to fade. She had imagined him being a miniature poodle with hair like silk. The hair began to be less silky than his mother's, although it was still very white and curly. His skin was like pure pink satin, but Keen kept growing and stretching up. An expert declared to the wonderful lady that he was not a purebred, that the little female, it was necessary to admit, had slipped. There was a cross breeding. Keen's father had mongrel blood, without a doubt. For this reason, the delicate Spanish–English woman had less regard for the dog of her dreams. Nevertheless, she had him taken care of and treated him like a prince, though no longer a crown prince. At first, because he was afraid they would throw him into the street into the life of a vagabond—something which horrified him because it is an almost impossible life for a dog unless he reverts to pillage and scandal—at first, as I was saying, Keen by his ingenuity and—let's speak the truth—by his antics tried to stay in the good graces of his mistress and attempted to make her forget the horrible crime of his hateful tendency to keep growing bigger.

A very young, talented author, Mr. Pujo, has recorded in a recent book a very correct idea, which does not surprise me, about how much elderly people who are respected for their good judgment are deceived regarding the intellectual gifts of children. The child, in general, is much more precocious than one thinks. For my part, I can say that when I was very young, I would laugh to myself about adults who did not think I had common sense or good judgment, two things which I had been keeping to myself for a long time. This is what frequently happens to children and this is what was happening to Keen who had come to understand human language perfectly in his own way, though he could not distinguish words from gestures and attitudes because he saw in all three an expression of ideas and sentiments.

Keen could not quite understand why people were so astonished at his intelligence, and he considered them ridiculous when he saw them take as some sort of wonderful talent his standing on his hind legs, carrying a cane on his shoulders, doing calisthenics, jumping through a hoop or counting out someone's age with his paw. All these petty accomplishments which kept him more or less in the good graces of his mistress seemed unworthy of his lofty thoughts and had come to be something of a farce which embarrassed him. If they loved him for his clowning and not for simply having been born in the palace, he believed he did not owe them much gratitude for their affection. Besides, in front of other dogs who were less pampered and who did not do tricks, it embarrassed him to let them see how he earned the good life.

He wanted to be loved, man's pet, because his nature required this affection and this mysterious alliance in which there were no explicit agreements and in which nevertheless there is often great trust, at least on the part of the dog. "I want a master," he said, "but one who loves me for being a dog, not a prodigy. One who will let me grow as big as I am supposed to be and who will not show me off as some kind of marvel, making me look ridiculous."

And he ran away, not without difficulty, from the palace in which he was born.

He passed by the front door of a barracks and the soldier on guard called him, threw him a piece of cheese and Keen, who had not eaten for twelve hours, because he still did not know how to find food for himself, ate the cheese and responded to the soldier's petting. Why go any farther? He could be his master if he wanted to. The life of a mongrel horrified him. If they would have him, he would stay there. And he stayed. He hid the tricks he knew from the regiment, which did not take long to adopt him, but he let his nobility and loyalty shine through. Everyone in the barracks was overjoyed with Keen, whose name they learned from the license attached to the fine leather collar he had escaped with.

From the colonel to the last recruit, everyone considered himself the single undisputed owner and friend of the noble animal. Keen had his talents and his intelligence, but he surpassed himself in good behavior. He was loyal, discreet and manly as far as a dog can be. There was nothing pretended or feigned in his loyalty to the regiment. He charmed the men of the barracks and they were proud of him. Life did not go badly for him there. Of course, he preferred living there to living in the palace. At least here he was not a clown and he could grow as big and get as fat as he wanted. He would not let them cut his hair down to his skin. He did not want to show off the skin that looked like pink silk. He did not want his aristocratic origin to be obvious. Long hair seemed better suited, more modest, and it kept him anonymous. He wore his hair the way a beautiful, chaste woman wears a habit. He tried to keep himself clean and that was all.

He made some friends in that part of the town and they introduced him to their companions in the street gangs and to a famous personality who had attracted public attention in Madrid. They introduced him to the famous dog Paco. Keen greeted Paco rather coldly. He disliked him immediately. He was a fake, a comedian, a public clown. Basically, Paco was a mediocrity. His talent and instincts which the people of Madrid admired so much were commonplace. The dog Paco had the cheek to do tricks which other dogs conceal for the sake of modesty and to escape the humiliating applause of men who were usually astonished to discover that dogs indeed do have some intelligence. Among dogs, Paco lost credit very quickly. The larger ones of his breed, whatever it might have been, disdained him the more as his triumphs became greater. He prostituted the honor of his kind. All his art was merely cheap tricks. He did everything for glory. He even engaged in histrionics and in some rather disgusting demonstrations of libertinism. Truly brave, serious and dignified dogs hated his bull ring bravura and looked at his tricks as Ajax and Agamemnon in Shakespeare looked at the satirical jokes and witticisms of Thersites.

Keen was among those who disliked Paco the most, without ever letting him know it. And Paco blushed every time he met Keen, as black dogs do with their eyes, and in his presence he pretended to behave naturally and to have grown tired of his life of constant travel, performances and the stage. So he would not have to see these things, Keen decided to leave the capital. "A dog who tries to be funny," thought Keen, recalling Pascal, "has a weak character." Besides, he began to find life in the barracks unworthy of his deep thoughtfulness. Some of the soldiers were crude and took advantage of his gentleness, and his wide reputation of faithful companion began to bother him. He wanted to live unnoticed, to escape to the country. But with whom?

A regimental commander who had declared Keen—if not his son—his adopted dog, was waiting for a decision on behalf of a close relative of his from the Office of Pensions and Annuities and often took our hero there with him. But of course, the dog never got farther than the gate where they allowed him to stay. He usually waited there for his commander to return and take him for his walk. There, where he had spent many hours waiting patiently, Keen met the person who would help him realize his dream of escaping to the country.

Keen observed that after arguing a little with the doorman at the Office of Pensions, everyone who tried to get in to see the office personnel succeeded. The dog noticed that the boldest ones with the worst manners were the ones who got in easiest, even though they did not enjoy any particular distinction. The shy ones suffered humiliation and embarrassment trying to overcome the resistance of a gold-braided Cerberus. And one slender young man with a sparse yellow beard, melancholy clear blue eyes and rather thread–worn clothes, in spite of never missing a day at the gate, which was defended like a fortress, could never get in. To judge from the look of anguish on his face each time they turned him away, he must have been suffering greatly. Keen, lying on a mat with his muzzle on his paws, watched the daily skit of the porter and the young coward with interest and pity.

The doorman at the ministry read in the eyes of the poor farmer, whose speech revealed his country origins, that he came with no more recommendations and with no greater spirit than on other days. The guard spilled out on him all the offended pride and despotism he had suffered from other more rash people. The anguish and desperation were evident in the young man's face. You could see flashes of energy which quickly disappeared leaving, in the shadows of weakness and timidity, his face abandoned to an expression of defeated sadness.

Keen came to recognize that the porter considered the young man inferior even to him, a mere dog. It is probable that he would have let the dog go in to make his petition to the office first.

The man with the brown pants, as Keen came to call the villager with the yellow beard, sat on a velvet couch and spent many tedious hours there, just as if he were wrapped in a burlap bag, for all the good it did him.

From a few snatches of conversation which Keen was able to overhear, he learned that that young man came from a distant city to try to clarify his father's military record so that he could get a small widow's pension for his mother who was poor and in bad health. He had no one to sponsor him. So, he did not have a chance. They would not even let him speak to the lofty official who insistently interpreted incorrectly the decrees regulating the functions of his office. Various mistakes, lack of good will, or whatever, were the cause of suffering for this young petitioner, a seeker after justice—the most hopeless of all.

Because they were alone together many times at the door, Keen and Sindulfo (which was the name of the timid young man) with their shared humility and exclusion from bureaucratic grace, got acquainted and began to like one another. Neither thought very highly of himself. Both experienced the constant, silent sadness of being considered inferior. Without speaking, they understood one another. So, with very few words, and a few demonstrations of deference, such as moving over for Sindulfo, and a couple of pats on the muzzle, they became very good friends. Then, while they shared in eternal silence the common misfortune of being insignificant, on one afternoon, a messenger boy with a telegram for Sindulfo came in. Sindulfo turned pale on seeing the blue paper. It was nothing important. His mother had died, all he had in the world. He fainted. The doorman went into a rage. They gave the young man a little water grudgingly, and as soon as he could stand up, they almost threw him out. Sindulfo never returned to the Office of Pensions and Annuities again. Why should he? The widow no longer needed her pension. She had died before they could take care of the necessary papers. Our bureaucrats never count on our being mortal.

But Sindulfo did not lose the friend he had made at the door. The afternoon of this misfortune, Keen left without saying good–bye to the commander and followed the orphan to his modest room.

In the loneliness of Madrid, a city he did now know, the man from the country, wearing brown pants, had nothing to weep into except, perhaps, the fur of a dog.

In a third–class coach the two went to the sad, distant city which was Sindulfo's home. (Keen, in order not to be separated from his master, crouched under a bench and made it to the country. This is what he wanted, anonymity, peace and quiet.)

The very little traffic and almost no noise in the streets enchanted Keen. It seemed to him that he had reached the shore after being bounced about by the waves on a rough sea.

He did not see many other dogs. He preferred to stay near the house. His master lived in a humble cottage which enjoyed the sun on the outskirts of the city. He lived with one servant. In the morning, he went to the store where he kept the books for a business that closed during the afternoons. Then he returned to the house and to Keen and worked silently and sadly on the beautiful pieces of wood inlay which were his pride and a help in meeting his expenses. The rapid, nervous noise of the little saw bothered Keen at first. But he grew accustomed to it and came to enjoy taking his naps rocked by the rhythm of that work.

He sighed. This is the life.

The first few months, Sindulfo worked on his inlay furniture quietly and sadly. Sometimes, tears came to his eyes.

"He is thinking of his mother," Keen said to himself. He wagged his tail a little, stretched out his muzzle and hid his head on his master's skinny legs which were covered with the brown slacks. One afternoon in May, Keen saw with a pleasant surprise that his master, after finishing a Gothic tower of yew, took a flute out of its case and began to play very sweetly.

What a delight. Those ancient little dance songs, those romantic, monotonous melodies played naturally with peaceful, heartfelt simplicity were wonderful to the dog.

Keen had never been in love. Bitches did not impress him. The brutal polygamy of the species made sexual love repugnant to him. Besides, how scandalously they behaved in the streets! And how sadly complicated physiologically the copulation of canines was. "If ever I fall in love," he thought, "it will be in a small town, in the country."

His master's flute made him think about love, not about love affairs. For a temperament like Keen's, friendship can be a warmly sublime, shared affection.

His love was for his master. He read the depths of the man's soul in his eyes, in his way of doing inlay, and especially in his way of playing the flute. He was very sad, not desperate, but definitely disconsolate. Sindulfo was born to be loved very much, but he was unable to try to bring love into his home beyond that of an insignificant personality like his dog. He had brought Keen. He would never dare bring a companion, a wife or a mistress.

But Sindulfo, like Keen, in peace had found balm. They understood one another by signs, by the harmonious order of their household. System, silence, order, efficiency and a chaste discipline of humility defined everything. This is how they both wanted to live.

Keen's affection was the stronger, the firmer of the two. The dog, being inferior, loved more. He was not afraid of a rival, however. "No," he thought, "there will never be a lady here to steal his affection from me. My master will never leave me for a wife. He is afraid of women."

"We are going into the country, my friend," Sindulfo came in saying one day. And off they went. A few miles from the city where his mother had left him a few small parcels of land which he rented to a former servant, Sindulfo went to fish and to change the terms of his tenant's lease.

When Keen saw the meadows, the woods and the green cultivated fields on the sides of the hills, he felt a thrill run down his spine. He remembered his old idea, "If I could fall in love, it would only be in the country."

"I wonder if I could still be happy with something more than sweet peace and resignation?" To experience this hope seemed to him an act of pride. Besides, it was an infidelity. Had he not promised in secret never to love anyone or anything except his master, his true master?

The august solitude of the shady valley was a valid excuse for his dreaming of being able to enjoy a sensual happiness there among the new, intense emotions which the country air evoked in him. With the delight of an artist, Keen considered the stages of his life: from the capital to a provincial city, from there to a village. And each step into reclusion seemed to bring him closer to himself. The more lonely he was, the more aware of himself he became.

When night arrived, the people left him in the yard in front of the house. What memorable hours! The chickens were roosting in the henhouse and there in the distance he could hear the mysterious noises they made in their sleep. The pigs in a stone pen were dozing and dreaming, making sensual grunts; the air softly moved the biblical leaves of the oriental fig trees, making sounds like lovers talking in secret. The moon ran through the clouds and through the valley; toward the hill facing them, there were echoes accompanying the silvery light, singing the song of eternal poetry about the miracle of mysterious creation, echoes of the barking of dogs who were dispersed about the countryside in the many farm yards. They barked at the moon like priests in some frightening primitive cult or like unconscious poets who held on in exasperation to their mystic illusions.

Keen felt joined by new bonds to this pagan initiation, to mother nature, to the cult of Cybele and to the passion of his breed. From the Indian chestnut trees there flowed a scent of prolific seed; love to him seemed a rite of universal faith, common to all living things. From the next alley, sunken in the darkness of the trees which formed a bower, Keen waited for the key to love's mystery to appear.

With the voices of the summer night, his entire being cried out to him that from that darkness there had to appear the mystery—the bitch.

He heard noise toward the street; two figures appeared. They were two mastiffs who could have swallowed Keen in one gulp.

Keen did not know the customs of the village. He did not know that there, dogs and men alike went wandering in search of females. They courted them.

Those mastiffs were two toughs from the parish who had smelled a new dog here in the Coto valley and had come to see if it was a female.

They sniffed Keen with their village rudeness and were disappointed. Grudgingly, they invited Keen to follow them. They were going looking for females, courting girls, or rather bitches.

Oh, the disappointment of it all! The bitch in the country lives in polygamy like the bitch in the city.

Keen, nevertheless, could not resist the temptation, and more from the anger of disappointment than the seduction of a night of lascivious scents, he followed the two mastiffs. Like so many poets with a virginal soul, after the icy death of that first pure love, he threw himself furiously into biting the flesh of the orgy.

Keen the Royal spent that night wandering.

He followed the mastiffs through the dark streets without knowing precisely where they were taking him, disturbed, full of remorse and repelled by sin. His ears burned and buzzed. But he went. The inertia of evil and the inheritance of a thousand generations of dogs compelled him.

They ran into the wide moonlit meadows which were covered by a light mist, which Chateaubriand calls a reminder of the deluge, that like a silver lagoon flooded the valley. In was Saturday. In the mysterious poetic darkness of the two hills, which to the north and south cut off the horizon, the young men of all the neighboring parishes were courting next to the farm houses hidden in the thickness of chestnut and oak groves.

The prehistoric cry of the Celtic villagers echoed in the depths of the foothills and under the bowers of the grove and was confused with the song of crickets, with the strident Wagnerian exclamations of the locusts and with the barking of dogs in the distance.

Never is the prose of crude vice as abhorrent as when it occurs in the poetry of nature.

In that valley of solemn silence broken by the cries of animals keeping vigil, those cries of desperation lost in the immense, silent solitude of earth and sky, in that expanse illuminated with the elegiac light of an eternally romantic sky, Keen longed for a chaste, pure passion and love! He quickly realized what was happening. There was a new bitch that had come to one of those rural parishes just recently. The scarcity of females is one of the hardships that most afflicts the canine breed in the country. Because of a deliberate process of selection, the weaker sex is not chosen to guard cattle and the houses on the farms. The bravest dog must fight a Trojan battle in certain competition with a hundred rivals to win the slightest amorous favor.

But those mastiffs made Keen understand on that night through the careful observation of the data that men behave even more irrationally. At least the dogs attacked and bit one another to win a female or be among the first in line for her favors; but the young men of the villages who shouted *ixuxú* and like the dogs crossed the moonlit meadows and hid in the dark canyons and river beds attacking granaries and ovens in the middle of the night, why did they beat one another with clubs and stab one another with knives and shoot one another with pistols and revolvers? Because they loved to fight. They could have peacefully divided among themselves the girls of marrying age who are more numerous than they and not usually so discreet as to hide away, but rather choose to flaunt their beauty with taunts such as those we hear in Moreto's plays, taunts thrown from their doorways in the light of the stars like Margaret's in *Faust*, less poetic, perhaps, but better armed with large fists to defend their putative virginity against no less than ten or twelve young men in one evening.

Yes. Men, like dogs, made a battlefield of the poetic valley on Saturday nights, fighting in the loneliness for love's captive. The difference was that the amorous adventures of the dogs were always consummated, though with a brief and repulsively polygamous union, while the major slips of the boys and girls in the valley were much less frequent.

At dawn, breathless, lost, with his tongue hanging out, his coat spotted with the mud of a hundred ditches, Keen returned to the door of the farm house where his master was sleeping. He regretted crimes he had not committed, feeling the revulsion and bitter aftertaste of furtive pleasures which he had not had. He suffered the shame of the bacchanalia and orgy without having experienced the material delight of its sensual pleasures. The happy bitch fought over by eight mastiffs that night had doled out her favors right and left. But Keen's timidity and coldness had not been suitable qualities to capture a moment of attention from that hunting Messalina; she was a hunting dog.

Finally, our hero returned to his master's door without having known a bitch that night, and instead, he returned humiliated by the scratches and nipping of other dogs who had believed him to be a rival and had treated him cruelly.

But the worst part was yet to happen. Sindulfo, his owner, more beloved than all the bitches in the world, had disappeared. He had gone fishing before dawn. Keen did not know where. He waited all day at the door of the farm house and his master did not appear. He did not return that night, either. On the following day, Keen discovered that an urgent message from the city had made him renounce his planned stay in the country and return to the store where his help was indispensable. The dog found out more. Sindulfo's tenant, the villager who was renting his four fields, had become very fond of the dog's good character and had begged Sindulfo to leave him there on the farm since he did not have a dog at that time. So Keen found himself on loan in the farmer's power.

The whole expanse of the wide valley seemed like a jail to him, an unbearable slavery.

He was humble, obedient and resigned, but he could not bear his master's ingratitude. How could it be that fate had become his enemy and was punishing him for his first mistake? Just because of one, almost involuntary try for a fleeting moment of sensuality, this terrible whip was falling on him, the punishment of being denied the one true affection he knew in the world. Keen did not realize that this was the form the most exquisite favor of grace often takes, that the mistakes of those who have been called not to make any evoke a prompt and harsh punishment so that the just do not become accustomed to wandering off the straight and narrow.

He sniffed the air with his nose toward the cool northeast wind as Ariadne would have done if she were a hound. Fleeing the farm house at a good trot, he looked for the road to the city and arrived at his house on the outskirts in a few hours.

Sindulfo did not receive him well, although he was proud of his dog's love for him and of his ability to travel so many miles without getting lost. But Keen had to return to the country because a man's word is his word, and the loan of the dog was a promise that had to be kept. The humble animal did not rebel. Before a final and direct mandate, he no longer dared invoke his rights to liberty.

His affection tied him to obedience. That master had chosen him from among all other dogs. He was the absolute master. He cried, in his own way, over the ingratitude and repaid it with loyalty, living among those rude farmers who treated him like a vile mastiff, no different from all the other dogs who lived there.

At first, the boring life of the village repelled him. But little by little he began to feel a new bond, the strength of custom. He began to hate himself for beginning to sink without any further displeasure into the half-living, plant-like existence.

And horror of horrors! He began to lose the memory of his past life and with it his ideal, the love for his master. It was not that he had stopped loving him, he just stopped remembering him. He forgot what he looked like and what it was like to love him. Veil upon veil, forgetfulness began to cover his mind. He forgot images and ideas. Sindulfo as his master disappeared completely from his mind, as did the concept of master, of the city and of the days gone by. Merely a dog after all, Keen was not free from any of the characteristics of his species and his mind did not have the strength to keep alive all the images and ideas. But he still had the pain of disappointment, of that which he had lost. He continued suffering without knowing why. Something was missing and he did not know that it was his master. He felt deceived, an immense radical deception that saddened the world and he did not realize that what he was suffering was the disappointment that comes from ingratitude.

Who knows? Many human sorrows that are unexplainable may have a similar cause. Who knows? Perhaps those hopelessly sad poets are exiled angels from heaven who have lost their memories.

Keen was getting drowsy and vague. Since he could not become a symbolist nor create a philosophical system or a religion, he let himself fall into relentless sensuality as into a well. He chose the most passive form of sensuality—sleep. Whenever he was left alone, he stretched out with his head between his paws. And with the patience of Job without a roof over his head, he watched the flies and worms crawl into his dirty, long, tangled and disgusting fur.

He spent many days like this. He was the laziest dog in the valley. He gave no sign of life and had no inner life. He did not live for anyone or for himself. He did nothing but sleep and experience a strange pain.

One afternoon, the French poodle was dozing on the top of a wall which separated the yard from the meadow, across whose green corn fields was a path leading with many twists and turns to the highway. It was the road to the city, and Keen woke up looking with half-opened eyes at the narrow ribbon of path, as was his instinct, without remembering anymore that that path was the one on which he had seen his master disappear.

Suddenly, he caught a scent which made him lift his ears, lift his head, growl, and afterwards let out two or three loud, nervous dry barks. He stood up. He heard a noise in the corn. That scent! He smelled a resurrection, an ideal that was waking, a love that was emerging from forgetfulness like someone disinterred. A voice followed the scent. Keen gave a leap and in that moment, there below, a few yards away, appeared Sindulfo, still wearing his brown pants.

With a leap, Keen threw himself from the wall onto his master. On his hind legs with his tongue waving in the air like a flag, he began to jump around like a clown, trying to reach the yellow beard of his master who appeared, breaking through the shadows of forgetfulness, through his latent nostalgic sorrow.

Keen understood everything! That is what was silently aching in him! That absence, that ingratitude, which was forgiven as soon as he took charge of it. I should say he was forgiving him! How could he do otherwise, since the ingrate was there again?

Keen jumped about, howling and trembling with supreme joy. He was jumping, and in one of his leaps into the air, he felt that someone caught him in the middle of his body with a trap of very sharp teeth and threw him to the ground. While his back pulsed with terrible pain, he felt his chest and stomach crushed by two huge beastly paws, and terrified, he saw above his eyes the terrible face of an enormous Great Dane, a gigantic dog who was opening his great bloody jaws threatening to swallow him.

Sindulfo came quickly and freed his poor Keen from the grip of death.

"Get away, Tiger! Damn you! Have you ever seen the like? He's jealous! Ha! He's jealous!"

When Keen recovered from his terror and confusion, he understood what was happening, that Sindulfo's new faithful friend had come with him, a purebred Great Dane, a beautiful and terrifying animal.

He would tolerate no rivals or enemies around his master, and when he saw the excesses of that French poodle, he had leapt to defend his master and free him from the caresses that offended him, the Tiger, so greatly.

Yes, it was the sad truth. Keen had caused Sindulfo to develop a love for dogs. The specific dog did not matter. But he could no longer live without a dog, and now he had another one who was bound to him by strong, close ties. There was nothing more natural!

Sindulfo petted Keen and looked at his terrible wounds. But secretly he was proud and satisfied with Tiger's behavior. His Great Dane was a wonderful watch dog.

Keen spent the night almost out of his mind with pain, with coals in the wounds on his back and fire in his outraged inner being.

So this is why his memory returned, this was why he recovered a clear awareness of his lost friendship! He could not fight off his anguish.

He spent that horrible night scratching at Sindulfo's bedroom door, and in the morning when they let him in, he jumped into the bedroom on a mad impulse and without noticing the mud and blood on his miserable coat, he threw himself onto the bed in which his ungrateful master was still lying, jumping over Tiger who missed when he tried to catch him in mid air.

Keen, trembling, almost sorry for his deed, took refuge in his master's lap, ready to die in the jaws of his hated rival, but die in the warmth of that beloved chest.

No one died. Sindulfo prevented any further attacks. But that afternoon, he left the village and returned with Tiger to the city. He said good–bye to Keen with three pats and forbade him to accompany him any further than the wall separating the meadow from the yard.

And Keen, wounded, humiliated and badly treated, saw them leave, saw his master with his favorite dog go down the path on his way to the highway, to the city and to forgetfulness.

It was the hour of the angelus; in a chapel next to the barn, the people of the village came together to pray the rosary. The farmers entered the church without seeing Keen, much less noticing his suffering.

The French poodle, when he lost sight of the ingrate, left his watchtower and walked about for a while in confusion, and when he heard the sound of the prayers in the chapel, he crossed the threshold and entered the sacred refuge. He did not understand what was going on. But the scent was a consolation. It smelled like the last refuge for good, long–suffering souls. But the moment when he felt these strange thoughts, he also felt a hard kick from one of the faithful, directed to his hind quarters to expel him from that shelter.

"It's true," he thought, and left hurriedly without protesting.

"What was I doing there? Dogs do not go to mass! I do not have an immortal soul. I do not have anything." And he returned to his watchtower, henceforth useless, on top of the wall which overlooked the path to eternal absence.

No longer able to bear his suffering, he let himself drop more dead than rejected. It was growing dark. The leaden sky seemed to come apart above the earth. He put his head between his paws and closed his eyes. There was no religion for him; there had been no love for him; he had despised vanity and ostentation; he had taken refuge in a warm affection, sublime in its opaque light and in faithful friendship. And friendship betrayed, outraged and disdained him.

The worst of all insults was that his dog's mind and canine soul would quickly bring him the forgetfulness of his lost ideal; and he would be left with only a mute, intense suffering without awareness of its cause.

Poor Keen! Since he was a dog, he could not console himself thinking that, all in all, in spite of so much unhappiness, so much suffering, just for having been humble, loyal and sincere, he was happier than many kings who have made history.

Satanmas Eve

His Serene Majesty of Hell was traveling incognito, his forehead clear of the fiery horns that are his crown, and his tail twisted around his thigh and between his legs under the tunic he wore as a disguise to hide all indications of his accursed power. He traveled over the face of the earth and at the moment was touring the Roman Empire, to whose grandeur he had entrusted the preparation, by force and by the humiliation of souls, for his dominion over the earth, which he already considered his as demonstrated by genealogical trees and by all sorts of Salic laws compiled with the help of hell's own lawyers.

He had reached Roman Judaea, crossing the Great Sea as if it were a ford. Lucifer's feet left tracks of smoke and sizzling water which boiled away at his every step on the waves. He came ashore in Ashcalon, moving northward along the sterile deserted beach, the ancient homeland of the Philistines, and from there approached Arimathea and Lydda at sunset.

But when the icy cold night came with its shining, trembling stars, many of which were particularly bright and glittering, he felt a certain superstitious fear, and like a bird which the changing wind moves according to its whim or like a ship caught in a storm, Lucifer felt impelled eastward, or rather toward the southeast on the road to Emmaus and headed in that direction against a current of a shallow, almost dry river.

The night frightened him more each step he took. It was a peaceful, clear night. But for that very reason, the devil trembled because each star was an eye and a shout. They all looked at him and cursed him, singing in their own way with their light the glory of the Lord. And moreover, Satan felt strange wisps in the air, supernatural vibrations and something like the apprehension of hidden voices of divine joy, nervous shimmerings of air and ether; the electromagnetic forces of the planet were active; the devil was suffocating in that atmosphere in which the imminent explosion of something prodigious seemed like a storm on the point of erupting. Just as the highest clouds sometimes lower their flight and roll over the mountains and descend to drink the water of the valleys, it seemed to the demon that that night, heaven with its angels had become humble and was clinging close to the earth. The river mists and the blue distances of the horizon seemed to him to be legions of the cherubim in disguise.

He left Emmaus behind him and guided by an instinct greater
than his will, he continued traveling to the southeast, leaving on his
left the city of Jerusalem whose walls looked to him like walls of fire.
He approached some shepherds who were awake and keeping watch
over their flock by night. Hiding in the shadows so that he was un-
touched by the light of the restless flickering flames, he did not approach their campfire. But suddenly, the blaze began to pale as if day
were breaking and the sun were stealing the power of its glow. The
shepherds looked about and believed dawn was breaking in the far-
thest reaches of the heavens and approaching them with its rosy tints.
It was not the dawn. It was the wings of the Angel of God fluttering in
joy and creating light by stirring the air. The shepherds huddled together trembling and lay prostrate on the earth, their faces hidden in
their hands while the devil sank his teeth and claws into the ground,
like the roots of an accursed plant.

Lucifer heard the confused sound of the Angel's words echoing
from on high like soft music captured in the folds of the air. But he
could not understand what the celestial apparition was saying to the
shepherds. He did not hear him say, "Be not afraid because I bring
you tidings of great joy which shall be for all the world. Unto you is
born today in the city of David a Savior who is Christ the Lord. Here
are the signs: you will find the child wrapped in swaddling clothes
lying in a manger."

Satan heard none of this clearly, but he saw that the apprehensions which he had had before were taking shape in reality, because
suddenly, like an ambush, legions of angels leapt from the waves of
the air, a multitude of celestial armies which were praising God and
saying, "Glory to God in the highest and on earth, peace and good
will toward men."

But all this transpired as in a dream. The campfire below and the
stars above began to shine again, but the demon was gnashing his
teeth. He remembered paradise, Adam's crime, and the promise of
God. The Only Born Son was going to appear! God was going to keep
his promise. His infinite love was delivering the Son to the cruelty and
blindness of men.

Hidden in his own shadow, which took the form of a dark cloud,
Lucifer followed the shepherds who, as if in a mystic rapture, left
their flocks and walked to Bethlehem.

They arrived at the inn where Joseph and Mary were sheltered
and there they were told that all the rooms had been taken and that
Joseph and Mary had the most humble place. They entered and saw
the Child lying in a manger.

And while the shepherds worshipped the Child, the Devil, overcome with envy of God's love, in the form of a bat flitted in and out
of the humble corral. But little angels also began to fly in and out,
models for Murillo, and since their wings bumped into the infernal

bat's wings, they were frightened and ran away, and Lucifer took
himself away from the Redeemer's cradle and went out into the loneliness of the night, into the sad frost, so pensive that when in the
darkness he returned to his natural shape, he forgot to remove his
wings which had grown to a size proportionate to his body. They
looked like an angular cape of repugnant, half–living skin; and instinctively, to protect himself from the dampness of the night, the
Demon pensively wrapped his wings about him.

"Oh, night!" he thought. "What a night! After losing my heavenly battle, after the first night in the shadows of darkness, this is the
most terrible night of my immortality."

His envy of charity tore his soul which, since it belonged to an
angel, though fallen, kept in his evil powerlessness to do good all the
delicacy of perception and of feeling which he had had in his pristine
seraphic state. The devil knows very much, and knows that the greatest and most noble thing is not physical beauty, power, genius or
fortune, that the greatest thing is love and abnegation. And so, he did
not envy God His dominion over the infinite starry firmament, His
wisdom, the beauty of His works created for His glory; he envied Him
that infinite love which delivered to the pains of the flesh a divine
nature and made from the Word a Man to speak to miserable mor-
tals.

His prophetic imagination, his greatest torment, presented to Lucifer, wrapped in his wings, the spectacle of the world after that terrible night which people would call Christmas Eve.

God saw into rebellious spirits; Christ would reign over souls and
peoples who seemed the most rebellious to His law! First, the humble
domain of a few ignorant Jews; then that mysterious attraction exercised on a distracted pagan world which was basically more frivolous
than perverted; then the conversion of barbarian tribes; dominion by
faith, by hope and by charity; an ideal kingdom without a sword. And
the demon smiled with bitter complacency imagining what would follow: a scepter–cross; a crozier–scythe which makes the wandering
sheep bleed with its edge on returning it to the flock; temporal power,
orthodox empire; afterward, the imperial papacy and the blind
strength of believing oneself Christian; the cross serving as a wall for
imperial edicts; state pasquinades nailed to the sublime beams; death
sentences nailed where once was read I.N.R.I. The devil smiled, but
not very happily, because he saw that that world would endure briefly
in comparison with the multitude of future generations. Again, the
spiritual kingdom! The resurrection of those fleeting splendors of the
thirteenth century, of the New Testament; the civilized world, with its
complex life and its intense culture extended over all parts of the
earth creating, simply, one large brotherhood which could be called
the Universal Confederation or the Third Order. Saint Francis eternally in fashion! The evangelical phrase, "The poor ye will have with

you always," explained not in terms of material poverty nor in terms of the egoism which it destroys, but by the constant imitation of Saint Francis.

The most distant, far–flung peoples, those most removed from Christian civilization, leaving their idols, their sacred books, first to copy secular Europe and America, their states, arms and frivolous laws of political formality, their art and industry, and afterwards imitating the conversion, the intimate depth of the essence of their culture, their basis in Christianity. All peoples will be Christian. The entire world seeing with new clarity and strength the profane meaning of those words: "The gates of Hell will not prevail against Her."

"Oh, yes!" thought Lucifer weeping. "What a wonderful idea God has had! To become man...to become man in the blood of the Son...to be the Son of God, born in a manger and preaching: 'Our Father who art in Heaven...give us our daily bread...Thy will be done...we are all brothers; God, Father of all; forgive our trespasses; give to the poor and follow me...Take up your cross...and die on it...forgiving...unforgettable!"

"On the other hand, I," continued Lucifer, thinking, "I am growing old; soon each day for me will be a century; my decrepit years will not be solemn or dignified; I will be a useless old man without dignity whom people will chide and whom children will chase, not a venerable patriarch guiding a people; I will be something less than that: an abstraction, a metaphysical ghost, a rhetorical commonplace; good for a metaphor. Oh, I do not communicate with the world! In my apparitions, I never abandon my diabolic prerogative, my spiritual inviolability; I am afraid to make myself flesh which men can torment. Sterile egoism will not let me reproduce myself. I do not have the Word; I do not have a Son. I will become useless, despicable, I will see myself paralyzed in a corner of hell without daring to show myself to the world, and my Son will not take my place. The Great King of the Abyss has no heir!"

And he continued feeling in the distance the joyful tremblings of the universe on Christmas Eve; those signs which the stars sent winking at one another in shared understanding of the sublime secret as if saying to one another: "Can you imagine what has just happened? There below, somewhere, in a corner of the Milky Way...God has been born!" Since the angels insisted on fluttering over Bethlehem and the heavens continued in low–lying divine mists covering the face of the earth confusing Judaea with the empyrean, Lucifer, whose immortal tissue of subtle spirit was torn by envy, made a supreme effort of will to violate his egoism and thought: "I, too, want to incarnate; I, too, want to have a son; I, too, want my Eve."

But in whom to engender the Son of the Demon? How can one perpetuate evil in human form, creating something which will last forever on earth, and make my nature a living thing, something tangible, imperishable and unforgettable! And spreading his bat–like wings which were now immense and reached the horizon, hiding the stars with their darkness, the night became blacker. And with the voice of thunder, Satan declared his desire to the shadows; he proposed to the night an infernal copulation in which Satan the man, a diabolical humanity, should be conceived.

But unfortunate in everything, his prophetic imagination made him see beforehand the portrait of his useless efforts, the constant failure of the prurience of a devil's love, the endless abortion of his attempts at an accursed paternity. What terrible luck! Before even beginning the deeds of his impossible triumph, he saw and understood the unrelenting disappointments. He saw his children dead before engendering them!

And he saw that the only children the night would give him were first fear, then superstition which, because it is blind, is taken for faith, sentimental error, impassioned and therefore false science; shallow reasoning, mad hypotheses, feigned humility which surrenders the power of reason to authority and makes the conscience a slave of unconscious pride. But all these pale offspring were dying little by little as if they had been born in cold, dark caves, a race of microbes which the light of the sun annihilates.

Lucifer, since he could not imitate God, tried to imitate Jupiter and took a thousand forms to seduce his Europas, Ledas and Alcmenes; and from prostitutes, evil vestals and corrupt queens he had bastards who lived for him very briefly; they were all weak, misshapen and frail. He took as his concubines doubt, madness, tyranny, hypocrisy, intolerance and vanity and they gave him children named Pessimism, Pride, Terror and Fanaticism. They all lived in hunger, devouring the good of the world which they ground up in their gullets creating corruption; but their destruction was in vain because little by little they were dying. The demon even took the portals of the Church to his bed; but neither the Inquisition, Ignorance, Absolute Monarchy nor pseudo–scholasticism was the son he was looking for, the immortal son, because they all died. Finally, he thought he had engendered what he was looking for in civilization, whom he had caught sleeping. From a forced union he engendered Materialism in all its egotistical, frivolous sensuality. But it too died at the hands of the legitimate children born of that chaste mother and Satan saw that the world returned to Jesus when it seemed that the devil's time had arrived.

Unfortunate father! After centuries and centuries of constant efforts to leave descendants, he wept in his sterile old age, surrounded by shadows, the memories of his infinite offspring now disappeared and dead. Thus Lucifer saw himself in that image of the future which his tormented imagination presented to him in the shadowy depths of the night in whose breast he tried to engender his first born, created

only to die. He, an immortal, could not give immortality to his offspring. Every year a child, every year a corpse.

Every Christmas Eve, Jesus was born in the manger and the shepherds saw him lying between the pure hands of Mary who wrapped
him in swaddling clothes.

And at the same time, in the loneliness of the cold night, the
devil buried his son in the depths, his son who had died from the
cold, wrapped in a shroud of snow, of snow born from kisses without
love given by a cursed father who cannot love; and since he engenders without affection, without a spirit of abnegation and sacrifice, he
engenders only eternal death.

Round Trip

Mother and son entered the church. It was in the middle of the country, half way up the side of a green hill from whose height, crowned with oaks and pines, the nearby Cantabrian Sea was visible. The temple occupied a hidden bluff like a fortification among great chestnut trees; the ancient tower with three recesses for three venerable dark bells which were covered with the patina of the mystic mineralization of their Sufitic, or stylitic aging acquired from constant exposure to the elements, from having surrendered themselves to their fate...was barely visible among the white fronds of the fruit to come and the shades of green in the glossy, noisy leaves rustled by the breeze like enchanted Hindu dancers in an unceasing ballet in solemn, holy rhythm. From the noble, rustic temple in its patriarchal simplicity there seemed to issue forth a saintliness like perfume which turned the surrounding woods into a holy place. Silence of a consecrated religious nature reigned. God lived there.

To enter the parochial church of Lorezana it was necessary to go through a portico, nursery school, and cemetery waiting room. On one wall, like some majestic adornment, was the paupers' coffin hanging from four posts. Beneath it were two shining skulls forming the bas-relief of the wall with words from Job.

The main door in front of the altar under the chorus was, according to the priest, Byzantine; a half-pointed low arch with three or four columns on each side with elaborately carved fusts and pilasters which more or less resembled fantastic animals. Those venerable stones were like parchments which attested to the noble heritage of piety in that country.

The temple was poor, small, bright and clean. It had a village simplicity mixed with august antiquity, which was enchanting. In the nave, the silence seemed reinforced by the hushed prayers of the spirits of the air. Outside, silence, within, even more silence; because outside, the chestnut tree leaves were dancing and colliding and whispering.

Two oil lamps, daylight stars, burned in front of the favorite altars. The Virgin on the main altar was illuminated by a sunbeam which entered through a narrow window of white and blue panes.

On the floor of large, badly aligned and uneven paving stones there were the remains of a carpet of large rushes strewn about a few days before during the celebration of a holy day. The breeze which entered through a lateral open door moved those withered long leaves like swords surrendered to the faith. A sparrow appeared occasionally in the side door. It approached the middle of the nave as if it had come to be converted and at the last moment, thinking it over, shot off like an arrow for the open air, the forest, and its joyful life of unconscious paganism.

In the presbytery on the right side, seated on a bench, the ancient priest meditated peacefully, reading his breviary. There were no other living beings in the church except the sparrow and the priest.

The mother and son entered, crossed themselves with fingers dipped in the holy water taken at the door.

After a few steps, they modestly kneeled, fearful of interrupting the good priest who thought himself alone in the house of the Lord.

They kneeled in the middle of the nave. The mother turned her head toward her son in a familiar sign: she was indicating to him that the prayer for the soul of his departed father, her lost husband, was beginning. She led the prayer and her son responded as a chorus with words which had nothing to do with those of his mother. It was a mystic dialogue similar to those paintings by certain primitive religious painters from Italy in which the figures of saints attend a scene without being aware of one another, without looking at one another, yet are all together and each one alone with God. That was the state of the priest, who was as unaware of the sparrow entering and leaving as of the mother and son who were praying nearby.

Then the miracle began.

The prayer had become a meditation. Each one meditated alone. The mother, because of the pain of her widowhood, reached God immediately through her graceful, firm, easy, smooth and pure faith.

The son was twenty years old. He came from the world and from the disputes of men. His father's death had wounded him in the most intimate depths of his being, in the nucleus of strength which enables us to resist, to hope and to venerate the doubtful mystery. Sometimes his mother's resignation before their common misfortune irritated him. He felt within him something of the bitterness of Hamlet. He saw in his mother's religious fervor the happy rival of his deceased father.

He was a student, a poet, a dreamer. His soul had not torn itself violently from the faith of his mother because of his indolence or concupiscence. Like the sparrow in this village church, his soul entered and left orthodox piety. He read, studied and heard teachers from all schools of thought. His absolute sincerity of thought obliged him to vacillate, to affirm nothing with that complete conviction which he would have been able to dedicate to something worthy of his unbreakable, definitive loving commitment. He was suffering in this state, consuming the generous energy of his youth on inner struggles. But at the moment, he loved only love, he believed only in faith without knowing what kind. He professed the religion of wanting to be religious. And meanwhile, he followed his mother to church where he knew he was doing a charitable act simply by pleasing someone whom he loved dearly. Besides, his poetic soul continued being Christian. The fragrance of the village church, its coolness, its simplicity, its mystic silence, its air of voluptuous reminiscence from his dreamy childhood of faith and belief gently inebriated him. And without hypocrisy, he humbled himself, prayed, sensed Jesus's presence, and reviewed in his mind the idea of nineteen centuries of great Christian victories. He was flesh of that flesh, a descendant of those martyrs and those soldiers of the cross. No, he was not irreligious in his village church, in spite of his changing philosophies.

The mother, from thinking about the deceased father went on to think about the son who was perhaps threatened with a more terrible death, a spiritual death in all its blind, doleful impiety. She remembered Saint Monica's tears and asked God to illuminate her son's mind into which so many things not transmitted by her blood, so many things which were not a part of her, had entered. In her painful doubts about her son's moral fate, her imagination stopped when she reached the idea of a possible condemnation. That infinite terror, sublime in the immensity of its torment, could not dominate her mind because she could not conceive of such suffering. Hell for her son! That could never be! God would take measures to avoid that. Men's souls were free, yes; they could choose evil and perdition, but God had his providence, his infinite goodness. The son would be saved. To prayer! One must pray to achieve it!

These two were so absorbed in their thoughts that they forgot about the time of day and escaped the shadow of the pendulum which swings in the eternal prison of the second which it measures. The power of foresight, or a fear which imagines future trouble, took shape for them in reality; their future life was foretold in those moments of profound meditation.

For the son, the poetic arguments of faith were withdrawing like martial parade music passing by. It speaks when it is near of patriotic enthusiasm, of happy self–denial and leaves in its place after disappearing into the distant silence the idea of a solitary death. To avoid thinking about the greater problems of reality in the context of his sentimental recollection of a beloved sacred tradition began to seem like a duty to him, an austere law of thought itself. Just as a soldier in war is alone with danger, accompanied only by the enemy's bullets, far from his own country which cannot see him suffering, far from the thrills of martial music and the incitements of patriotic rhetoric, alone with the austere destructiveness of war as Shakespeare's *Coriolanus* paints it, so that sincere thinker remained alone in the desert of his ideas where it was ridiculous to ask his mother for help or to seek refuge in the purity of his childhood, as ridiculous as it would have been in a duel or in a battle.

Good or bad, favorable or unfavorable, there was no other law except for the laws which govern thought. One must believe whatever might be true, no matter how horrible. Like a valiant man who is truly brave believes he has no amulet to protect him from bullets but faces them convinced that they can pass through his body as easily as they pass through air, so was the bold mind of the woman's son. But his youth was dying in his logical proofs. His heart was becoming shriveled and small. His life was escaping him amidst such doubts. Sensual dreams were losing their attractiveness of unconditional worth, and instead were becoming precarious and relative, a cheerful comedy from the point of view of the plot and sad from the point of view of the fatal brevity and vanity of the senses. He was unable to enjoy anything very much. The dream of a true love, of the ideal woman, was fading also. All that remained of her were traces of a dispersed dream floating freely, torn apart at ground level like the smoke of a locomotive fleeing through the countryside on giant spider's feet, dissipating a little more after each leap across the meadows and among the hedgerows.

Logic wanted him for its own. If the great idea were problematic, perhaps an illusion, the ideal woman was a puerile phenomenon, a fortuitous vulgarity in the meaningless and graceless game of natural forces.

Nature remained. And the thinker, who no longer expected anything from love, turned from the fantastic cloud–sculptured sky to lean his head over the soil, in love with his humble land and its fruits. He was a geologist, a botanist, a physiologist. The natural world without the beauty of its apparent forms can still appear great and poetic, but sad, sometimes horrible in its Oedipal destiny. Nature began to represent an infinite abandonment to him, a universe without a father was frightening because of the uncertainty of its fate. The blind struggle of things against things, the unconscious desire for life at the expense of the life one has, the battle of the so–called species and of individuals to conquer, to be on top for a moment, killing a lot to live a little, made him tremble with terror. The eternal classic tragedy certainly has its sublime and mysterious beauty, but is no less the terrible for it.

Life passed by, and in a kind of rational myopia, his spirit began to feel separated by mists and veils from the physical, plastic world. With more force than when he was involved with his academic studies, idealistic theories began to cast into doubt and hide among the subtle arguments of logic the objective reality of the world. And again the worst kind of metaphysical anguish returned, stronger than ever, an uncertainty about his ability to judge, a lack of confidence in reason itself, which is perhaps the threshold of madness. A painful skill with destructive intuition and sharp analysis was destroying like a nervous fever the most intimate fabric of his unified and consistent conscience. Everything was reduced to a kind of incoherent moral dust which, because of its worthlessness, caused vertigo and spiritual agony.

Meanwhile, in their own way, his mother's thoughts also flew around regions which, though very different, were also dark and sinister. She was losing her son. He was separating himself from her and was becoming lost. Very far away, she felt, he was living in blasphemy, forgetful of God's love, and enemy to His glory. It was as if he were mad. But he was not mad, because God asked him for an account of his actions. He was a wicked man who did not kill, steal from or dishonor anyone. He did not harm anyone, and in God's eyes he was wicked. And she prayed and prayed again to extract him from the abyss, to bring him back to the lap where he had learned to believe. It was strange. She saw him kneeling on the ground in a desert like an anchorite, without eating or drinking, without flowers to admire, love to experience, completely sad and alone, always kneeling with his hands raised toward heaven, his eyes fixed on the dust hoping without hope, cursed and yet innocent in his way, a blameless reprobate, a painful absurdity in the eyes of his mother and in the heart of her faith.

"It would be better to bury him," she thought. "Let him live very briefly and very quickly, if he must live this way." And she herself was building his tomb for him, throwing snow around the immobile body of the condemned anchorite—not earth, snow. Snow was falling on him, was now reaching his shoulders, was now covering his head. "Lord, save him, save him, before he disappears under the snow I am burying him in!"

In his spiritual crisis, things began to have a double meaning which the son had not noticed before. There was a background accompaniment which was, one might say, like music. While men spoke of things, the things themselves were silent. The man curious about reality, the one who believed in the mystery and who approached it on his own to spy on the world's silence, heard what voiceless things were singing in their own way. They vibrated, and this was a kind of music. They complained of the names which men had given them. Each name was an insult. Doubting reality was an infantile game appropriate to the childhood of human thought. Men of other better days were hardly able to imagine such subtleties. Everything was becoming clearer as it was becoming more confused. The printed signs in that botanical garden of the world began to disappear, and evidence of a nameless truth was becoming clear. The Greek names for the branches of science were lost and no longer had any purpose other than to provide a cool shelter where one could take the pleasant, safe nap of an idyll. Faith was returning in a different way. Symbols continued being venerable without being idols. There was a sweet, unwritten reconciliation without stipulation, a peace treaty in which the signatures were placed below the ineffable.

What did not return was ardent enthusiasm or the graceful innocence of belief. There was a home for the soul, but the surrounding air was winter cold. The years did not repent.

The mother felt a horrible weight lifted from her soul. The nightmare ceased. The breeze brought to her face the perfumes of the neighboring woods. While enjoying that sweetness, she thought about her son, not as she had seen him in her dreams. She thought about the son who meditated next to her. She turned her head softly toward him. The son also looked at his mother. They hardly recognized one another. The son was an old man with gray hair. The mother was a decrepit ghost, a living, pale shadow. The son, stooped with years, stood up with difficulty. He stretched his hand out to his mother and helped her rise with great difficulty also. The poor octogenarian could not walk without the support of her beloved son who was old also, though not decrepit.

She kissed him on the forehead. She crossed herself with a trembling hand in front of the main altar. She understood and was grateful for the miracle. The son believed again. He had made the round trip of thought. There was nothing left except for the fact that he had spent his existence in the battle. He was now an old man and she, by another portent of grace, lived in extreme decrepitude near her last breath, but happy because she had lasted long enough to see her son again in the lap of maternal faith. Yes, he believed again. She did not know why nor how, but he believed again. They approached the door of columns carved with strange figures. The mother took the holy water from the font and offered it to her son, who wet his wrinkled, snow-covered forehead.

They stopped at the portico. The mother, worn out by fatigue, could no longer walk. She smiled, stretching her hand out to the paupers' coffin, a dirty pine box spotted with mud and candle wax, hanging from the white wall.

And with a hushed voice, the happy old woman exclaimed on losing consciousness: "On that morning, on that day in the morning..!"

Trap

Was the highway a good thing or not? First of all it was a novelty, and it had that against it. Manín de Chinta, moreover, was sorry to leave the old road behind, the royal highway which had in reality never even become noble, because in spite of the many fortnights the parish had spent laboring on it, it had always remained common, narrow, arduous and uphill with gulleys for culverts, and with boulders, puddles, and mud holes for a surface. In the winter the animals sank their hooves up to their hocks. In the summer, the mud which was petrified in rising and falling swells like the sea still kept deep imprints of cows' and calves' hooves which adorned the motionless waves with arabesques. It did not matter. Manín's father, his grandfather and all his ancestors from time immemorial had driven their carts over that royal highway.

It took Manín de Chinta three hours to bring his cattle to town. That was a long time for such a short journey. But it had taken his father and grandfather three hours, also. Besides, the highway divided his pasture lands, that cool fragrant path of green, a gift of the corral, exactly in half. Manín resisted as long as he could. He held up the expropriation as far as his influence reached, but the invincible tide of progress, the role of civilization—as the district congressman had said at his own testimonial dinner—the torrent of the future, the highway, was stronger than Manín. And the enemy ran right through the meadow, filling the grass and trees on the left and right sides of the highway, running across Manín's land, with a dust which made them wither.

The romanticism of these villagers is never so excessive that they continue fighting against anything useful for very long. Manín dedicated a few nostalgic moments to the abandoned royal highway which was quickly covered over with grass. But like all his neighbors, he used the new road which, little by little, became rustic and earned its place in the community, becoming something familiar and beneficial. Along the side of the road, freshly painted small houses were being built, cleaner and more solid than the huts on the nearby hillsides. Taverns and small stores were numerous along the new highway. The traffic increased and it was not long before Manín saw his neighbors abandon the typically heavy carts of his country with their horrendously squeaking wheels which must have been used by the Huns for centuries for their own trips to the villages. They had begun to adopt

light, springy two–wheeled surreys which were painted in such lively
loud colors, that on speeding over the road it seemed that they made
almost as much noise with their green, red, and blue painted planks
as with their gravel–throwing tires.

Manín de Chinta felt envious and finally came to want his own
painted cart. He was something of a carpenter and between him and
the neighborhood blacksmiths, he managed at no inconsiderable expense to leave at the Chinta corral gate a blue and red vehicle with a
canvas top, pine seats and even a step on the back. The only thing
wanting was a horse.

Manín's family consisted of his mother Rosenda, his wife Mara
Chinta de Pin de Pepa, two marriageable daughters, and a son named
Rafael or Falo, who was a discharged army cavalryman.

After thinking it over carefully and taking out, counting, and
weighing the coins which the housewife had saved in a green purse—
money from the forced sale of parts of their meadowlands—family
members decided that Falo should go to the next fair on the Feast of
the Assumption, traveling all the way to the capital of the province to
buy a draft animal, a strong one, for about fifteen hundred *reales*,
one accustomed to work and able to pull the entire family up the
Grandota hill and beyond. Falo understood that if not he, then no
one could carry through the dangerous task of bringing home another
mouth to feed, someone with unknown habits and whose usefulness
had never been demonstrated.

The entire family was already suspicious of the intruder, even
before it had appeared, when Falo set off for the fair.

Cows, pigs, chickens, goats, ducks, and rabbits—everyone was
already familiar with them; they were almost like members of the
family, one might say. The donkey that they took to grind corn was a
humble guest and polite. But a horse was a different matter! And a
carriage horse, no less! The novelty was too great, too annoying, almost painful.

"You will have to make a place for it in the corral, next to the
cows," said Mrs. Chinta.

And Manín, rather disdainfully, shrugged his shoulders and said
between his teeth, "Bah! Whatever you say. We still do not know if
Falo will find anything suitable. There is always time."

And the family almost hoped that Falo would return without the
animal he had gone to buy and for which the cart leaning on its shafts
at the door was crying out.

Falo came back astride a mare. She was a tall animal, a bay, with
a fine head, good gait, and lively when she shook her bridle. And she
was not at all skittish. She was neither too skinny nor too fat. The
only fault she might have was that whenever they left her alone, she
was very sad. She would straddle the ground, stretch out her neck

and every now and then make a noise as if she were sighing deeply, trembling from the innermost part of her being.

She was from Castille, from the plains. Perhaps the mountains depressed her. Her age? That was where the mystery lay. Like any good strong country woman, her mouth would never give away her age. But she could not have been very old. Or perhaps she was. Perhaps she was like Ninon de Lenclos.

Falo had not bought her at the fair. He came back from the city with the money almost satisfied that he had not found anything suitable. Everything was either too expensive, of bad quality, or questionable. The truth was that the ex–cavalryman did not understand very much about horse trading and had been somewhat frightened by the gypsies who offered him so many bargains.

Where Falo did make his purchase was right outside the town near his very own house. He bought from a neighbor who lived in the same district, the artilleryman, a northern gypsy, more of a gypsy than those who run all over the world. The artilleryman recognized Falo as soon as he saw him looking at the mare he was riding, the mare the cavalryman had fallen in love with. Falo, much later, understood why he had taken such a quick liking to the horse. It looked like a horse that they had shot out from under him during the Carlist wars in a famous charge. But Manín de Chinta's son did not realize this right away. He liked the mare, he thought, because he liked her, because she was handsome, pretty, a nice color, had a good gait, and was not skittish.

Falo arrived home at dark and put the mare in the cow barn. This trained cavalryman understood immediately that the people at home would not thank him for his purchase at all. The old folks, thinking about the money, the three hundred pesetas which had been left elsewhere, rather regretted their daring decision to drive a surrey. Besides, a true mount was so new and different in the undifferentiated life shared there by man and beast! Manín's mother, a very old woman, unable to do anything but smoke, eat and shout orders, orders which sometimes were obeyed and other times were not, but which were always respected, this eighty–year–old Rosenda thought it was terrible that the pony, or rather the burro, who was the oldest animal and had served the family longest, had to be content in the little corral and learn to get along with all her neighbors, the smaller animals, and that the intruder should get half the corral for herself! And food? Heavens! The best grass from the meadow, even straw! Pure gluttony and luxury!

As the days passed, everybody's silent anger, except Falo's, against Chula, instead of diminishing was increasing. Falo spent hours with her, cleaning her, currycombing her, trying to console her for the indifference she was suffering and for the scarce amount of feed they gave her.

The Castillian mare became more and more sad. Every now and again, she would turn her head suddenly as if she expected to see some piece of familiar scenery on the plains of Castille which she was dreaming about half–awake. She would close her eyes tightly, trembling, and the flies rushed to her eyelids as if wanting to drink up the tears of homesickness from this resigned and melancholy beast.

Chula was growing thinner. Next to her sagging spine a hard lump appeared. Falo, filled with terror, hid the sad discovery from Manín and the women. He cured the animal secretly with vinegar and salt.

The day of the test arrived. The surrey was hitched, and Manín, his wife and son began the ride to town. Nothing unusual happened. Chula had pulled a lot in her life. The shaft and the noise of the wheels striking the rocks, the frequent collisions with carts loaded with hay to the point that they were invisible under the moving green mountain of grass, collisions with herds of swine and with bicycles did not disturb her. She seemed to be used to everything. She belonged to that school of horses which look straight ahead and probably do not even pay attention to what is going on around them. She would walk and dream, like so many poets exiled to the prose of the everyday world. They work and they dream.

Once in a while, as if coming back to reality, she would lift her head as if she were looking for freer air, wider horizons. Those green hills so close by on the right and the left seemed to oppress her, to suffocate her. At least this is what Falo, who was driving her, imagined to himself. Every few minutes, the boy would look, without his father noticing, at the swelling on her leg. It was getting worse. And another unfortunate thing was that the mare had overexerted herself and the harness had drawn blood on her chest and shoulders.

The famous Grandota hill appeared ahead, a formidable test! Chula, discreetly switched by Falo, started up the crest at an extended trot. Halfway up the hill, the surrey ran into a cart that was coming down and the mare suddenly stopped.

Quel giorno più non vi legemmo avante.

That day, Chula would not take one more step toward the village. Everything was to no avail—whips, sticks, caresses, persuasive arguments from Manín, his wife's complaints, the help of passers–by who came to lift the wheels of the surrey off the road. She just would not pull. She did not buck or grow impatient. There was no kicking or nipping—just silence, patience and resignation, but not one step. The blows rained on her back. The bay just closed her eyes, her lids trembling sadly. Suffer, chin up, dream of Castille! Everyone would have to get home as best he could.

The following day, at dawn, Falo saw with terror that her leg was much more inflamed. The wound kept bleeding, and on her back and chest the straps had rubbed her hide and it was shining, distilling a liquid mixed with blood, making great harness sores. It was neces-

sary to tell Manín de Chinta what was happening. The man shook his
fists at the heavens. The women went outdoors to shout, to grieve like
the mourners at a funeral. The life story of the artilleryman was
shouted out in the manner of a comedy by Aristophanes.

If that man had the nerve to cheat the Chinta family, he should,
they shouted, be sent back to jail where he belonged.

Chula was going from bad to worse. She was falling like the
stocks at the exchange when there was a panic. More and more flies
attacked to divide her up. Falo saw in fear the next transformation of
that animated figure, which he had begun to love without knowing
why, into an inert mass, putrid and repugnant. He foresaw the terrible "every-man-for-himself" reaction of matter which flees any organism abandoned by the mysterious breath of life. Besides, since
Falo did not believe in the immortality of mares' souls, that putrefac-
tion which his new friend was about to become seemed more horrible
and for this very reason he felt even greater pity.

He began to cure and take care of Chula with all the concern and
enthusiasm of a young, stubborn and energetic villager. He wanted
her to get better.

Meanwhile, Manín was quickly taking steps to go back on the
purchase. "Fortunately, I did not buy her at the fair. The artilleryman would have to give back the money and take the Trap back
because he had really cheated them." He did not know whether he
had a right to the rescission or whatever it was. But he knew one
thing for certain—that it was a question of power politics, of bossism,
that the judge would force the artilleryman to take the mare back if
the gentleman insisted.

The gentleman was the political power in the village, the boss to
whose party Manín belonged, someone who had taken Manín's
money to loan it out at interest and from whom Manín had rented a
little land. The artilleryman also had someone protecting his interests.
It was a fight between political bosses. The judge officiously had the
question placed in the hands of those who could solve the problem
without bringing it to court, letting everyone know that he, the judge,
should it come to that, would solve the issue in the same way. He
wanted to serve the more powerful party by delaying or without having to make compromises. The stronger political boss, the gentleman,
Manín's connection, won his way. The artilleryman was frightened
and gave up before presenting his case to the disreputable village
court.

But this entire pseudojuridical war of influence, intrigue, anger
and vanity lasted weeks and weeks and meanwhile, the mare neither
improved nor died. Little by little, some intelligent neighbors began
to come to Falo's aid in curing her, because of their love for veteri-
nary medicine. Rosenda and Chinta also began to take an interest in
that animal and its sufferings. Manin was the last one to come, but he

too came and turned out to be the most solicitous and the most determined one to alleviate Trap's suffering.

Chula was becoming more familiar to everyone, just like the highway. Even the cows noticed her. The chickens especially spent the
entire day around her hooves. The idea that she was one of God's
creatures gave the corral the atmosphere of a charitable hospital.
Falo beamed triumphantly.

The mare, finally, began to improve somewhat, but very slowly.
The family was becoming attached to her. Even the parish priest
came to visit her one day. The priest, like Chula herself, was also
Castillian, a grave, noble, sad, and courteous man. He, too, missed
the wide plains of Castille. The priest declared, patting the horse's
flank, that she was a fine animal, that she would get better eventually
and that the only problem she had was her age and some imperfec-
tions inherited with her blood. He suggested that in a way it was a
duty of conscience to take care of the poor animal which seemed to
be grateful for the pampering and the medicines she was receiving.

One day, the artilleryman appeared cursing, carrying a leather
purse in one hand and a bridle in the other. He was coming for the
mare. "They put one over on me, but they will pay for it during the
next elections. There will be hell to pay." He threw the money at
Manín's feet, went into the corral and began to untie Chula from the
barn like someone who had come to claim what was clearly his. He
led her into the barnyard, put the bridle on her and leapt upon her
bareback and without saying good-bye, dug his heels into the animal's flanks to get her to move. But Chula would not take a step.

Without noticing this important detail, kicking the bay's sides as
hard as he could, the artilleryman shouted, "This is against the law!
This is an offense against God! If the whole lot of them were not a
pack of thieves, I would go to the town hall personally and claim my
three hundred pesetas from the judge. But a poor man will never find
justice anywhere. Giddy-up!" And slash! How he kicked and beat
the poor animal!

Falo stood in front of the artilleryman to block his way and
looked at him. He turned and bit his lip. Manín, standing behind
Chula and surrounded by the women, was standing with one foot on
the artilleryman's money, which the latter had thrown on the ground,
and was turning over great ideas in his small brain.

The artilleryman was mistreating the mare in such a manner that
she would not move. Indignation was about to overtake everyone in
the group. The family watched the cruel treatment silently. The
eighty-year-old woman, the handsome Rosenda, was the first to cry
out.

"You brute! Don't you see that she doesn't want to? Don't you
have any feelings? Leave the bay alone or I personally will grab your
legs and pull you off that horse and onto the ground!"

"And if she doesn't do it, I will," said Falo, taking a step forward.

"The mare is mine. That is why you won your case at the gentleman's house. Hell! And they call this justice!"

"The mare is yours," answered Manín de Chinta, more calmly than Falo, "but since the animal apparently has taken a liking to the house, and since she does not want to leave, as far as I am concerned, let her stay. And so, dismount and take your money, right here where you left it, and Chula goes back to the barn." Manín took his foot off the money packet and put his hand on the horse's back.

After thinking it over, the artilleryman stopped mistreating the animal and said in a conciliatory tone of voice, "What you say is all right, but you'll have to pay the costs."

"What costs, if everything was decided among friends?"

"Friends, huh? Like hell! The damages to my peace of mind and the time I spent running back and forth to town! Five pesos more and mare is yours!"

After a lot of haggling, doubts, reversed decisions and veiled insults, the deal was made. Chula went back to the stable, Falo went to take care of her, the artilleryman went off with his three hundred pesetas plus twenty-five more which he had not brought with him.

Chula, after a few weeks, was able to return to pulling the surrey. She did an average job, like a veteran who deserves to retire. The wagon was not loaded too heavily. Everybody got off when they came to a hill. Chula took the grade little by little. No one pushed her. She stopped often and no one pretended to notice. She tried to do the best she could. The family put up with her natural weakness, her terror of hills.

And so they lived tolerating one another, just as they tolerated the old woman who no longer could work and did nothing but complain, like everyone who has something to tolerate, to forgive one another for. Such is life among those who love one another and must cross this valley of tears together, holding hands so that the winds of misfortune do not scatter them.

Chula always stopped at the Grandota hill. Chinta would sit down on a pile of gravel and calmly smoke a cigarette which was not wrapped in paper but in half a dried corn husk. And Falo would wait whistling, passing his hand over the back of the bay mare that looked like the horse they had shot out from under him on the battlefield.

Don Patricio or the Grand Prize in Melilla

"I wonder why they named me Patricio," Mr. Caracoles had often asked himself silently while he thrust his hands deep into his pockets, which were always weighed down with gold and silver coins, and he wriggled his fingers to make the vile metal jingle and tickle him by bouncing off his thighs.

"Patricio Clement Caracoles Cerrajera! My two last names," he continued thinking, "are fine. My mother's maiden name makes me especially proud. It sound like a guarantee. Cerrajera. *Cerrar* means to close; a *cerrojo* is a lock. Wonderful! This name is a treasure chest, one of those that explodes when a thief tries to break into it. Caracoles is not too bad. A *caracol* is a snail. I rather like the life of a snail. Someone once said that no one is without friends. I would say that no one is without a shell. If you are not a crustacean, you die. But Clement? Where could that name have come from? And Patricio! It sounds like *patris*, fatherland or patriot. Now there's a real joke!"

Patricio Clement had made his fortune—a bundle—in Havana where he had achieved a daily income of over twenty dollars. He had begun as a doorman and bouncer in a gambling casino and had ended up as the owner and had almost become one of the most important people in the city, at least as far as the colonial records were concerned.

Afterwards, he had had a series of successful business ventures which all had turned out very well for him, and since at his first job he had acquired the custom of charging admission, as he would say, collecting "the gate," he had come to the conclusion that every transaction had to have a fee which had to be collected. He always had to collect his ten percent fee for every contract, however he could get it. And he always got it. To ease his conscience, he said that it was simply the price of admission.

He had also begun to make millions in entrance fees in his own city as soon as he returned, called back by a love for his homeland and by certain business deals he had made from Cuba. As soon as he had reached the port, instead of beginning to sing like a tenor in a comic opera, "My land from o'er the bounding main, etc.," he recited to himself, "Service charges here have to be a gold mine, if I can only milk them right." And in effect he took charge of the tariffs on goods shipped in and the doors of his native city became just so many more gates to hell, each one guarded by its hound wearing a gold braid cap with an insignia which, though it read "Customs" meant "Abandon all money, all ye who enter here."

The time that Patricio did not spend working, that is, exploiting his fellow man, he spent in a social club. Clement's recreation consisted of playing in all the usual ways the part of a high–living, good–time buddy.

High life with its various altimeters paid well and was another gold mine. Yet it was also his recreation.

Patricio's true recreation was to visit his banker and merchant friends' places of business on the days when they prepared their cash for deposit, just to put his hands on the gold and silver coins and paper currency. He would grow pale, lose his power of speech, and with a vague smile on his face, stare at the sacks of coins and bundles of bills. He could not hear what anyone said to him. He would approach slowly and noiselessly like a cat and sink his hands with fingers spread wide into the boxes of coins and bills. He stirred and stirred. He weighed and counted it silently like someone murmuring silent prayers in some mysterious religious cult. And, in a hoarse voice heavy with emotion, he would finally manage to mumble, "Heavens! You cannot imagine how much of this stuff I have handled in my lifetime!"

He would then grow tender with his memories of gate fees collected at doors as numerous as in the city of Thebes.

Afterwards, he would blush, recover his awareness of his surroundings and, pretending to grow serious, shaking his open hands in full view of the clerks, would say, "Look here, gentlemen. Do you see? I have not taken anything. I do this just for the sheer pleasure of it, since I have counted so much money in my day."

Well, it was to this particular Patricio Clement that the Outdoor Recreational Society made the proposal that he contribute something for the relief of the wounded, of the widows and orphans of soldiers killed during the recent trouble at the Spanish outpost in the African city of Melilla.

"And so, how much are you going to contribute, Mr. Caracoles?"

"Me? I will contribute nothing because no one knows what it will come to."

That is how Patricio answered, a man from the border of Galicia and Asturias who talked like a dance hall comedian.

"But why won't you contribute something?"

"First of all, because of what I say. Anyway, I don' know writin'."

"Well, sign with a cross!"

"That's a good'un. The devil's ahind the cross."

Tired of being bothered about the contribution, Patricio went to his club one afternoon with an idea and dirty hands, as usual, and after winning a few bets, went very contentedly to the room where no one gambled, where people just talked, people disenchanted with the fickleness of cards. And Patricio delivered a speech to them which more or less went like this:

"I don' give money, now, and no hard feeling; but I give somethin' worth more 'cause it's worth it...or might be. Let's see, men; you who talk about the generosity of all social classes in Spain, patriotism and the train of the great old lady Spain who bleeds for her children and plays the castanets like this, what will you bet that my idea won't go over in that holy nation, as you call it, of Recaredo and Catachinchi the Fifth? And it won't cost anybody a penny, now, and in all honesty. The thing is you gotta make things go your way, like I did in Cuba and it went good; and since the lottery is the biggest thing in Spain—the Christmas lottery alone takes in every Spaniard because of patriotism, and, no bull, that's *all* the Spaniards—no matter how much they bet on the Christmas drawing, they promise to hand the winnings over to the wounded, the widows and orphans of the Melilla campaign—one half of their prize if they win the grand prize. What I mean is, just figure that prize reaches eight million *reales*, four million would go for the wounded and others in Melilla. By promising what I say, all the players, they could take care of those defenders of Spain who, without even betting, would win the grand prize. And four million ain't hay. It ain't no big sacrifice. It would be, if the offer was made after somebody won. But when what somebody's givin' up is just his half of a very remote chance, the sacrifice ain't no big deal. Put my idea in the newspapers. What'll ya bet nobody will take you up on it? What'll ya bet nobody will give you his half of the grand prize if he wins it?"

Patricio's idea was received with applause.

"Wonderful! Wonderful!" everyone shouted, and Caracoles's idea, properly edited, was sent to the papers.

The majority of the people who had some extra cash played the lottery and promised on their word of honor to give up half their winnings if they won the grand prize.

Patricio Cerrajera, using his mother's last name, declared that even he had succumbed to the temptation of buying an entire ticket, an extravagance completely unlike him. And he, too, swore solemnly that if he were to win the eight million, four million would go to the wounded and others in Melilla.

"An' I don' min' puttin' it in writin' that, of course, if I get the big one, I give four million for the needy."

And to be absolutely certain, Patricio told everyone who asked him the number of his ticket.

The day of the drawing arrived, and the club wanted to play a joke on Mr. Caracoles to test his patriotism. They contrived a telegram with everything necessary to make the trick seem authentic;

they delivered it to Cerrajera, who was astonished when he read it. "The grand prize is number XXXX." Caracoles exclaimed, "That's a good–un, fellas."

"And what do you say now, Clement? Will you give your four million to Melilla?"

"No, siree! 'Cause I promised only if I won the grand prize."

"Well, that is the grand prize."

"No siree! It ain't. It's one of your tricks; you're real funny. But I'm funnier yet, 'cause I don' play nothin' on the lottery, never will in my life, until I can get my cut. Ha! I know what a gate is!"

The Substitute

Biting the fingernails of his left hand, a very old habit unworthy of a person who assured his public of his talent, he had just written the following verse on a clean piece of paper:

> I want to sing, so as not to cry
> Your glories, dear homeland, seeing you die...

That is to say, Eleuterio Miranda, the best poet of the particular political faction that inspired his muse, was biting his fingernails and meditating in a very ill humor. He was almost ready to break, not the lyre which he lacked, to be truthful, but the quill with which he was writing his most recently assigned poem, which might be either an ode or an elegy, depending on how it turned out.

The country was in very serious straits, or at least that is what the people of Miranda's town were being led to think. The most illustrious citizens, led by the mayor himself, had come to ask Eleuterio to write a few lengthy verses, which should be as grandiloquent as possible and which should include references to the battles of Otumba or Pavia and to the various famous generals suggested by the council, for a patriotic rally to raise money to pay the expenses of the war.

Although Eleuterio was not a Tyrtaeus or a Pindar, he did not lack an occasional attack of maliciousness or of good sense and he understood clearly how basically ridiculous it was to contribute poetry in heptasyllabic or endecasyllabic verses like those of Quintana for the purpose of raising money to save the country if, indeed, it were in any kind of danger.

Granted that if, as in other times when he was about sixteen years old and had never been to Madrid and had not yet subscribed to the Parisian paper *Le Figaro*, he had truly been an epic poet and had sung the political and moral interests of his homeland, he was now a very different person and did not believe in patriotic verse nor in any kind of "objective" writing. He believed only in intimate poetry, and in the prose of everyday life. For this reason, for the sake of beans and bread, he decided to pluck the lyre of the Pindaric ode, especially since he had his eye set on the post of secretary to the town council and it would be prudent of him to be in the good graces of the councilmen who asked him to sing. Considering this, he bit his fingernails again and reviewed the first two lines of his poem:

> I want to sing so as not to cry
> Your glories, oh homeland, seeing you die...

And he stopped again, not because of any technical problems, because he had a superabundance of rhymes for cry and die. He stopped, rather, because suddenly an idea occurred to him in the form of a recollection which did not take long to become a regret. It was simply that, farther along, at the conclusion which he was already planning, he intended to write something like the following climax to his ode:

> But how vain to try
> To raise my flight
> And reach the sanctuary
> Of patriotic love
> In the regions of heaven far above
>
> But if I fail
> With fainting voice
> And exhausted fancy,
> Let my blood and my tears
> Flow in the battles of the years.
>
> War! Let no more be said.
> My muse will not permit it.
> Rather give me a sword
> Since my life I give
> Which is nothing,
> Oh homeland, not already yours;
> Because if I spill my blood
> It is merely my grateful debt repaid.

Just as he was about to sit back and enjoy the results of his labors, in spite of the lack of rhyme, something tormented him, something in his brain, a voice shouting, "Raymond!"

Eleuterio had to get up. He paced about his office. Passing in front of the mirror, he noticed that he had turned very red.

"Damn it! Damn Raymond anyway! Well, I don't really mean that. Poor Raymond. I mean just the opposite. He is a very good person!"

A good person, and a brave man! A coward! Because chicken is what everyone in the town called him because of his shyness. But he turned out to be a very brave chicken, like anyone when there are baby chicks to defend.

Raymond had no children. On the contrary, he was the child; but the one dying of hunger and cold was his mother, a poor woman who could no longer see well enough to work to give her children their daily bread.

Raymond's mother, a widow, rented a certain small farm which belonged to Pedro Miranda, Eleuterio's father. The poor woman could not pay her rent. How could she pay, if she did not have any money? Every year her debt became greater, to the point that she no longer had any hope of repaying it. Don Pedro was patient. But one day, since times were bad for everyone and taxes and contributions began to affect both great and small, he claimed his rights, and as he himself said, took a stand. He swore that Christ himself went no further than the cross and that he was not going any further either; that Mara Pendones had to pay her back rent or leave the farm. "My rent or leave the property." Don Pedro called this his ultimatum and Maria called it the end of the world, the death of her and of her children, all four of them. Raymond was the oldest.

But at this point, the army drafted Eleuterio. Eleuterio was Don Pedro's only son, his family's pride and joy. He was a jewel who wrote for the newspapers in Madrid, a privilege that no other individual below the age of thirty enjoyed in the town. Since not Miranda's but his enemy's party was in power at that time, there was no way for the town council or the provincial clerk's office to have Eleuterio declared unfit for military service. Being a lyric poet was not a sufficient exemption. The only solution was to pay a fortune to free the boy from his duty. But times were very bad. God knows where there was any cash. However, there was one happy solution.

"The oldest of Pendones's children! Exactly!" And Don Pedro changed his ultimatum saying: either quit the property, or pay me the back rent by having Raymond take Eleuterio's place in the king's service. Said and done. The Pendones widow wept and begged on her knees. When the terrible moment of his departure arrived, she preferred to abandon her house and live in the street with her four children, but with all four of them and not one child less. But Raymond, the chicken, the most sickly child of the family who had suffered from fevers and rheumatism, showed some life for the first time in his life and, without his mother's knowledge, sold himself to Don Pedro, liquidating his mother's debts. The price of his self sacrifice was enough to pay the back rent and current charges as well. He commanded such a large price that he was even able to leave his mother enough money for food for several months and to buy his fiancee, Pepa de Rosala, a silver locket which cost him a small fortune since it was no less than gold–plated silver.

Why did Pepa want a lock of Raymond's hair, a sad, dull curl of very fine, ash blonde strands, a testimony to his miserable health and physical weakness? Who knows? One of love's many mysteries. Pepa certainly did not love him for his money. No one knows why she loved him. Perhaps because he was true, faithful, sincere, humble and good. The fact was, to the great consternation of the lads of the town, lovely Pepa de Rosala and the chicken Raymond were engaged. But they had to be apart for a time. He went into the service. She kept his locket and every once in a while would receive letters written in the hand of some lieutenant, because Raymond did not know how to write. He availed himself of a transcriber who usually charged him something. He signed his letters with a cross.

This was the Raymond who was becoming an obsession to the town's epicolyrical poet as the latter worked the final lines of his patriotic elegy or ode. And his remorse, sarcastically, suggested an idea to him. "Don't worry, friend; just as Don Quijote ended each stanza of a particular poem to Dulcinea by adding the half–line 'from el Toboso,' in the interest of serving his scrupulous concern for truth, you can place as a coda to your poem the lyrical offering of your own sacrifice, saying something like this:

> Homeland, I wish to offer my blood
> Instead of the songs of my lyre.
> Since my country has cost me to date
> No more than a financial sacrifice.

Such cruel sarcasm! What terrible shame! Singing to one's country while the poor coward fought in the front lines, in Moorish territory and in the post that actually belonged to the fine young gentleman."

He tore up the ode or elegy, which was really the most decent thing he could to to serve his country at the moment. When the mayor, the chief town councilman and several officials came to collect the verses, they raised their voices to the heavens when they saw that Eleuterio had none to give them. They made veiled allusions to the secretaryship. His fear of losing his future job was so great that the Miranda boy had to agree to substitute (a terrible word for him) the missing verses with an improvised speech which he could declaim as well as the next man. They took him to the theater where they celebrated the patriotic rally and he actually spoke well. He paraphrased in prose, but in a prose which far surpassed the uneven verses of his shredded elegy or ode. The audience was thrilled; he himself became excited. In his rather emotional concluding remarks, he envisioned the pale figure of Raymond again. And he offered among hoorays and applause from the audience, to sign in blood, if his country required it, all those words of love and sacrifice. He swore silently to himself to leave that very night, any way he could, for Africa to fight next to Raymond as a volunteer.

And he did as he intended. But when he reached Malaga to embark, he discovered that in the hospital among the wounded who had just arrived two days earlier from Africa there was a poor soldier from his hometown. He had a presentiment and rushed to the hospital. There he saw poor Raymond Pendones on his death bed.

He was not seriously wounded, only superficially. His wounds were not killing him, but his usual malady, his fever, was. The unhealthy life of the army camp had caused his fevers to increase and between fire and ice he was consumed in ashes. For one long month, he had been the hero of the hospital. How he had suffered! How badly he had eaten, drunk and slept! What pain, pathetic chills, intense cold, anguish and homesickness! How had the wound happened? Well, very simply. One night, when he was on guard suffering from, well, what they called dysentery, which he could not restrain, he left his post out of consideration so as not to offend anyone and squatting down in the moonlight—bang!—a little Moorish soldier had evidently seen him and had taken aim. But he did not hit anything serious. The wound was insignificant. But the cold, fatigue, fear, sadness, especially the sadness, and fever, his worst malady, were killing him remorselessly.

Raymond Pendones died in the arms of the fine young gentleman, very gratefully entrusting the care of his mother and fiancee to him.

And the young gentleman, more of a poet and more creative than he himself had imagined, but once again an epic "objective" poet, left Malaga, sailed across the puddle and went straight to Raymond's captain, a talented, good–hearted and imaginative mad man.

"I have just come from Malaga where Raymond Pendones has just died. He was a soldier in your company. I have come to take his place. Please act as if Pendones has regained his health and as if I am Pendones. He was my substitute. He took my place in the ranks and now I want to take his. Do not let his mother or fiancee know that he has died just yet. Do not let them ever know that he died unsung in a hospital, from homesickness and a fever."

The captain understood Miranda.

"Agreed," he said, "today you will be Pendones, but once the war is over...you understand..."

"That will be my concern and my responsibility," Eleuterio replied.

And from that day forward, when Pendones was called to muster, he answered roll call again. His friends noticed the trade and thought the young man's idea was a good one and the substitution was the regiment's secret.

Before dying, Raymond had told Eleuterio how he used to write his mother and fiancee. The same lieutenant who had written the first letters continued writing the ones Eleuterio dictated. Since he did not want to write them himself for fear that someone in his town would recognize his handwriting, Eleuterio signed them with a cross.

"But all of this," asked the lieutenant who wrote down the letters, "what good will it do the mother and fiancee if, when it's all over, they will have to be informed?"

"Don't worry, don't worry," said Eleuterio very much alone. "It gives them some relief. Afterwards, God only knows."

Eleuterio's idea was very simple and the means of putting it into effect were even more simple. He wanted to repay Raymond the life he had given in his place. He wanted to be the substitute's substitute and leave Raymond's loved ones a glorious memory which might eventually help them.

And he watched for the opportunity to act heroically, but like a true hero. He died killing several Moors, saving an outpost, turning a retreat around and making an imminent defeat by his glorious example into a splendid victory.

There was a reason for his being an epic poet and an unusually brave man. His recollection of the *Iliad*, the *Ramayana*, the *Aeneid*, the *Lusiads*, the *Araucania* and the *Bernardo* filled his mind with the inspiration necessary for a heroic death. Heroes must have an imagination, as do artists and actors. He did not die as Raymond would have done in his place, but with elegance and distinction. His death became famous. He was determined not to be an anonymous hero. And although he was only an enlisted man, his deed thrilled the entire army. The chief-of-staff gave him a public eulogy. He was promoted posthumously. His name appeared in bold print in all the newspaper headlines: "Raymond Pendones: Hero," and his mother received his pension for the rest of her life and could pay Pedro Miranda's rent, whose only son, certainly, had died too, probably in the war also, as the people of the town suspected, but nobody knew where or how.

When the captain, years later, confided this story to his closest friends, many of them usually replied: "Eleuterio's sacrifice was exaggerated. He did not have to go to such lengths. After all, the other man was a substitute. He had been paid and had voluntarily agreed to go in Eleuterio's place."

That was true. Eleuterio had exaggerated. But he was a poet, after all, and if most young gentlemen who pay a soldier to take their place, one who eventually dies in a war, do not do what Miranda did, it is because there are very few poets. Most young gentlemen write prose.

Mr. Insula

If you could see him now! Once, he believed in God, in his fellow man, in the laws of history ruled by divine providence, in art. He believed in science, in the value of action and in the miraculous results of the spirit of cooperation. He was thin. His fat disappeared as he ran from place to place getting involved in everything.

He was a member of such and such a commission, he participated in debates at Congress and at clubs where literature was made and unmade. He went to the gatherings of theater people and to bookstores. He wrote for several newspapers and magazines and he published books. Finally, he even presented a sociological drama in which he berated the present organization of the civil and economic sectors of the country with such beautiful poetry that God alone knew how much work it cost him.

If one did not know the Mr. Insula of those days personally, one would believe, judging from the verses of his play, that he was a desperate man, steeped in bitterness, that he was a Proudhon on the verge of throwing himself headfirst at the first opportunity into the great pond of the Retiro Park or into the Manzanares River. But no! In those days, especially after they had applauded his inflammatory verses, Insula was very pleased with himself. He loved everything and he believed in that very same justice which none of his characters seemed ever able to find.

It was only necessary to see him smiling, shaking hands with actors, senators, newspapermen, musicians and dancers to recognize his contentment. And he was the most admirable and enviable for the sheer happiness he felt when he would walk out onto the stage among the actors and actresses to receive the public's applause, that same public about which one of his characters had just said:

> Society, in constant struggle
> With me even before I was born,
> I would owe you nothing,
> Not even my existence. Let me die!

He was never a pessimist nor a demagogue for more than three acts and in verse. It looked good for him to come to the theater and fight against the reigning ideas and claim justice for someone whom he was not certain even existed. But in any case, there must be someone who was hungering and thirsting for justice. If so, Insula was there to satisfy the hunger and thirst of those unfortunate people whom he did not know, with brilliant scenes, wonderful stage effects, profound monologues and incredible spirit in the last few climactic lines of each play:

> Yes, dear Conscience, in vain I fight
> In this most fierce of battles
> Against you who are so foolish
> While society is so wise.
> The rabble will conquer me
> If I heed you.
> So I heed you not.

As a social critic who redeemed justice for the weak, he claimed what was rightfully his, received his applause and lived quite well.

He went everywhere. Everything interested him. The day's event, whether religious, economic, scientific, political or artistic, bullfights and lotteries, everything impressed him so much that it always seemed that everything was going his way.

There was always someone who swore he had seen him at a wedding on the very same day and at the very same hour that others swore that they had spoken to him at a funeral.

But, my friend, little by little people began to tire of seeing, hearing, smelling and touching Mr. Insula so often. The newspapers and magazines began to hide his articles in the deepest recesses of their editions. Editors looked for reasons not to accept his books. In literary and political circles and at artistic gatherings, in the cafes, he was becoming just one of the many others like him who, no matter how much noise they made and how original they pretended to be, still formed part of the chorus. It was terrible! Insula began to suspect that perhaps the characters in his plays were right when they said such horrible things about society.

Just to be sure, he wrote a play in which pessimism was bandied about desperately. His serious drama was no better or worse than a comedy. But time had passed and the audience had seen so many different things. The fact was that his inflammatory, sententious poetry no longer had any effect. Once the drama came to an end, it died in silence.

The following year, Insula appeared again on stage with a high comedy full of bitter irony, with mysterious characters who spoke with a prophetic concision that made the audience's hair stand on end. Every character could have been called Apocalypsis.

And this high comedy fell from its lofty domain directly into the tomb.

The same thing happened with another play which he produced two years later. It was not enough that the characters spoke a flowery prose and perceived a ray of hope. The public simply refused to appreciate those hopes for society's salvation for what they were worth.

As his comedies were becoming happier and less pessimistic, Insula himself was turning more and more bitter. The poet did not use verse to complain about his fate, rather he used interjections that were poetic in their own way. He complained about his luck, the audiences' bad taste, their fickleness and their inability to recognize true art. He was growing old, out of style and was beginning to repeat himself. Society was not. It was impossible for them to see eye to eye, of course.

For these reasons, for vengeance and as an insult to his audience, he took a house in the suburbs so far away that it was beyond the reach of public transportation.

And in that rustic retreat, which still was rather expensive per square foot, among fields which a rascally society would soon invade with paving stones, roof tiles and boards, Mr. Insula (who was getting fatter and fatter to hide his heart and spirit from the surrounding world) despised all creation and went to bed early.

He went to bed early as his own kind of protest against the latest tendencies in a theater which would no longer have anything to do with a sociological, three-act, poetic Juvenal such as himself.

He never missed the opportunity to let everyone know that he retired with the chickens, stating his opinion that to stay up all night was criminal decadence, and breathing the infected air of the theaters was deleterious to one's health and well-being.

"The theater!" he would say, "Humph! It is a pseudo-genre, bad for your health, sickly, artificial and childish. Nature! I prefer the great outdoors!" And he would stretch his arms out to the vacant lots which were for sale all around him.

He was pleased when someone came to him asking for a few lines of poetry, to be included in a commemorative album to be presented to some prominent citizen or other, or for his signature for another album, or his signature for some other type of homage, or an interview dealing with some current event. He was pleased to turn them down flat. His opinion? He did not have opinions about such nonsense, so everyone should simply leave him alone. The world was hopeless, so everyone must simply leave him alone. And that was his opinion.

He forbade his name to appear anywhere. The only thing which might have pleased him would have been for the *Gazette* to publish a news item next to one about the king's state of health such as the following: "Mr. Insula retired last night at 8:15 p.m., so when the curtains rose in the theater, he was already sleeping soundly."

On one occasion, a newspaper put Mr. Insula's name on the list of writers who had gone to the cemetery to attend the funeral of a certain literary giant.

He was outraged! He almost published a protest statement, but he decided not to in order to avoid calling attention to himself.

He never inquired about which government officials were rising to prominence and which were falling out of favor. He never asked about national catastrophes or about the latest artistic triumphs. He read only foreign books and books which were always very old. No one was allowed to come to him with information about current events.

He aspired to a kind of nirvana in which everything simply disappeared, everything, of course, except for Mr. Insula himself. His huge paunch was very current, as were his memoirs which he was collecting for a book about his satirical–sociological three–act verse plays.

He believed he was living a full and natural life. He planted a garden which would never bear fruit because afterwards he always forgot where he had planted the fruit trees, flowers and vegetables, so he did not bother to think about them anymore.

"Yes, nature! Nature!" he would exclaim looking at his sad brown fields and vacant lots with eyes heavy from boredom and bitterness.

His hair turned gray and his soul grew a protective cover of scales and spines.

He believed himself to be a practical philosopher, a Saint Paul in the desert.

What all this meant was simply that he did not know how to grow old.

He did not know how to move aside and gradually relinquish his place in society. He wanted to stop time and fill all space.

He insisted so much on being an island so that he could consider himself, all by himself, a continent.

Snob

Rosario Alzueta was beginning to tire of the great triumphs her beauty was enjoying in Palmera, a flourishing port on the Cantabrian coast. It was always the same: first, general public admiration, then the spoken homage of hundreds of adulators, after that the silent tribute of envy, the least flattering but most eloquent expression of respect for one's merit, and finally, the boredom of a satisfied ego and the pangs of a vanity wounded by rivals whom apprehension makes fearful. Besides, the natural waning of emotion had a double effect: in the one admired and among those who admired her, the results were inversely related: the more they admired her, the less Rosario enjoyed it since she had become accustomed to their flattery; and the public, once they had memorized her attractiveness, after a while praised her routinely, but without the same feeling as before. Their frequency in seeing her had gradually diminished the pleasure.

On the beach, at the resorts, during the morning concerts, while strolling on the pier and through the parks, in the casino pavilion on the fairgrounds where there was a continual dance, during tours of the so-called high spots of Palmera and neighboring towns, Miss Alzueta always came first, and whoever saw her the very first time considered her the only woman worth looking at. She never went to the theater. She despised the theaters in Palmera where, she said, it was impossible to breathe. She preferred to allow herself to be seen by people taking their evening stroll while she sat under the electric lights which graced the Indian chestnut tree.

They called her the Moorish girl. She was very dark-complected and was proud of it. She wore no powder or make-up. She was a burnished bronze of the finest quality. She affected the naturalness of an English garden planted by a continental *parvenu*, one of those gardens which are an imitation of nature by virtue of their extravagance, lack of plan and comfortable design.

Rosario, who was nothing but appearances to the depths of her soul, pretended to a simplicity and sincere candor as if such great gifts were easy for a girl such as herself to acquire. The upshot of it all was that she was simply very ill-mannered. Assured of her physical beauty, she believed that in addition she was entitled to the charm of an innocent gracefulness. She was a splendid hothouse plant who wanted to be taken for a violet hidden in a crannied wall. Most of her admirers were taken in by her appearance and affectation; most of them admired her obvious statuesque feminine beauty—a naturalness they believed in with the same stupid faith which they gave to the idyllic love scenes at a garden party given by some skirted Theocritus with the assistance of either a Mosco or Bion, designers of drawing rooms.

If Rosario had been a bluestocking, a writer, even an outdated romantic, she might have had more substance, though rather unpleasant, to lend to her false natural formality of pristine, paradisiacal simplicity. But her spirit was given over to social vanities and to the all–too–common sensual inclinations of egoism. A frivolous, empty-headed life in which she had been caged from the day of her birth, ruled by the routines of instinct and her basic sensuality, had made her spirit somewhat less than noble.

She loved crowds and was little else than the noise of their applause captured in a museum piece which had the shape of a goddess. She believed that she was distinguished, different, exceptional, the muse of silence and of solitude, something in the nature of a musical presentation on the program during the holidays.

The days had not yet arrived in Spain when certain literary fantasies were popular, so she would not imitate the heroines of poems nor feign to be affected by the moonlight shining on the dead waters of her soul—in her case a poor puddle with neither mysterious depths nor poetry growing on its banks. She knew nothing of those things which so many people imagined to make life more interesting and occasionally transcendental. It was even funny to see the contrast between her poses, gestures, and other mannerisms and the horrible triviality of her judgment, opinions, thoughts, desires, taste and preferences. For example, she would affect simplicity, sincerity and naturalness mixed with a certain charming grace to say that she liked comic opera more than grand opera or that she preferred one of Taboada's articles to the poetry of Felipe Pérez, or that she was not pleased with where they had placed the statue of Cybele in Madrid.

Miss Alzueta had of course visited a foreign country and she was very proud of it. She had also acquired several annoying habits because of it. However, she knew only the most superficial things about any country, things which appeared in the guide books, particularly in the illustrations and engravings: styles, holidays, militant causes, life on the railways and at expositions, things of that nature. This was all that Rosario could see, in her own country as well as abroad. For this reason, she was not even able to imitate those women who perhaps were worth no more than she, but who knew how to acquire a certain distinction in the world with their idealized affairs, their study of theosophy and their strange charitable or socialist campaigns, with their worship of art and their fetish of adoring genius, or what is less an evil than all of these, with their great exaggerated and extravagant passions of the heart. Rosario knew nothing of this kind of spiritual grandeur which, while false and harmful, was still less common and pedestrian.

She talked a great deal; she argued often; she was an unconquerable debater but only in the defense of a cause under attack. She was never at a loss for one of those answers which admit no reply simply because of their meaninglessness and emptiness. She more or less understood a little about everything, like those numerous journalists of today who, depending upon their circumstances, become theater critics, art critics, court reporters, sports writers, book reviewers and political and social columnists. She defended Wagner loudly at the royal theater without having heard or allowing others to hear what it was she was praising. She was the muse of the bad taste of the day, the inspiration for a universal suffrage favoring the reigning climate of opinion. Her manner of speech was the same as those foolish newspaper writers whose only grace consists of using certain meaningless quotations marks, clichs and slang. It was painful to hear that mouth made for keeping the divinest secrets of poetry express some foolishness wrapped in numerous conventional expressions and other similar examples of low speech: "I prefer..., I abhor...," this skirted judge would say at every opportunity, forgetful of her beauty, mindful only of the logic of her arguments. She either did not "see the point" of things and despised them if it "were expected" of her to like them. That beautiful woman made one's head swim like one of these newspaper articles which, though pointless, makes the readers happy.

Like many other women of her class, she based her national identity on her ability to speak openly about anything shocking. She prided herself on avoiding all euphemism and periphrasis, even when speaking of things that require an understatement for the sake of decency. There are few things more distasteful than those crude forms of expression that certain sectors of aristocratic women and their imitators use as a sign of their nationality. The results of these bad manners, of this inopportune breaking and tearing of the more special forms of elegance, delicacy and ceremoniousness are, from their sheer shrillness, scandalous. Rosario, imitating certain elegant ladies, carried this fault to extremes and acquired a particularly outstanding and unfortunate originality in the field because of her insistence on being natural and simple in a highly artificial way.

This woman who, because of one of reality's more unfortunate sarcasms, was beautiful in body and ridiculous in soul, although very few noticed the latter—this woman after a brief period of time was becoming bored with Palmera at the height of her triumphs because, to be brief, none of her newest admirers seemed worthy in her opinion of her attention for even one day.

However, one afternoon while walking along the beach she saw a very elegant yacht arrive from the north, carried forward by huge, taut, triangular sails spread over a long, narrow hull which was as subtle as the spirit of the waves. She saw the Lohengrin of her dreams arrive.

He was a young Englishman, Aleck Bryant, the son of a very wealthy landowner from Pembroke. This ruddy Alexander had sailed on a whim from Milford out to sea. He reached Palmera by chance simply because he had sailed a straight course. After a few days, he became acclimated and liked northern Spain, which was totally un-like anything his reading had led him to expect. It seemed more like the Emerald Isle that he had left astern to the northwest. The most select of the elegant colony who spent their summers in Palmera wel-comed this noble Englishman with open arms, as if he were one of them. The most elegant sportsmen fought one another for his friend-ship and company, and, of course, the most seductive young women of the highest social classes made him into a kind of extraordinary prize in their constant display of flirtations.

Bryant was handsome, strong, wealthy, learned, elegant, a great traveler, a man of the world, a sportsman. He had *esprit*, which meant all those little gifts in the catechism of foreign affectations compiled by the highest society, the *crême de la crême*.

Rosario Alzueta quickly saw that he was a worthy prize, equal to her self–esteem. They introduced him to her and she, in an effort to seduce him, called up from the bottom of her trunk of feigned natu-ral English simplicity all her tricks for winning hearts. She also used her abundant natural grace and exotic abilities. Very soon, Aleck Bryant learned that Miss Alzueta had ridden a bicycle across the sands of Battersea Park. She spoke of the famous Mrs. Humphrey and of the illustrious cyclists, the Duchess of Portland, the Countess of Dudley, the Marquise of Hastings, as if they were her personal friends. She even intimated that she had some connection with Prin-cess Maude of Wales, the Duchess of York, and the Queen of Italy herself.

Bryant was forced to learn that in the famous debate with these bicycling ladies about what the proper attire was for such an activity, that Rosario Alzueta sided with the aristocratic party, which favored the skirt.

The noble Englishman smiled and listened silently to the beauti-ful Moorish girl, devouring her with his blue eyes which reflected a certain sweet maliciousness. He could barely understand what she was telling him in a French that seemed like bad Castillian. Doubtless she was the most beautiful woman at the beaches, and as long as he postponed the remainder of his trip, there was no reason to be apart from her. Except for the time this valiant traveler spent exploring that picturesque part of the country, he spent his vacation with her.

Rosario no longer doubted the choice. What a triumph!

One night, however, during the evening stroll made pleasant by the music of a military band, Rosario was sitting on her throne like the goddess of the city park, if not exactly under an oak tree, at least under the branch of an Indian chestnut. She overheard nearby, a few chairs behind her, a conversation in French which she vaguely understood and which interested her very much. A foreign gentleman, a new friend of Bryant's from Biarritz was talking about her with the Englishman. She was certain of it. She could not catch all the details of the conversation, but she did understand the general idea—that the foreign gentleman, without suspecting that they were being overheard, asked Bryant if it was true that he was really interested in that extraordinarily beautiful, dark Spanish girl. When the most important part of the Englishman's reply was about to be uttered, Rosario discreetly turned her head a little in order to observe his expression, the look on the face of her most ardent admirer. How strange! Miss Alzueta of course expected to hear praises of her beauty expressed in the British traveler's French. But the young man must have said something else, because the sound of his voice and the nature of his gestures accompanying his words did not signify enthusiasm, but rather a certain sincere but disdainful compassion confused with a tenuous and discreetly mocking tone. Finally, she was able to hear that Alexander Bryant was calling her, Rosario, a snob.

"Snob!" Miss Alzueta was familiar with the ugly word but was uncertain of its exact meaning. She feared it was not very good.

A terribly powerful emotion made her blush with shame. A presentiment told her that "snob" meant the same thing as the Spanish word for "common."

That night she could not sleep because the question about the specific meaning of that word kept sounding in her brain.

Finally, on the beach, she asked a friend of hers, a professor of rhetoric, the meaning of the word "snob." The professor outdid himself in explanations. According to his dictionary, it meant a vulgar, pretentious person. Thackeray in his famous novel *Vanity Fair* used the word in the sense of foolish, stupid, a show–off and other such things. Rosario left the professor in the middle of his speech. Bryant had not called her foolish, common nor presumptuous. That was not what he meant. Snob! When she met the Englishman that same afternoon at the garden party given by the Marquise of X, Rosario immediately read in his smiling eyes the translation of the ugly word.

Oh, yes, in the dictionaries the meaning was not exact. But it was in his glance and in the sweet maliciousness of his blue eyes which shouted "Snob! Snob!" but meant "common and ordinary."

Knight of the Round Table

It was now cold in Thermo Alto. Everyone missed their winter clothes and rooms furnished to prevent colds and pneumonia. The dining room, which was as long and wide as a cathedral and had bare walls painted such cheerful colors that they made one sneeze because of their freshness, was acquiring the atmosphere of an indoor market-place.

People came to lunch and dinner wearing jackets. Women wrapped up in shawls and stoles. Every few moments someone shouted: "Please close, close that door!"

The few remaining diners gathered at the head of the center table as far from the fearful entranceway as possible. Behind the glass doors that opened onto the columned vestibule painted in the national colors, one could see as in a store window the languishing figure of a Piedmontese musician with long hair, wearing a threadbare dinner jacket and strumming the strings of a harp with his skinny dirty fingers. The sad notes were lost in the roar of the wind and rain which intermittently lashed against the long narrow windows.

Ten or twelve guests, the last sickly swallows of that sad summer spent at the beach resort, were having lunch quietly, huddled together trying to keep warm. Once they began their lunch, they spoke only occasionally to demand in an imperious tone some piece of silverware or other. The waiters, whom everyone now knew well enough to scold for their mistakes, suffered the guests' ill humor silently during what they called the autumn season. The day was not far off when everyone must give them a sizeable gratuity. This fact contributed to the guests' bad mood, to their audacity and despotic tone of voice and to the servants' patience.

There, no one's bad manners or ill-timed requests were taken wrongly. People expected it; it was a natural law. Porters, doormen, and waiters had been observing how, at the end of the season, this law was obeyed every year. Besides, those fits of misanthropy were figured into the bill also, without anyone's knowledge, of course. The owner of Thermo Alto was able to live from his income, that is, off his guests. He presided over the table. He heard the complaints of the sickly without becoming disturbed, without really hearing them. He did not take the complaints seriously nor did his boarders refrain from unburdening themselves in his presence. There was a silent agreement that they could rid themselves of their ill humor by complaining and he could choose to pay them no attention whatsoever. He neither undertook the improvements they suggested nor did they refrain from demanding their rights in requesting them.

That the place was in ruins, the building falling down, drafts entering everywhere, that the mineral baths were simply cold and not even remotely warm, that it rained there too much in the fall perhaps because of Mr. Campeche (the owner of the spa), were all commonplace in every conversation. Sometimes even Mr. Campeche forgot himself and, not knowing what to say to a stranger, would tell him confidentially and quickly like someone repeating a lesson from memory: "But have you ever seen a more terrible climate anywhere? It's always raining. And how boring it is here!"

No one would believe that it was the same Thermo Alto that had opened to the public in the spring. Mr. Campeche arrived full of energy, happy, whistling, and tapping his ample stomach with the ivory handle of his cane. He jumped down from his two-wheeled carriage painted a brilliant yellow, and he inspected the baths, the inn, and the gardens, which were already populated with birds who sang madly; they were the first guests to arrive. After checking his accounts, he decided to begin what he emphatically called his improvements.

The improvements consisted only of whitewashing the entire building and painting the green friezes blue and the blue friezes green. He also repaired the plumbing, if it was totally nonfunctioning, covered the cracks in the plaster and patched a few broken simulated marble sinks. As his most important improvement, he painted the hospital white, the hospice which proudly displayed on its miserable door a presumptuous sign in large red letter, GERONTOCOMIA. That ugly word frequently appeared in the nightmares of the sick who came to visit Thermo Alto.

The first jokes of the newest arrivals always were made about the Greek sign. Most people left without ever knowing what it meant. Even Mr. Campeche was not sure whether a translation was possible. One woman who had been coming to Thermo Alto for over thirty years had come to be known as Lady Gerontocomia.

There was a lot of scrubbing and cleaning, moving furniture from one place to another, and general disorder. Of course, when the first guests arrived, they would find everything rearranged from top to bottom. Workmen and maids hurried about. It was impossible to lean against any of the walls or touch any of the doors because they were all being painted. The noise of hammers and saws thundered throughout the building. Everything smelled like strong detergent. The floor of narrow pine boards was either covered with puddles or sawdust, because as far as scrubbing and making everything shine were concerned, Mr. Campeche made no compromises.

Lifting her skirts a little and leaping over puddles in the constantly damp hall, Lady Gerontocomia always said, "Much ado about nothing!"

The fact is that in spite of all the repair and cleaning paraphernalia, which made so much noise and inconvenienced everyone, Mr. Campeche spent very little each year to improve his establishment which, according to the guests who were there in the fall, was in ruins.

It was always the same: the guests who stayed during the spring were cheerful, confused, optimistic, and found everything brand new; it was the best spa in Spain and for that matter in all Europe. And the water? Whoever took the baths and did not improve must indeed be in a very bad way.

And Mr. Campeche! What a gentleman! How attentive! How zealous in defending the reputation of Thermo Alto! It was true that his improvement projects bothered people considerably. No one could sleep late or take an early afternoon nap or wear slippers about the house because of them. But after all, the improvements gave the place a little life, animation, cheerfulness and were an indication of prosperity and pleasant activity.

"Ladies and gentlemen," Campeche would say smiling and shrugging his shoulders which seemed stooped under the weight of so much responsibility, "Please forgive us; the work has gone much slower this year, I know. There has been so much to do! Since January we have been building and cleaning like mad. Especially the new roof for the convalescent center."

The amusing part was that the same people whom Campeche deceived in the spring, or rather who allowed themselves to be deceived, were the same people who in the fall shouted down the establishment and at the same time arranged for their next visit right in the owner's face. This practice no longer surprised anyone. It was universally accepted. When people visited in the spring, everything was fine. When they visited in the fall, everything was terrible.

In the spring and during part of the summer the guests suffered one another's practical jokes and always played a few of their own. There might well have been better hydrotherapy than the baths there, but there could never be a better place for greater pranks. Since everyone is different, in spring as in winter, more than once, actually rather often, there were threats that never came to any dire consequences, fortunately. Often each season, however, someone slapped someone else, or at least resorted to the most atrocious insults.

But usually people tolerated the jokes because they felt free to return them twofold. One would notice that the young people, who all winter long in the neighboring capital had distinguished themselves by their quiet, peaceful and taciturn demeanor, surpassed themselves as soon as they came to Thermo Alto in thinking up the most outlandish jokes and the most horrible atrocities.

In this regard there was one young man suffering from a liver ailment who became famous for many years afterwards, a youth who was the color of Cordovan leather and who in the city never spoke to anyone.

One rainy afternoon, the young hypochondriac arrived at the spa on horseback. He dismounted, approached a friend and asked in a voice that sounded as if it came from beyond the grave: "Is it true that people commit atrocities here?"

"Yes, sir, it certainly is."

"My doctor has ordered me to take the waters and enjoy myself for a while. I have seen Niagara Falls and found them no more impressive than a mountain spring. Nothing. I am going to see if, by enjoying myself, I am going to commit my own atrocity. This liver of mine!"

And in effect he went to the stable, mounted his horse, spurred him on and rode into the inn and into the dining room, greeting most formally those present.

The joke created quite an impression. Some of the women fainted. In the end, everything turned out exactly as he wanted. The young man suffering from a liver ailment—he had visited Niagara Falls in vain—improved, received cordial congratulations, and confessed that he had not had such a wonderful time in many years. Nevertheless, a few envious people began to mumble, saying that his feat was not completely original. They had forgotten the thirteenth-century poet Raymond Lull, who, according to legend had followed a woman into church, mounted on his horse. And they had forgotten that into that very dining room, there once rode a man mounted on a sturdy burro. It was all the same. The man on the burro was a provincial deputy who had won fame with this act, and because he had stabbed an elector in the groin several years earlier.

The young man with the liver problem discovered that the guests were grumbling and decided to outshine all the provincial deputies in the world. On the following day, he made such an impression that he left a lasting memory of himself in the spa.

What he did was to place, with no little effort, a huge chest of drawers on top of the railing of a balcony which overlooked the dining room. He dropped it suddenly on the table where approximately twelve women and twenty gentlemen were having dinner.

No one died, but only by luck. The man with the liver problem had done what he could!

The table and the chest of drawers were broken into splinters. The dining room floor caved in, destroying all the dishes, silverware and crystal. More than twenty people fainted. Three threatened to kill the man. Fourteen guests got up and left the spa immediately.

The most recalcitrant had to confess the evident fact: there had never been a practical joke like dropping the chest of drawers. As far as the owner Mr. Campeche was concerned, he had the good grace not to say anything to the perpetrator of the joke. It was the custom of the establishment.

No one could explain to anyone's satisfaction why, in the cheerful months of May and June and even during the heat of the summer, Thermo Alto was an Arcadian spa, when during the fall it was a boring, cold and sad hospital where everyone was constantly in a bad humor.

Probably, the climate contributed to this difference. The scenery was perhaps the most beautiful on the northern coast. It was green everywhere with hills like flower vases, little brooks, forests, a real lake and such romantic surprises as caves, islets, waterfalls and even a crater at the top of a conical mountain, which Mr. Campeche swore was an extinct volcano. He threatened those who did not believe him with written testimony from the town hall, which was a mere league away from the hotel.

The crater was the legendary element in that topography, which the owner of the spa had turned into a lucrative business.

But if the countryside offered such natural delights to the guests, as soon as September arrived, spirits were dampened. Fog, wind, showers, endless days of cold, sad rain, a leaden horizon and damp chills that reminded one of the tomb were the attacks made by the weather on that delightfully scenic landscape. It was useless for Mr. Campeche to show his new guests photographs of the crater and waterfalls.

They replied to him that that would be fine, if the crater were erupting. At least then one could get warm! As far as the waterfalls were concerned, the sky was making them everywhere. Then why did people come to Thermo Alto in the fall at all? Because doctors in the entire province, whether they had been paid to by Mr. Campeche or not, swore that the best and most healthy, hygienic and therapeutic time for taking the waters was in September and October.

Therefore, those who wanted to enjoy themselves came in the summer; those who wanted to cure their illnesses came in the fall. Perhaps this factor, no less than meteorological variations, was another cause for the differences in humor among the guests who came at different seasons.

II

During those sad days in the month of October when the guests at the grand hotel of Thermo Alto huddled together at the head of the table in the cold, damp dining room over dessert, the conversation that had languished and turned bitter regained a little spirit, even if only to curse with renewed vigor the unbearable life everyone was

living, exploited by servants seeking gratuities in that huge, old building. Everyone discussed the medicinal value of the water, a topic of
conversation which during the first season was considered almost in
bad taste. The majority of the sick declared that they were not convinced. Some were totally skeptical and denied the usefulness of any
kind of spa; others were skeptical only of the water at Thermo Alto.

The first morning when we saw the miserable Piedmontese com-
pete in vain with his harp against the wind lashing the windows for the
privilege of pleasing the guests' ears, the bitterness of the conversation had increased considerably, far beyond the silent, ill-humor in
which the lunch had began.

Everyone was doubting everything; the crater, the waterfalls, the
improvement to the buildings, the humor of the practical jokes, the
beauty of the scenery, the very existence of the sun on the northern
coast and even the reputation for beauty and audacity of the young
country women in that part of the country.

A couple suffering from tuberculosis, each one over fifty, each
one with a perpetual bitter countenance, assured everyone that the
village girls in that region were ugly but honorable because they were
so savage; all the amorous adventures that everyone talked about
were made up by Mr. Campeche to attract customers and vacationers, that is, robust bachelors who came there just to cause trouble.

"It does not seem very proper to me," pronounced the little old
man whose words were seconded by his wife's nods, "it does not
seem very proper at all, I say, for anyone to malign the reputation of
the weaker sex in an entire district for the simple purpose of attract-
ing attention and bringing people of questionable morals to the spa."

The gentleman who had spoken was a district attorney in the
capital and his wife helped him count out on his fingers the years to
be added or subtracted from prison sentences by virtue of aggravating
or attenuating circumstances. His wife had become so accustomed to
the technicalities of the penal system that when someone asked her
how she was enjoying the spa, whether she found the water too cold
or too warm, she replied: "Do you know? I like it from the minimum
to the maximum."

As always, the district attorney denied the beauty of the young
women in the region and the ease of consummating love affairs in the
surrounding green countryside.

"Well, sir," Don Canuto Cancio, an old attorney who respected
the district attorney but hated him for what he called his pedantry,
dared to reply, "well, sir, Don Mamerto does not have the reputation
of a liar. And, by your leave, Mr. District Attorney, and respecting
your superior judgment and your knowledge of the law, Don
Mamerto assures us in all confidence, of course, that he, that the
Galinda girl and the Rico Paez girl and the miller's girl...."

"That bit about the miller's girl is a fact," another diner interrupted.

"And I saw the Paez girl with Don Mamerto along Pancho's fence this year in July when it was getting dark," another guest chimed in.

"You, Don Canuto," replied the district attorney, ignoring the other guests' interruptions since he had not been introduced to them, "would believe anything anyone told you."

The district attorney's wife, balancing her spectacles on the tip of her nose looked disdainfully at Don Canuto and in a defiant manner challenged him to contradict her husband. "Anything anyone told you!"

"That Mr. Mamerto...."

All conversation ceased. No one moved. Even the waiters stopped to hear what the district attorney was going to say against Don Mamerto, the idol of Thermo Alto. Mr. Campeche, who listens contentedly while they malign his spa, frowns, fearing that the district attorney might be overstepping this time.

"That Mr. Mamerto...."

He hesitates. He doubts his authority will extend far enough to risk saying something against the reputation of Mamerto.

"That Mr. Mamerto," a retired colonel roars out in a thunderous voice from the seat next to Mr. Campeche, "is a model gentleman, incapable of lying and much less incapable of showing off with made-up adventures and imaginary good fortune. You do understand that, my good man."

The district attorney and his wife turn their chairs around to look at the colonel, who from this moment has assumed all responsibility for whatever may transpire, as is his inveterate custom whenever the discussions turn particularly violent at the table.

Don Canuto always provokes a response and will not let a question expire; not fearing their insults or disrespect, he turns to the colonel as if to say, "What do you know about it?" and the colonel, who never throws a stone, because he is very wise, never denies his ideas once stated, either. He usually uses his remarks carefully to strike out against the person who is irritating him.

Don Diego, with his gout and other ailments, defends the traditions of the table, and there is no tradition more respected than Don Mamerto Anchoriz, our hero.

Don Mamerto Anchoriz appears every year in Thermo Alto to spend one week in May or June and another during the worst weather of the fall, when there is the most rain, to keep those people company and liven things up a bit. The district attorney knows this quite well and therefore is mistaken in criticizing a man who is so well respected in Thermo Alto.

Of course, the district attorney has not said anything yet, but he has spoken his name twice, and according to the colonel, one does not impute anything to Don Mamerto; therefore, he assumes responsibility for whatever is about to transpire. "And I hope something happens, because anything is preferable, even the death of a district attorney, to this horrible boredom!" many of the guests think to themselves.

The district attorney foresees the conflict, but neither his character, his dignity nor his social position allow him to retreat or unsay words that he has begun to utter. He wife is even more daring and, highly irritated, she casts violent looks about the table, ready to defend her husband's dignity by fighting on her back like a cat, if necessary, should he be unable to defend himself.

But he is very able, for he says, picking up a knife by the blade and tapping the tablecloth slowly with its handle and revealing the tenacity of his character, the unmovability and rigidity of his opinions, and the calmness of his spirit: "Colonel, sir, I have said nothing to offend you or Mr. Mamerto. But every time you anticipate my statements with a desire to inhibit the free expression of my opinions, I must say without ambiguity or indirectness absolutely everything I think about Mr. Anchoriz."

"You will of course take care to say nothing against him."

"I will say, do say, hold and maintain that the man under consideration, Don Mamerto, is a dirty old man...."

Not even the chest of drawers falling from the balcony onto the dining room table produced a more obstreperous reaction that the one produced by the words of the representative of the administration. The general indignation was so great, even among the servants, that the colonel's rage was lost in the general wave of scandal, and for once, the colonel was unable to assume responsibility.

The district attorney and his wife were victims of everyone's upbraiding and learned to respect the opinion of the masses and the weight of tradition before which even the prestige of law is helpless. It is amazing that the district attorney did not know that customs, that is, tradition and history, are more powerful in Rome than written law. The colonel began to pity them and did not challenge either the district attorney or his wife.

But a waiter, one Perico of much less refinement, a fanatical admirer of Don Mamerto, dealt the *coup de grâce*, speaking modestly with the strength of consummated acts: "Mr. Anchoriz has just arrived this morning. He is bathing at present and has said that he will come to have lunch at once."

The response was electric. Tears came to Canuto's eyes. He imagined that the rain has stopped and that spring has returned. He forgives everything and with no irony whatsoever greets the district attorney and his wife, who, after nodding respectfully, take themselves off to their rooms.

The colonel insists that no one tell Anchoriz anything about what has happened. He prefers that Anchoriz not know the little favor they have done him by defending his honor.

"These things are not done to win thanks, but because they come to one naturally."

"Agreed. No one will say anything. But how wonderful! Don Mamerto has come back! He could not have let us down. And how considerate! Exactly when the weather has turned the worst. Such generosity!"

The Piedmontese in the doorway rises suddenly and with a firm, powerful wrist, plays the solemn cords of the Royal March.

"It's him! Everybody stand up! Hooray for Don Mamerto!" They wave their napkins like pennants. "Hooray!"

III

Don Mamerto Anchoriz, accustomed to these receptions, did not lose his composure for one moment. With his round, narrow-brimmed, black and white, fine straw hat, he greeted the group, while his majestic, benevolent rosy–lipped smile flashed under his well-trimmed moustache between his black shining sideburns.

He was tall and strong, with smooth white skin and small delicate hands with shining fingernails. Over his ever–so–slightly protruding stomach, a vest of the finest white material reflected the light. A hunting jacket and gray wool trousers completed the suit of this arrogant figure of manhood, whose appearance during the entire constitutional history of Spain, excluding the first two constitutions, of course, had attracted the admiring glances of women from all social classes.

From the time he was fifteen years old, Don Mamerto had been the best looking man in his part of the country. According to the gossips, he had been seducing married women, single women, widows, nuns, marquises, seamstresses, village girls and dancers for over fifty years. Don Mamerto could not be anywhere near seventy–five years old, but he was definitely much older than he appeared. No one knew for certain how old he was because no one had ever heard him speak of age.

What was certain is that the generations came and went and Anchoriz was the same man for every one of them, with his black sideburns, rosy lips, soft, brilliant eyes, fists as smooth and white as snow, English cut trousers, arrogant bearing and discreet elegance. The serious, solid Anchoriz was the eternal archetype of the good-looking man, welcomed at all parties, a spectator at every show, a participant in public frivolity, a lively spirit and an uproar at all times and at all places.

No one had ever seen him at a funeral. He did not visit the sick. He had never given alms, lent a penny, reduced a bill, voted for anyone or stopped deceiving every husband, father or brother he could, seducing their women. And in spite of how well–known his character was throughout the province, there was no man there better loved. Everyone said, "Oh, Anchoriz! A perfect gentleman! And how well he always looks!"

Everyone also said that had he ever done any reading, he would have been a great intellectual because there was no natural talent quite equal to his. He knew everything there is to know about the world.

He was not very wealthy, but he lived as if he were. For many years he had neither a job nor a pension but got by thanks to the generosity of a wealthier brother with whom he did not reside (because he had always preferred the best inn in town) but who apparently paid all his bills. This was due to an inheritance which had never been divided between them. The brother did not complain and no one seemed to mind. When his relative died and the inheritance was distributed, Mamerto's share was evidently scanty. But he continued in the same style of life, eating well and living elegantly without denying himself anything. Eventually it was discovered that Anchoriz for a long time had been the general administrator of the Duke de Ardanzuelo's estate. There was nothing to administer, however, because the duke's various foremen did everything prior to obtaining Anchoriz's signature.

The grandee's palace was put at the disposal of his general administrator and because of vanity, ostentation or something similar, Anchoriz went to live in the huge mansion. Nevertheless, he continued having his meals brought to him from the inn. Six months passed and his public noticed that Anchoriz was getting thin and pale.

Anchoriz in bad health? Was the world coming to an end? The most distinguished doctors of the city thought it their duty to study the patient, without alarming him, of course. But they could not discover the cause of his illness.

It was Mamerto himself who diagnosed and cured his infirmity. One afternoon, he appeared in the kitchen of the Eagle Hotel, his former residence; he approached the cook and smiling, after patting him on the shoulder, said: "Perico, put little pieces of ham in the soup today."

"In what soup?"

"In the *soup du jour*, everybody's soup!"

"But, are you going to have dinner with us today?"

"Yes, today, tomorrow, and everyday. Please put in some ham."

Mamerto loved little pieces of ham in his soup because they reminded him of his parents' home. He, who had become a perfect gentleman in his eating habits, who had learned to dislike Spanish cooking when he was still very young and made fun of stews and roasts, ate whenever he could an oily soup with pieces of ham, the one luxury of his father's dinners which he had been fond of all of his life. This was the only practice he conceded to family tradition. He did not believe in the religion of his father (although he neither attacked nor defended it, as he was fond of saying); he did not believe in the validity of monogamy or in the natural affections that stem from blood relationships; he did not believe in his country. The only thing he believed in was oily soup with diced ham. It was his only relic.

When Mamerto stayed at the inn, everyone often had his kind of soup.

When the news of Mamerto's return became generally known, the cook grew sentimental as did the dishwasher. The cleaning women either wept or sang for joy, depending upon their temperament. Room six, which had been Don Mamerto's for many years, had remained vacant since he had left it. He returned to it that very night. The widow Uriah, owner of the hotel, said solemnly to the servants that this was a historic day for the establishment.

When the beloved guest took his place at the table in the dining room, a place reserved for him for a long time, there was a respectful, eloquent silence, a profound emotion among the servants and guests of long standing.

The newer guests also looked respectfully at the hero of the evening. Don Mamerto simply smiled, unmoved, fixed his eyes on his soup bowl, cooled the soup with the pieces of ham with the same natural modesty and tranquil parsimoniousness that had always been his custom.

It was obvious that the man always, in any similar situation, kept his mind on his own business.

The simplicity with which this perfect gentleman was able to return to his former way of life reminded one guest of the story of Fray Luis de Len who after a long stay in jail returned to his classes in Salamanca with the words, "As we were saying yesterday." Mamerto seemed to be saying, "As we were dining yesterday...."

As soon as he returned to the inn, his improvement was evident with each passing hour. In a few weeks, he had become the same Mamerto as always and the city slept peacefully.

IV

He had never been ill and he never intended to be. Many and very complicated causes contributed to his perfect health and Anchoriz's supreme ambition was his health, perhaps his only concern. But if someone asked him, "Sir, what advice do you have for staying in such good health?" Mamerto would reply, smiling, "Do not read anything after eating."

And if the person asking the question deserved more clarification, Anchoriz would add, "Or before, either."

Of course, this was the prescription he gave to get rid of people who were bothering him. His system, his philosophy, was no more than common sense advice which any doctor would give. There was nothing to it. Why ask anything about one's unfaltering health?

Of course, abstaining from reading was one of the items in his program. But it was a very secondary one.

Why should he read? Reading presupposed a certain harmful curiosity, a spiritual impatience, a disequilibrium, all of which were in opposition to true well–being. Strictly speaking, not reading was an effect of his good health, not a cause. He was not healthy because he did not read; he did not read because he was healthy.

Nothing a writer could possibly have to say interested him at all.

Anchoriz did not underestimate knowledge and literature, of course. He simply disliked them as one dislikes pharmacies, pharmacists, doctors and sick people. Mamerto would smile with pity when he saw someone suffer an attack of nerves, an attack of abnegation or of insight. It all came down to the same thing: disequilibrium, a sign of an early death, a mistaken idea about existence. He could not conceive of a challenge, a bad word or a good deed. His principal concern in life was himself. To sacrifice for others was something which went beyond the mere servility demanded by courtesy and was foolishness. To never do anything good for your fellow man was a difficult rule to follow, almost impossible. Of course, for this reason, Mamerto had never met but one happy man: himself.

Upon this principle of absolute egotism were based all the rules for his personal conduct, which explained the pleasant existence that Anchoriz planned to continue indefinitely. Must one die? We would all see when the time came. Every absolute statement annoyed him. There was nothing known for certain about anything. The fact that everyone he knew to date had died eventually was not an absolute proof that everyone henceforth would die.

Science states that every organism eventually wears out, that everything perishes. Salvation! Science says many things. He did not deny the possibility, even the probability, of death. But after all, it was not really certain, what one could call absolutely certain, and this type of thinking was sufficient to keep him tranquil. The important thing, besides, was not this abstract and metaphysical aspect of the question, but rather its practical aspect, that of not dying.

"As long as I am alive, it matters little that I am mortal. It is one thing to be mortal and quite something else to be dead." He remembered having heard that according to Buffon, every man, no matter how old he is, can legitimately hope to live another year. Buffon was a great, wise man, doubtlessly worthy of not having to die. Anchoriz intended to keep his body fit to live another year for as long as possible. So if death, as far as he was concerned, was only a word, a threat, or a creation of the imagination, and would continue retreating, life would continue gaining ground. Besides, he knew how those old people died, the ones who are examples of longevity. They ended like little birds or like newborns. They disappeared without sorrow. Their stomach and health outlived their brain and everything else indicative of existence of the soul.

Well, to die in that way was not exactly the same thing as dying. He expected, supposing the worst, that he would die after all and go on to a better life when he was no longer aware, expiring like a little old man he had known who had cried out, "Villalon cheese! The cheese man!" from his death bed, swearing over and over again that it was dinner time. And when one was about one hundred and twenty years old, maybe more, hell!, it was not too hard to take. At any rate, he would think it over.

And meanwhile, he lived tranquilly, peacefully, *sub specie aeternitatis*.

V

This was the man whom the diners in Thermo Alto received with such joy and solemn praise, people who were dying of boredom in that cold, damp dining hall that sad autumn morning.

At first, no one said anything about the incident with the district attorney and his wife. Everyone was interested in hearing the latest gossip that Mamerto had brought fresh from the city.

Weddings, dances, scandalous love affairs, excursions, retreats— the eloquent personage told everything and was very pleased that he was able to satisfy those people's curiosity (many of whom he knew only slightly). The colonel asked him afterwards what was taking place in the civil wars and what had happened after the explosion in the Langreo coal mines. Anchoriz made a face, wiped his mouth with his napkin and declared that he did not have the least bit of news about such a terrible catastrophe nor about the fighting our brothers were doing.

And a little while later, smiling, he played bridge in the recreation room (a recreation room where four vacationers played the piano at the same time!), certain to win bets from some newcomers who considered themselves honored by the presence of such a fine, jovial companion to whom no one could possibly be rude.

In the evening, thanks to Anchoriz's influence, the Virginia Reels and the round dances resumed after the silence that had reigned since the end of July. Don Mamerto usually did not dance. But on that memorable evening he deigned to invite a woman who was hiding in a corner behind a card table, knitting, with a very unsociable look on her face, apparently disapproving of all those mundane frivolities. Yes, she was unabashedly knitting at a dance.

It was the district attorney's wife. Anchoriz already knew (they had told him over coffee) about the incident at lunch. For this very reason, he went directly to his enemy, sure of conquering.

In effect, after an initial rejection and several hesitations and protests, the good woman herself went out onto the floor on Don Mamerto's arm. A burst of applause greeted the couple. It was truly glorious! The wife's face radiated joy.

Vanity filled her little spirit. Very little vanity was necessary to fill such a narrow place. With no more than a very refined invitation, one glance from a gallant gentleman, a few smiles in which good health and blood take the place of poetic spirituality, Anchoriz had conquered the district attorney's wife's attention. This lady, on feeling her arm on that of such a gallant man, one who always seemed young and vital, now saw the world, and particularly Don Mamerto, from a different point of view, "from the perspective of the flowers," and she pardoned Anchoriz because he had loved greatly.

For four or five days, our hero provided the guests of Thermo Alto with delightful entertainment. And those who had remained there definitely needed consoling and encouragement because those who had left the spa seemed to have taken all joy with them.

"What do you suppose it is?" the district attorney's wife asked Don Mamerto, whom she had made the confidant of a certain hysterical romanticism that she had hidden under the penal code, which had come to overtake the greater part of her heart. "What do you suppose causes one to become so attached to people whom one has known for so short a time and who upon leaving seem to take part of one's soul? Could it be the familiarity of living together every day, the extraordinary nature of the friendships developed here under these circumstances?"

"Yes, madam," Don Mamerto answered smiling, "something like that. But the main cause of this sentimentalism that overtakes one at the end of summer is the great quantity of fruit and tomato sauce everyone has eaten. These foods weaken a person and stimulate the nerves. And from these causes come this sudden love for one's fellow man and this tendency to see in everyone who comes and goes a motive for melancholy."

"Tomatoes? This sadness that comes from seeing people leave comes from tomatoes?"

"Yes, ma'am; but especially from fruit; fruits with pits particularly. Peaches cause bile and bile causes sorrow for no good reason."

Besides, it was not hard for Anchoriz to make people happy because he was as lively as castanets. In spite of the fruit, it did not matter to him at all that people were arriving and leaving. As long as there were still people around, it did not really matter very much if it was one group of people or another. For this reason, he could not understand why some people became so upset when someone died.

"Why do people weep over death and celebrate every birth? Just look at the newspapers," he explained. "The town registry: today: four deaths and six births. We are winning by two points. And it is always the same."

So it was that when a guest announced he was leaving, Mamerto saw only cause for celebration. No matter how ill-liked the guest might be in the hotel, Anchoriz always organized a demonstration, a practical joke in good taste which consisted of making an agreement with most of the guests to pretend to be distracted when the hour of departure arrived and so cause the people taking their leave to become angry at everyone's indifference, forgetfulness and lack of courtesy. And just at the moment when they were about to board the coach which would take them to the train station, the group would come out onto the porch in a solemn formation singing the Royal March, playing an accompaniment by tapping stones from the river together. The guests who had been annoyed would leave most happily, assured of their popularity at the spa and convinced that they were leaving behind numerous good friends who were no less firm because they had never been tried.

And Anchoriz, who was such a good friend of this type, as faithful to friendship in good times as he was determined not to accompany anyone in their sorrow, what did he think of the others' friendship for him? Was he a skeptic? Would he deny himself all hope that the others would be more charitable with him than he had been with them? No. He did not think about it. He considered these comparisons totally meaningless as he did the whole idea of death. He did not want to involve himself in such deep questions as seeing just how far others' egotism would extend. These investigations did not suit his own.

If man were evil and egotistical, the best recourse would be not to allow oneself to be in a situation that would verify it by experience. For this reason, without having resolved the question in a pessimistic vein, just in case, Anchoriz treated friendship as Don Quijote treated the second visor for his helmet. He did not put it to a second test. And his egotism, closely aligned with self-interest and with possible profit, under the auspices of law which assures one of what he has earned with or without charity, tried to live without needing anyone by means of doing nothing for anyone who might in turn need the cheerful and cooperative Don Mamerto.

This cheerfulness was rather affected because everyone was naturally afraid of the sadness and loneliness and of the bad weather which was getting worse. The cheerfulness had reached its peak, thanks, as usual, to Mr. Anchoriz, when one morning, which was exceptionally beautiful because of the brilliant sunshine and warm breeze, a waiter announced in the dining room that Don Mamerto was not coming to dinner at the round table because he was somewhat indisposed.

Everyone present turned toward the bearer of such bad news.

"He's in bed?" many asked.

"Yes, in bed. And he has asked that Dr. Casado come to see him."

"Anchoriz in bed! And at mid-day!"

General consternation. Even more than that, astonishment, as if the sun at midday had not yet left the soft plumes of his classic bed nor abandoned the arms of the goddess with whom mythology would have us believe he lies.

VI

Without finishing dessert, a committee composed of the most select members from the round table went to visit Don Mamerto in his room. This was done without preventing the other guests from going in one by one to fulfill their common duty, as it was called by the public official who, though grudgingly, had reconciled himself to the injured Don Juan thanks to the influence of his wife.

The hotel doctor who was very fond of joking and treated medicine lightly, particularly the value of hydrotherapy, had hardly wanted to take Mamerto's pulse and check his throat. "What could Anchoriz possibly have wrong with him? Nothing. By eight o'clock the next morning he would be taking a bath." But he was not. Instead of taking a shower, he had to suffer patiently the 101 F fever with which God had wanted not to try him, because He already knew quite well the kind of man Anchoriz was, but rather to mortify him.

For the first two days of his illness, with the greatest delicacy in the world, the gentleman would not permit his friends to come to see him in his bedroom. They were permitted no farther than the dressing room which was, like every other one in the hotel, first class with one difference. The table and chest of drawers resembled a display case for cosmetics: dozens of combs and brushes for the hair, fingernails and teeth; dozens of syringes, hundred of bottles, bars of soap, tablets and flasks; triangular cloths to tie up the ends of his moustache; boxes of soap, mysterious chemical artifacts applied to a stubborn old age; a thousand little pill boxes and cosmetics suitable for an actor's dressing room.

His visitors spoke to him from the dressing room. Only the waiter and doctor could enter his bedroom. At first, Mamerto answered very kindly the charitable souls who had come to ask about his health the very moment he had lost it, forcing his voice so that they could hear him clearly outside speaking with the same correct, refined and jovial tone as always. He seemed to be asking his public's pardon for the annoyance of his having inopportunely taken to his bed and interrupting the general good cheer which he had revived in them. He did not believe his illness was anything serious either, in spite of the fever. He was in total agreement with the doctor on this point. Him, seriously ill? That would be the last straw!

Since the situation was becoming more serious, the fever refused to go down and a general weakness began to overtake him. His body ached and boredom attacked him. Don Mamerto, because of the inconvenience, and the doctor, because of the fever, became alarmed.

People invaded the bedroom and the sick man no longer had the strength to resist them. Moreover, although he had his reasons for not letting anyone come in, the desire to see other human beings was more powerful, to see friendly faces who would show him some gesture of sympathy and who shared in his displeasure, even though it might be insignificant. He wanted to tell everyone about that interesting illness, Anchoriz's sickness. He even wanted others to feel his pain in order to see if that would ease his mind.

The guests, seeing Don Mamerto suffering in bed, mentally made the sign of the cross. How delicate we are! That is, how delicate Don Mamerto was! After four or five days of fever and after not grooming himself, he suddenly aged twenty years.

He looked decrepit. He looked like his father brought back from the grave. He knew very well the effect he was having, but he was in no mood for vain pretense. All he wanted was for people to feel sorry for him. And they truly did. They kept him company for too long. His sick room had acquired the spirit of a retirement party. What comings and goings! Everyone wanted to sit with him. Everyone wanted to keep track of the time to give him his medicine, the correct dosages and proper prescriptions. They took turns applying the poultices to his legs and it turned out that no one could do it as neatly and as efficiently as the district attorney's wife. This woman did not hesitate for a moment to put them on neatly with the hands of a tender, loving nurse. She was one of the more assiduous women about visiting the sick man. But Anchoriz had already noted that she took precautions not to make noise in order not to bother him, which everyone else had not remembered to do.

When he felt her apply the poultices, he noticed in the softness and calmness of this angular woman's movements, in her manner of changing the bed clothes something like a tender recollection of his distant childhood. He thought of the mother he had lost when very young. Although she was so ugly and particularly ridiculous because of her expression, her stuffiness and her funny little manias, he became attached to her and insisted that she and no one else arrange his blanket and pillows. It was delightful to feel her arrange things with such delicate and efficient movements that they seemed like caresses and a balm.

Don Mamerto, because of his weakness, had become more ob-
servant and began like every good critic to be rather pessimistic about
the minutiae of everyday life. Everything that glittered was not gold.
He noticed that most people took care of him as a form of entertainment. Many only pretended to hear. And not a few began to tire.
Some had already begun to slacken in their attention and decrease
the number of their visits. Others said good–bye to him because their
stay was coming to an end and they left him alone—that is, bereft of
the great wide world which they, those egotists, were going to travel
across, see the sights and enjoy!

It was the strangest thing! The sickly Anchoriz finally noticed a
great similarity between the character of all those people who were so
healthy and who were abandoning him and the character of the robust and healthy Anchoriz he had always been. They treated him as
he had always treated everyone. But it was not the same. It did not
suit other people to behave in that manner.

VII

The good weather that seemed to have brought Anchoriz with it
gave up the cause. Showers began to lay siege to Thermo Alto again.
Many of the embattled regiment surrendered to the enemy, bore-
dom, and left the field without honors of any kind because Don
Mamerto was no longer there at the door to bid farewell with the
Royal March to those who were escaping.

Some said good–bye to him; others did not. He noticed the loneliness. He felt the terror of remaining there, tied to his bed while,
little by little, the guests went parading by. It was now a case of every
man for himself.

In his sickly manias and apprehensions, he began to regret the
lack of company, as he said, as much as suffering from the sickness
itself. His fever made his isolation more unpleasant. There was more.
Staying there so alone in that room in the spa was associated in his
mind with his breathing and each time they told him that someone
had left, he imagined that he was short of breath.

He wanted to hear noise, even if it bothered him.

The doctor advised quiet and darkness and he sought noise and
light. He made them move his bed to the dressing room. At night, as
long as the gathering of the few remaining guests lasted in the salon
which was closest by, Don Mamerto ordered them to open the doors
to his room so that he could hear snatches of conversation. They
were playing bridge and what he heard most was: "Two hearts,"
"three clubs," "three spades," "pass," and other such lovely remarks.

It did not seem possible that there could be people in the building
who gave so much attention to a card game while he was as ill as he
was undoubtedly becoming.

Yes, he was very ill. Let the truth be told. He sensed it and besides, he understood as much from certain symptoms: he noticed that the doctor, Campeche and the servants were taking care of him with that angry concern which a seriously ill person inspires in the strangers who must watch over him.

This was not what they had bargained for. The healthy Mr. Anchoriz, as cheerful as castanets, would always be very welcome. Anchoriz who was simply indisposed would be acceptable and even rather amusing because of the unusual nature of the situation. But an Anchoriz in danger of dying, demanding days, nights and countless hours of care, frankly was a painful surprise. A bad joke.

Either to lend importance to himself or because it was true, the doctor let it be known that perhaps, just maybe, that illness would degenerate into typhoid.

The statement, particularly with the word "degeneration" could not have come from the doctor but the fear of typhoid indeed did originate with him.

A few days later, Anchoriz could not hear the voices coming from the salon. It was useless for him to have the door opened. He could no longer hear: "One club," "three no-trump," "pass." It did not seem possible but those words which were meaningless, unimportant and cold to him had come to represent company. They spoke to him of a humanity that existed, though very very far away, like a ship which a man fallen overboard sees on the horizon, a hope that passed by many miles from where he was drowning.

The bridge game ended. The gathering of players ended. Everything ended. Mr. Campeche had to leave. There were no guests left. The extraordinary French chef had been dismissed and the servants were greatly reduced in number. It was now like winter must have been there, if it were not for the inconvenient sickness of Mr. Anchoriz. The doctor also was growing impatient. Officially, he no longer had any obligation to be there. Someone spoke of moving the patient to the capital. Impossible.

The only trip was the one returning him to his bedroom, which to him seemed a waiting room for the tomb. In that atrium he hardly knew the few people who approached him. He did not recognize the district attorney's wife except by her touch, by the maternal sweetness of her way of arranging his bed clothes and pillows. The district attorney and his wife had not left. He had a great deal of freedom in his work, and his wife for whatever reason controlled her husband. They were ridiculous, formal and old-fashioned Spaniards. They had backward ideas and were slaves to legal formula in questions of law. They were harsh and bound by custom in questions of a legal nature because that was the nature of the law. But evidently they were very good people. Perhaps he was nothing more than a husband dominated by his wife. But she, whether or not she was in love with

Anchoriz, as some had suggested without respecting her age, was, at least to judge from the results, a very charitable soul.

Without her, Anchoriz would have died like a dog, like a dog attended to by stewards.

He did not die in that manner. It was quite different. One night, while a kitchen boy who was supposed to watch over him was sleeping and snoring like a log, Don Mamerto suddenly felt very ill. He called out, shouted, but not very loudly, and it was useless.

As if he were already buried and had awakened in his coffin, he began to thrash about and kick at the wall. He did not want to die without a witness, without pity. The boy did not stir; he was sound asleep. The poor child had risen at five in the morning and had worked hard.

Anchoriz—who during his lifetime had not needed to dream in order to have appear before him voluptuous and enchanting visions worthy of dreams in the form of beautiful healthy women wearing very light gowns who approached his bachelor's bed unexpectedly— now saw, either dreaming or delirious, that out of the darkness there appeared a figure whom the light of a lamp merely made seem more pale, a skinny, angular ghost, death with her hair in pin curls, a vision from the Dance Macabre.

It was not death; it was the district attorney's wife in her night- gown, her hands placed as dictated by a posthumous modesty; horri- ble in her midnight ugliness but moved by a spirit of charity which had not been completely destroyed, even if gossips were correct and she came to him with the strength of a certain useless lascivious curi- osity which was perhaps ridiculously loving and romantic. The fact was that he had to be content with what there was.

Humanity did not give Anchoriz in that moment of supreme trial anyone but a toothless, ugly, solemn and ridiculous old woman who was very fussy and a little pious.

Such as she was, she approached the dying man. Since there was no time to call a doctor, priest or even any of the servants, in the great egotist's last moments of strange lucidity, she spoke to him of celestial consolations. She let him hold tenderly a squalid hand which he grasped tightly as if he were holding on to life itself. As he wept, she wept. There are Christian traditions which, in certain moments, regain the always newly discovered sublimity understood only by those who find themselves in the most supreme suffering. Perhaps what transpired between the old woman and the libertine, between the honorable wife of the district attorney and the dirty old man, was the most interesting interlude with a woman this confirmed bachelor would ever have to tell his fellows at the round table...if he had been able to tell it.

Queen Margaret

At night, one would see her during rehearsals when there was no show—that is, on Mondays, Wednesdays and Fridays—sitting in the shadows in a seat in the fifth or sixth row, wrapped up in her threadbare gray shawl. She would remain motionless for hours, silent and without smiling when her companions on stage laughed without noticing that she was there. During performances she would usually go to a third-level balcony as if she were hiding, as quiet as ever, taking up as little space as possible. She did not enjoy looking at the public, who were all strangers, indifferent and often almost hostile.

They were always the same to her in every town the theater company visited: a distracted enemy who, without thinking, injured her. She would not look at them. It was enough for her to have to look at their cold insensitive faces when she had to appear on stage and sing without losing her place or forgetting her lines, and express with gestures and certain poses passions that were not her own and sorrows that were not the ones that tormented her.

She looked at the stage. She preferred to see the same scenes and hear the same songs once again even if it were for the thousandth time. At least that boring and monotonous spectacle repeated over and over was something familiar, like a portable hometown. The opera traveled with them. She looked at the stage as gypsies look at the wagons or tents that accompany them across new and unknown lands. In her imagination, the stage was the land and the public a stormy sea. At least so it seemed when she looked at the stage from the perspective of the audience. Because when she was on stage, the public continued being a rough sea and the stage a fragile, floating board at the mercy of the waves.

She went to the theater, not because she enjoyed the show, but to escape the loneliness of the hotel and because of habit, to be with her own kind. After all, she was part of the company although they treated her rudely, coldly, offhandedly and usually rather indifferently. She had grown accustomed to this treatment since she was a child. Her mother had been a singer; her father, an orchestral musician; she, as a little girl, simply wanted to sleep, but not alone in her room. She would go to the theater and suffer from cold, fatigue, tedium and boredom in the wings. She preferred this to the fear of being alone in the hotel at night. She now had no parents to follow. She went to the theater just to be with people, to flee the dimly lit

room in the poor guest house, to run away from the cold, the silence
and the isolation which consumed her soul with hours of yawns as
deep as wells.

She could not remember how she had become an artist. It had
begun as one of her mother's dreams. One day, it was necessary to
find a child to play a particular role. She was available; the public
applauded her and from that day, she became a member of the
troupe. On one occasion, the musical director, something of a voice
teacher and rather fond of Marcela's mother, discovered that the girl
had a beautiful voice. Her parents believed it; no one denied it and
the girl learned music and began, when she was old enough, to sing
very small parts in the company in which her mother worked. That is
how it began. She was a singer because she had never been anything
else. She was fond of the theater, just as people who live in an ungrateful and poor country have a fondness for their homeland. She
had that warm affection which derives from seeing the same thing
every day. But she no longer had any aspirations of being an artist.
She had almost forgotten the dreams she had had at the beginning of
her cloudy, rather sad career. The public had gradually disillusioned
her. Besides, she was not beautiful. She had been eighteen years old
like everyone. But neither triumphs nor love had woven any crowns
of happiness for her. A commonplace silent disillusionment was all.
She had been in the company she was with now for many years due
to the friendship her deceased parents had had with the directors of
the organization. And since Marcela was a good stand-in, they put
up with everything. She had no pretensions; she did not get in anyone's way and she was satisfied with the salary, which was far below
minimum requirements. She had never played anywhere but in the
provinces.

The reviewers, who were always badly dressed and not always
very polite, but who always represented Aristarchus on matters of
singing, usually treated her with that provincial kind of disdain that
one must experience in order to appreciate its total humiliating bitterness. They left her with her life. At best, they would say she had not
destroyed the show. But their most frequent statement was to affirm
that Miss Marcela Vitali (Vidal) had made praiseworthy efforts to
control the emotion that visibly oppressed her.

Yes, this is true. She had an uncontrollable deerlike fear of the
public, a fear the years did not diminish. Her benefactors, the owners
of the company, were growing accustomed to tolerating her as a mere
charity case who did have some rights. In order to avoid hurting her
feelings and in order to avoid endangering the plays any more than
they already were, the company gradually began calling on her less
and less to perform. They continued paying her her miserable salary
and she understood that she hardly earned it. But she was silent in
this sad humiliation and almost grateful. In general, the other singers

neither loved nor hated her. They regarded her as an inoffensive appendix to the company. But when egotism and envy no longer have anything to say, malicious joking still does, thanks to its horrible frivolity. No one knows who gave Marcela the nickname everyone in the company called her from that day forward: Queen Margaret.

The reason was as follows. Each day, the public was less kind to Marcela, no matter how insignificant a role she played in the operas. But there was one exception. In a certain classic composition, which was well received everywhere, Miss Vitali played the rather fantastic role of Queen Margaret, a queen who did not reign but who was as constitutional a monarch as possible because in everything and for any reason whatsoever she would allow another soprano to surpass and eclipse her. A singer who was not even a duchess would put her in the shadows completely and would devour with her stronger voice Margaret's voice and steal from her a lover whom Margaret secretly adored. Everyone ruled there except for the queen, who disappeared in the third act after pardoning a series of crimes committed by a number of chorus singers, never to appear on the stage again. She was a sad, modest and slight monarch who listened at court to a series of arias, romanzas, duets and trios. She spent half an hour seated with no one paying any attention to her and when she was allowed to sing her two or three brief arias, she did so in melodies of painful resignation without making much noise. Finally, she allowed herself to be dominated by more powerful voices which in concert drowned her eloquent, sweet, monotonous laments.

Without knowing why, she had fallen in love with this part. The public, the director and the company found a certain grace in this role which she revealed in no other. Marcela Vidal looked almost pretty as Queen Margaret. The only compliments she ever managed to overhear from the select subscribers to seasonal balcony tickets were owed to Queen Margaret. So that she could always look the same, since she had done well in this role, Marcela made herself a dress for this particular opera and never used the company costumes, only the one she had spent her own money and labor on. Sometimes, the public not only found Vidal to be pleasant and discreet in this role, but occasionally they rewarded her with applause when she finished a duet with the soprano who later surpassed her completely. In the fourth act, no one on stage or in the audience remembered Queen Margaret at all. But this did not keep her from returning to her hotel room, alone but happy, and less melancholy than usual, not exactly making any new dreams for herself—that illusion had disappeared a long time ago—but with the satisfaction of having earned her bread, at least for that night.

Nevertheless, that impression began to wear out also and Marcela noticed the irony in her companions' references to her as Queen Margaret as they alluded to the relative success the modest singer had

had in that role. She herself finally saw the humorous side of her
rather limited specialty. The company took it much more seriously. It
was understood that in that particular opera, the role of the queen
went to Marcela. The lights would go out before there were any
changes made.

The company came to a city in northern Spain in the middle of
winter. The singers were bored and afraid of losing their voices. The
dampness reached their very bones. They shivered huddled together
and the entire wardrobe was not enough to protect their throats. The
tenor, who believed himself a man of the future, would have liked a
silver velvet–lined case for his larynx and would not open his mouth,
except to eat, until it was time to sing. It was a sad cathedral town,
but wealthy, and considered operas a luxury rather than an art. The
illustrious citizens bought all the tickets but left the theater practically
empty on many days. There was no love for music there, only money,
and all art for them was a justification for their own pretentiousness.
They did not understand it, but since they were rich, they believed
they had the right to be demanding. Besides, one must not break a
contract. They would be very unhappy if they were cheated, not because of the bad notes in the score, which did not matter to them,
but for the great injury done to their interests if they paid for eight
singers who were, if you please, worth only four. So they restlessly
consulted the few experts or people who pretended to be experts in
the town and listened to their answers as if they issued forth from
oracles.

The actors, as usually happens, stayed in a special part of the
city. There, they hardly interacted with anyone. They were not interested in the monuments, the customs or the beauty of the countryside. They went from the inn to the theater for rehearsals or shows
and back again. All they knew was that it was raining, the sky was
gray, the public cold, reserved and afraid to compromise its reputation for being knowledgeable by applauding something that might not
deserve applause.

This was nothing new for Marcela. Every audience was the same
to her—an enemy, judge and executioner, somewhat like a policeman
who pursued her for the crimes of not having a good voice, for becoming embarrassed and not taking control of the stage. The rain,
the dampness that got into her very bones, the low, ash–gray sky
made her sad. She felt more like a stranger there than in other cities
in her region of Spain, which she no longer considered her home.
Since she was unable to go out and look around, her only recreation
besides the theater, she was deathly bored in the hotel. She sewed,
repaired the silk fringe and the glass pearls on her costume, played
solitaire with a worn deck of cards and slept a lot. She sang the role
of Queen Margaret for two or three nights. For the first time, stern
reviewers named her personally. They had no difficulty declaring that

Miss Vitali had been discreet in the modest and lovely role of the queen and had received well-deserved applause in her duet in the second act. That was all. Marcela returned to her usual inactivity, wrapped in her gray shawl and hidden in the shadows in the sixth or seventh row during rehearsals and in the third balcony during shows.

There from the third balcony, on the far left-hand side, she witnessed a very painful spectacle which made her hair stand on end and caused her to hate the monstrous enemy, the public, more than ever.

The first tenor had just lost his voice because of dampness and because the company had forced him to sing. The newspapers complained. The subscribers threatened to withdraw their support. Counting on their fingers, those worthy businessmen proved that the tenor's cold was cheating them of so many *pesetas* and *céntimos*. "It is simply mathematics," they growled to the company.

The company raised its hands to the heavens and did not know what to do. As if fallen into their laps from above, there appeared in the town, no one knows from where, a tenor who came from the chapel of a certain famous cathedral. He knew a little more music than most. He had a small but well-tuned voice over which he had great mastery. Actually, it was much more pleasant to listen to him sing than to the other little tenor in spite of the latter's presumptuousness. The newcomer declared that the libretto he had mastered best was that of Gounod's *Faust*. He did not have the costume, certainly, but he knew the role flawlessly from start to finish. The problem of proper clothing was resolved as well as possible by borrowing from other Fausts in the company who were larger than he and then by stitching and hemming. Mr. Myrth—the new tenor's name was Myrth, who knows why, because there was no less amusing nor more serious man in the city—Mr. Myrth refused to be confirmed in Italian by taking the name Mirtolini which the company wanted to give him. "Why not take Scherzzo? Why don't you call yourself Scherzzo? It is a rough translation of Myrth," they told him. But no, he was pleasant enough and cooperative, but he would not give in. He would not change his father's name. And since they were in such great straits, the company conceded and the posters read: Faustus: Mr. Myrth.

That was not the worst part. Mr Myrth had a funny manner of walking, stomping down on his heels rather hard. He wore out the heels on his shoes quickly and resembled a strange animal because of his peculiar gait. Besides, he usually wore his hat too far back on his head and to be perfectly frank, though it is rather hard to describe, he held his arms in such a manner that his sleeves were always too long because he was always shrugging his shoulders. The company did not notice this and the director and the orchestra conductor failed to notice that their new Faust had never played the role except dressed as a bumpkin and looked more like a seminarian than anything else.

The night of Myrth's debut arrived and then came the slip, as a student of pharmacy from Madrid who was in the audience said. The public had a wonderful time because all night they laughed openly at Mr. Myrth. When they played for him to sing, the poor chapel tenor reminded one of an angel who truly knew his art. Suddenly, when it was time to snatch away his scholastic gown by pulling a rope, they left him in his shirt sleeves with his beard falling from his face. They made the necessary repairs as best they could. In the first scene with Marguerite, Faust revealed nothing else than his vocation for the ecclesiastical life. He was a martyr. The poor man, who undoubtedly needed the money badly, suffered well. They laughed at him and he smiled. He tried to be gallant with the flaxen haired Marguerite who was on tenterhooks standing next to a seducer who looked at best like a deacon. Myrth grasped the song like a burning sword. If they had let him sing with his hands in his pockets, it would have been better; if they had let him sing from behind the scenery, it would have been better still; but while he sang, the laughter stopped and they even applauded him somewhat. But he went back to miming, and the cruel public, like a pagan, continued to raise an uproar and one could easily hear the hoarsely shouted jokes that rang from balcony to balcony. It was an orgy of regional humor at the expense of a poor hungry provincial.

The other Margaret, the queen in the balcony, felt an infinite pity. The voice of Mr. Myrth, whom she had not had the pleasure of meeting, touched her soul, seeking compassion and consolation. In her mind, everything that Faust sang came to mean: "Those of you who travel the road of art, through this calvary, tell me if there is suffering equal to mine." Tears flowed down her face. If she had had a bomb, she would have thrown it into the audience where those fine gentlemen sat skinning alive a man who knew more music than all of them together. Marcela left the theater before the apotheosis, that is, before the *consummatum est*.

Feliciano Candonga Myrth and Queen Margaret did not take long to become good friends. They met backstage in a dark corner during the rehearsal of an opera in which Miss Vidal sang a few notes and Myrth sang nothing. They liked one another immediately. They were attracted to one another like a magnet by their common fate. Feliciano, after playing the famous Dr. Faustus, did not go back on stage. The company did not dare dismiss him because the other tenor might fall ill again. But neither did the company dare defy the public's indignation by putting the chapel tenor on stage again. He was always waiting in the wings while they warded off his hunger with a pitiful salary. Apparently, he was very short of funds, because in spite of the humiliation of his job, he did not complain. He smiled at everyone and pretended not to notice that he was shunned while waiting for a turn to return to the stage.

Marcela and Feliciano understood that their situation of half-qualified artists was very similar. Their common lot drew them close together. Besides, their personalities were similar. They sought out the shadows; they were shy. They were resigned.

Queen Margaret occupied her seat in the darkness of the seventh row during rehearsals and shortly, the hopeless tenor came to sit next to her. They spoke very softly, only occasionally, when the orchestra conductor did not insist upon absolute silence. At other times, they listened enraptured to the music, happy to hear it, sitting so close to one another. They coincided in their opinions about the merit of the operas and the talent of the singers whom they might have to replace. They both were free of envy. The duet of charity and justice in which their spirit was so harmoniously tied was a new and delicate pleasure full of consolation. They admired the same beauty and pardoned the same affronts.

What they talked about most was themselves. Marcela particularly found unknown pleasure in telling another person her troubles, the gray monotony of her existence. Their conversation for all appearances was not very poetic. The terrible colds the poor singer suffered from was the topic of the greater part of their discussions, at least at the beginning. By a tacit agreement they had adopted the custom of sharing everything they had done, suffered or enjoyed during the day. They spoke softly, with a certain mystic intonation which sounded like a lovers' dialogue, about the cold, the frost, the dampness, the lack of adequate blankets in the hotel and other such sad trivia of daily life. Myrth discovered that Marcela spent her free time playing solitaire with an old deck of cards. He offered her a new set. Myrth for his part played dominoes a lot in a caf in the suburbs.

What they never discussed was their art, as far as their own accomplishments were concerned. There seemed to be no future for them, either good or bad. Myrth, who was very honest, firmly believed that that charming young woman knew very little about music and sang only passingly well. He would give her his last dollar and share all that he had with her, but he would not flatter or deceive her. Marcela, who considered Feliciano an acceptable musician, understood more and more that that natural man, so good a musician among his family and friends, would never be extravagant enough to be a success on stage. No. They saw no future and never spoke of one. If Marcela insisted on talking about theatrical matters, always referring to the others, it was not because she wanted to, but because she had nothing else to talk about.

One day, Myrth noted with astonishment that Margaret the queen was not certain about who Martínez Campos was. She knew nothing about the world. In her opinion, it consisted only of a hostile public, an implacable judge. When the topic of their problems with boredom, colds, congestion and other such daily annoyances began to dry up, Feliciano little by little animated the conversation with references to other of life's horizons which were unknown to Marcela.

The favorite topic became how one could earn a living without having anything to do with the theater public. There were people who earned a great deal more than they, for example, by buying flour, storing it in a warehouse and selling it at a profit afterward. One bought a hundred units, sold it unit by unit and earned from each hundred a sizeable sum. "How wonderful!" thought the queen. And the people who came in to buy or sell did not have the right to whistle at anyone. Either there was business to do or not, but no insults were permitted. If people did not like what one had to offer, they had no right to make fun of the merchant. And Vitali sighed thinking about a paradise of percentages which was peaceful, sedentary, private, serious, honorable and humble.

And from one point to the next, Myrth finally confessed his secret to her. The reason he found himself in such a state was because he had been foolish and vain. Certain compliments had gone to his head and he had insisted on becoming an artist, even if that meant only in church. Because of this ambition, he had abandoned an uncle of his who would have sent him to a town in Palencia to work in his wheat business with a great possibility of prospering.

Queen Margaret, astonished, advised the tenor to write his uncle and sing his palinode. And that is exactly what he did. When, one month later, the company pulled up stakes and took its music elsewhere, Feliciano, after the last show, standing in the darkness on the ramp to the balconies, informed Queen Margaret that Dr. Faustus was breaking his pact with the devil of the arts and was going to Grijota where the fruitful sacks of his uncle Romualdo were waiting for him. The queen congratulated him with a trembling voice and said little for the rest of the evening. Feliciano believed it his duty to accompany her to her hotel where she told him she was retiring immediately because she did not feel well. In the dark, sad, damp street they hardly spoke. When they reached the entranceway to the hotel where Marcela had suffered such boredom and loneliness, the two stopped short. They did not know how to say good–bye.

"And you?" Faust finally said.

"Me? Tomorrow Queen Margaret catches the seven o'clock train and rides third class for eight hours and that evening she will be in Z... where there will be a show. She will perform for her esteemed public and will try her best not to ruin everything."

Then Faust Myrth, who left the theater because he did not know how to worship Margaret (the commoner) as he should in the balcony scene, Faust Myrth, as best he could, stumbling over his words, offered Margaret the queen his hand whitened by flour from the sacks of his uncle Romualdo together with everything he might earn in Grijota. Finally, he declared himself by jumping into the flour. The happiness of their honeymoon was translated into a definite and legal profit which they would enjoy together far from the stage, the public, opera glasses and the imposing expressions of the cellists and the tyrannical baton of the conductor.

A few years later, the town of Grijota celebrated the election of its provincial representative to Congress, Don Romualdo Myrth. There were parties, fireworks and even a theatrical production. The best part of the show was, of course, that Mr. Feliciano and his respected wife Marcela Vidal appeared on the stage set up by the town hall and sang like angels, dressed in costumes equal to those one saw in the theaters of the capital. It was delightful to see the wheat merchant and his wife, the industrious Marcela, one after the other, side by side, impress their neighbors with warblings, trills and singing sighs which gave great delight. Myrth stomped on his heels as always and his costume, made for Faust by his own wife, fit him no better than one of the flour sacks from his house would have. But his singing was remarkable. And he sang alone, without Margaret getting in his way.

Then Queen Margaret performed, wearing her own costume which she had saved. She rose to great heights, uneclipsed by anyone.

The following day, the town musicians thought it a shame that the happy couple did not dedicate themselves as professionals to the theater, because they could be sure of winning applause and contracts.

"How horrible!" Marcela and Feliciano said to one another laughing. "If every audience were like the people of Grijota, our friends and relatives!" And just in case there remained a slight temptation deep down in their souls, Myrth dressed a scarecrow like Faustus to frighten the sparrows away from his garden.

When the Sunday before Lent arrived, the first day of Carnival, all Grijota noticed one reveler at the Maritornes dance wearing a silk dress embroidered with gold and pearls. It was Sinforosa, the illustrious kitchen maid of the Myrth family whom Doña Marcela had given the costume which one day had been her only dream of artistic triumph, the court dress of Queen Margaret.

Notes

The Priest Of Vericueto

3   RAMON DE CAMPOAMOR During the Spanish Restoration (1874) Campoamor (1817–1901) wrote poetry which tends toward sentimental, philosophical skepticism.

3   SPENCER Herbert Spencer (1820–1903) applied the methods of positivism to ethical theory and developed the theory of social evolution. Clarín was introduced to Spencer's thought in reviews written by August Laugel for the *Revue des Deux Mondes* in 1864.

3   *GIL BLAS* Alain Renee Le Sage's novel *Gil Blas* (1715) is the first realistic novel written in France.

3   VOLTAIRE François Marie Arouet Voltaire (1694–1778) attacked the privileges of the Church in state affairs. Probably the most widely read author in Europe during the second half of the eighteenth century, he pointed to the abuses to which theological disquisition could lead.

3   KULTURKAMPF The conflict between Otto von Bismarck and the Catholic Church began in 1873 as a debate over the teaching of theology at the University of Bonn, then grew into a question of who should supervise instruction in the public schools, and finally was resolved in 1882 by Pope Leo XIII in a dispute between Germany and Spain over the Caroline Islands.

4   LUCRETIUS Titus Lucretius Caro (ca. 94–54 B.C.) wrote six books of poems, each exactly one thousand lines long, entitled *De rerum natura*, in which he develops the ideas of the Greek philosopher Epicurus (ca. 336 B.C.) whose atomistic theory denies the immortality of the soul and exalts the pure, serene pleasure of contemplation as man's greatest good.

4   ROUSSEAU Jean Jacques Rousseau (1712–1778) was a French philosopher whose ideas on education, romantic love, the noble savage, and social harmony create hope for a just society.

4   ZOLA Emile Zola (1840–1902) sought to relate the novel to the sciences by virtue of a common factor: the minute observation of detail as applied in the medical theories of Claude Ber-

nard's *Introduction a l'étude de la médicine expérimentale* (1865).

4   MATERIALISM This doctrine denies the existence of the spirit as a determining factor in historical evolution and affirms that discourse is meaningful only when limited to the observation of physical phenomena.

4   HEDONISM As an extreme form of epicureanism, this doctrine affirms that physical pleasure is the greatest good.

4   ETHICAL SKEPTICISM The assertion that the truth of any statement about the morality of action will never be apparent to one's judgment appeared in the teachings of Pyrrhon (365–257 B.C.) and was developed by Sextus Empiricus (220 A.D.) into a disquisition that concludes that one can neither assert nor deny the validity of any conviction, the *Hipotiposis Pirronica*.

5   HARPAGON In Moliere's *L'Avare* (1668), Harpagon personifies greed.

5   WHITEWASHED SEPULCHRES Matthew 23:27.

6   VERONICA The woman Veronica wiped Jesus's brow on the road to Calvary.

7   EPICURUS This Greek philosopher (341–170 B.C.) established a community in Athens where he taught that sense data are the primary basis for knowledge and that pleasure and pain are reliable keys to distinguishing good from evil.

7   IPHIGENAEA Agamemnon sacrificed his daughter Iphigenaea off the coast of Aulis to placate Artemis who was preventing his fleet from landing. In Aeschylus's *Orestia* there are two versions of her death.

7   *THE GOLDEN LEGEND* Jacobo de Varaggia (1230–1298) wrote hagiography.

7   PERRONE Gian Perrone (1794–1876) stimulated a vigorous revitalization of the study of theology with his definition of dogma regarding the Immaculate Conception.

9   HABIT OF DOLORES It is a custom in Spanish–speaking countries for women to wear a religious habit for a period of time to fulfill a sacred vow.

10   COLUMELA Lucius Junios Moderatus Columela (4 B.C.–54 A.D.) wrote twelve volumes on agriculture, *De Re Rustica*, in Cadiz.

11   CENOBITES Cenobites are members of religious orders that share dwellings under an appointed superior.

12   A CERTAIN DIPLOMAT Martínez de Campos (1831–1900) served in North Africa, Mexico and Cuba, against the Carlists in Catalonia, and against the city of Valencia, winning the last-

ing gratitude of monarchists. He reputedly was infallible in his predictions of the rise and fall of well-known political figures.

13   TIRSO DE MOLINA Gabriel Téllez (1571-1648) was a Mercedarian friar who wrote approximately three hundred plays. His most famous work, *El Burlador de Seville* (1618), brought the medieval legend of Don Juan to European prominence.

17   SAINT THOMAS Saint Thomas Aquinas (1225-1274) perfected scholasticism in the *Summa Theologica* harmonizing the philosophy of Aristotle with the doctrines of the Church.

20   BOSSUET Jacob Benigne Bossuet, Bishop of Meaux (1627-1704), was the most powerful counselor in the court of Louis XIV.

20   BOURDALOUE Louis Bourdaloue (1632-1704) was a Jesuit in the court of Louis XIV, "the orator of the King, the king of orators."

24   DURO A *duro* is a coin worth five pesetas.

25   GO AND SELL WHAT THOU HAST Mark 10:21; Matthew 19:21.

25   NI JUDICATUM SACIT Article iii of Table III of the *Twelve Tables*, this Roman Law was engraved in bronze and displayed in the forum of Rome during the Republic (ca. 449 B.C.) to ensure consistent and fair treatment of the plebeians by the patricians.

26   NALON The Nalón is the largest river in the province of Oviedo.

26   BASTIAT Claude Frederick Bastiat (1801-1851) created agricultural leagues to protect the interest of French wine growers, directed the *Journal du Economiste*, and wrote numerous books on the political economy of England and France.

26   WARS OF RECONQUEST From 700 A.D. until 1492, Spain fought periodically, winning back the ninety-five percent of Spanish territory which had been lost to the Moors during a seven-year siege.

28   VIRGIL Publius Virgilius Maro (70-19 B.C.), the Prince of Latin Poets, wrote the *Eclogues* (42-37 B.C.), the *Georgics* (37-31 B.C.), and the *Aeneid* (30-19 B.C.).

28   CATO THE ELDER Marcus Porcius Cato (234-149 B.C.), the Father of Latin Prose, described Roman agriculture in *De Re Rustica*.

30   GREGORIAN MASSES Gregorian masses are characterized by the monophonic music collected and codified by Saint Gregory and continue in their present form since the reign of Charlemagne (786-814 A.D.).

Breaker's Conversion

37   AUSTER The auster is the south wind.

37   ALCACHOFA FOUNTAIN This landmark in Madrid is located on the Paseo de las Estatuas near the Estanque in El Retiro Park.

43   CARLOS VII Carlos María de los Dolores de Borbón y Austria–Este (1848–1909) was claimed by his uncle, the Count of Montemolín, to be the legitimate heir to the Spanish throne. The Princess of Beira, Doña Maria Teresa of Portugal, his grandmother, published a "Carta a los españoles" in 1863 proclaiming him Carlos VII. He never returned to Spain after 1869, however, but died in exile in 1909.

Numero Uno

45   HEROD Herod I (73 B.C.–4 A.D.) was Judea's most powerful ruler for thirty–two years. A practicing Jew of Arab descent, favored by Mark Anthony and Julius Caesar, his progressive mental deterioration led him to have his family murdered.

46   PASCAL Blaise Pascal (1623–1662) through his philosophy and mathematics revealed to Spanish readers during the second half of the nineteenth century the compatibility of profound religious sentiment and rigorous scientific thinking.

46   ACHILLES The hero of Homer's epic *The Iliad* exemplifies Greek valor. Given the choice of a long, uneventful life or a brief glorious one, he unhesitatingly chose the latter.

46   THE CID Ruy Díaz de Vivar, conqueror of Valencia, provides the historical background for the anonymous Spanish epic, *El poema del mío Cid* (1140).

46   NAPOLEON Napoleon's invasion of Spain in 1808 precipitated the Spanish American Wars of Independence. In his *Memories de Sainte Hélène* (1820) he wrote that his greatest mistakes were his attacks on the Vatican and on Spain.

47   THE SEVEN LEARNED MEN Parmenides, Pythagoras, Heraclitus, Empedocles, Socrates, Plato, and Aristotle established the intellectual tradition leading to the disciplines of philosophy, modern science, and metaphysics.

50   SANCHO PANZA *Don Quijote* I, xx.

Bad Habits

51   COLLEGE OF CARDINALS The principal counselors and assistants to the pope and to the papal electors, the Sacred College consists of the permanent clergy of the See of Rome and of clergy from churches elsewhere subject to the four main Roman basilicas.

51   THE CONGREGATION OF THE INDEX The congregation, established in 1562, examines books to prepare a list of those which are forbidden to Catholic readers.

51   THE POOR Mark 14:17; John 12:18.

51   THE SAINT VINCENT DE PAUL SOCIETY This lay organization was established in Paris in 1833 to serve the poor.

51   LITTLE SISTERS OF THE POOR Founded in 1839 at St. Servan in France, this mendicant order was established to care for the indigent elderly.

51   INQUISITION Pope Alexander III instituted the Inquisition in 1179 in response to a plea for help from French noblemen in Languedoc who were attempting to defend the people of Toulouse and surrounding towns against repeated armed attacks by the Albigensians. In 1233, Domingo de Guzmán established a Spanish tribunal in Aragon which became instrumental during the Wars of Reconquest as a means to guarantee the religious unity of a culturally diverse medieval Spain. In Spain as in Sicily, the Inquisition was particularly powerful because its decisions were automatically valid to civil authorities. Queen María Cristina abolished its authority in civil matters in Spain in 1830.

51   ARGOS Entrusted with the care of the maid Io, Argos died when Mercury stole her, whereupon Juno transformed his many eyes onto the tail of the peacock.

53   SAINT ISIDORE THE LABORER Patron saint of Madrid since 1622, Isidore discovered that the more grain he gave away, the more his mill prospered.

Lucius Varius

61   LUCIUS VARIUS Roman poet of the Augustan Age, friend of Virgil and Horace. Lucius Varius together with Plautius Tucca was entrusted with editing the *Aeneid* after Virgil's death.

61   SCRIBERIS VARIO FORTIS "Thou shalt be heralded by Varius, a poet of Homeric flight, as valiant and victorious over the foe...," from "Ode VI" dedicated to Agrippa in Book I of Horace, *Odes and Epodes*, translated by C.E. Bennett (Cambridge: Harvard University Press, 1964) p. 21.

61   CLIVUS CAPITOLINUS The road to the top of the Capitoline Hill in Rome was paved in 174 B.C.

61   JUNO MONETA The temple, build in 271 B.C., dedicated to Juno, mother of the muses, served as the Roman mint.

61   DII CONSENTES Jupiter, Apollo, Mars, Mercury, Neptune, Vulcan; Ceres, Diana, Juno, Minerva, Venus, and Vesta are the Roman pantheon.

61   TEMPLE OF SATURN Built in 497 B.C. above the Forum on
      the Capitoline Hill, the temple was the depository for Roman
      treasure until Caesar's Gallic Wars.

61   TULLIANUM The Roman prison.

61   BRUNDISIUM Roman expeditions embarked for Greece from
      this city on the Adriatic.

61   PAUSILIPPUS Pausilippus is a promontory on the coast to the
      southwest of Naples.

61   CONCORDIA The Concordia was built in 367 B.C. to com-
      memorate the ending of a dissension over the rights of plebe-
      ians to elect their own consul.

61   TABULARIUM The Roman archives.

61   PAPYRI Paper manufactured from the leaves of the papyrus. A
      DIPTYCH is two carved wooden tablets of equal size joined by
      hinges to form a book. PUGILLARES are small diptycha which
      fit the palm of the hand. TABULLAE are wooden writing tab-
      lets. MULTIPLICES are folded papyri.

61   LIBITINARIUS The Libitinarius was the public official presid-
      ing over funerals; POLLINCTORES embalmed the dead; DIS-
      SIGNATORES assigned places in ceremonies; TIBICINES
      played flutes; PRAEFICAE were hired mourners; a FUNUS
      PUBLICUM was a public funeral; a CAPULUS a coffin of
      CESTRINUS, fragrant wood.

61   MOLLITER CUBENT OSSA Ecclesiastes 10:33, "Molliter ossa
      quiescant."

62   FORUM The Forum was the Roman market between the
      Capitoline and Palatine Hills where the praetors gave their deci-
      sions; a COMITIUM was a political assembly convened by mag-
      istrates to decide through secret ballot whether or not to ap-
      prove a proposed course of action; JANUS BIFRONS, the most
      popular of Roman gods, opened the heavens to night and day
      and protected departures and arrivals; the FATES Cloto, La-
      quesis and Atropos spun, measured, and cut the thread of each
      man's life; BASILICA PAULI AEMILII were two basilicas in
      the Forum built by the consul Aemilius with money Caesar sent
      from Gaul; a VICUS was a village outside Rome which de-
      pended upon a major city for its well–being, or a district within
      the imperial city. The Vicus Janus was the literary hub and the
      Vicus Sandaliarius was the book dealers' street.

62   NIDI The nidi were pigeonholes for documents; the VIA SA-
      CRA, Rome's earliest highway; PORTIA BASILICA, the first
      basilica, built by Cato the Censor in 184 B.C. after the Second
      Punic War; CURIA HOSTILIA was the Roman senate;
      ROSTRA, the speaker's platforms in the Forum.

63   PALATINE The seven hills of Rome are the Palatine, Quirinal, Viminal, Esquiline, Caelian, Aventine, and Capitoline; VESTALS were girls dedicated to Vesta, goddess of the hearth; the MANTUAN SWAN is Virgil who regarded Mantua, a town on an island in the Mincius River, as his birthplace, LIBURNIA is a district on the Adriatic coast famous for ship building; LATIUM is a plain between Etruria and Campania; the VIA CAMPANIA joins Rome and Naples; VENUSIA is Horace's birthplace; IAPYXYGIS is a combination of Iapygia, the country in Italy including Calabria and Apulia between Tarentum and Brundisium, and Iapyx, the son of Daedalus, conqueror of Iapygia.

63   ILLYRIA Illyria is Dalmatia in Yugoslavia; CAONIA is a city of Epirus, located between the Acroceraunian Mountains and the Ionian Sea; EPIRUS forms part of the Balkans between Greece and Albania; MOLOSSAS are part of the Pindus Mountain range; CORCYRA is Corfu; CHIMERIUM is a promontory on the coast opposite the island of Paxos; ACHERON is the principal river of Epirus, the gateway to hell, according to legend.

64   AUGUSTUS In 27 B.C. Augustus reestablished the system of *res publica* while governing the provinces of Gaul, Spain, Syria, and Egypt.

64   APELLA "'...credat Iudaeus Apella, non ego' that frankincense melts without fire at the temple threshold, because if Nature works any marvel, the gods do not send it down from their heavenly home aloft when in a surly mood." Horace, *Satires*, I, V. in *Satires, Epistles, Ars Poetica*, translated by H. Rushton Fairclough (Massachusetts: Harvard University Press, 1966) 73.

64   PENATES The penates were household gods; the LARES were deified spirits of a family's ancestors; VESTA was goddess of the hearth; MITHRA was the Persian god of light and the protector of truth; CYBELE was the mother of the gods; ISIS was the Egyptian deity, wife and sister of Osiris; SERAPIS was the god of curing whose temples became hospitals; COCYTUS was one of the four rivers of hell whose waters were the tears of the damned and along whose banks the unburied dead were condemned to wander; the AVERNUS is a volcanic lake west of Naples near Cumas; the SIBYL OF CUMAS was called Amaltea, Demo, or Deophobea and reputedly lived in the depths below that city where one could hear her rumblings when visiting the temple of Apollo. She was one of many sibyls whose writings Roman commissions collected and consulted to decide matters of state until Augustus ordered the sibyls' writings destroyed.

65   ZOILUS Zoilus was a Greek grammarian who accused Homer of lying for having included fables and legends in his epics.

65   TACITUS Publius Cayos Cornelius Tacitus (ca. 54 B.C.–13 A.D.) wrote histories of Roman contemporaries in an austere and powerful style exalting republican traditions.

66   GALLUS (69–25 B.C.) introduced the erotic elegy into Latin; ASINIUS POLLIO (75 B.C.–4 A.D.) established the first public library in Rome; CALVUS (82–56 B.C.) wrote over twenty books of which only fragments remain; MEVIUS and Bavius were detractors of Virgil and Horace; ENNIUS (b. 239 B.C.) was a Greek from Calabria who collaborated with Livius Andronicus to introduce the Greek muses to Rome and who wrote over twenty tragedies, winning the reputation as the most pathetic and best creator of character and of natural dialogue. Ennius's tendency to sententiousness made him Cicero's favorite source; he wrote eighteen volumes of history which Virgil quoted in the *Aeneid*; CINNA (d. 39 B.C.) was praised by Virgil and Catullus for his epic poem *Smirna*; VARRO (b. 32 B.C.) wrote three books of verse, which have been lost.

66   POMPONIUS ATTICUS Titus Pomponius Atticus (109–32 B.C.) was a Roman–born Greek scholar who spent his fortune building his library; SAMMONICUS SERENUS (d 212 A.D.), sentenced to death by the Emperor Carcalla, left his library to his student M. Antonius Africanus Gordianus.

The Imperfect Wife

68   LOPE DE VEGA Lope de Vega y Carpio (1562–1635), Spain's greatest dramatist, created the national theater with approximately nine hundred plays.

68   FRAY LUIS DE LEON Augustinian friar, poet, professor of ancient languages at the University of Salamanca, and Biblical scholar imprisoned by the Inquisition for having avowed the value of the Hebrew text of the *Song of Solomon* above the Latin, Fray Luis (1527–1591) wrote *La perfecta casada* (1583) which continues to be a popular treatise on the duties of married women. See: *La perfecta casada* (Madrid: EDAF, 1964) 349–50.

69   SANTIAGO The shrine of Santiago de Compostela is in the archdiocese of Galicia in northern Spain.

The Engraving

73   TAINE Hippolyte–Taine (1828–1893) in *La Fontaine et ses Fables* (1861) established the positivistic method of literary analysis. In his *Histoire de la littérature anglaise* (1863) he developed his thesis that race, time, and environment are the three principal factors determining culture.

74 WUNDT Max Wilhelm August Wundt (1832–1920) was a historian of German philosophy at the University of Leipzig who established the first laboratory of experimental psychology to identify the elements of consciousness and to state the principles by which these elements are combined through observations of social behavior in customs and language systems.

74 CHRYSOSTOM John Chrysostom of Saint–Lô (1594–1646) was a French Franciscan, confessor to Marie de Medici and to Anne of Austria, respected and admired by Louis XIV and Cardinal Richelieu.

77 GREGORY Edward John Gregory (1850–1909) was a well-known British portrait painter and illustrator for *The Graphic*; Arthur HOPKINS (1848–1930) was a landscape painter for *The Graphic* and *Punch*.

Windows

89 PEDRO RECIO In *Don Quijote* II, xlvii, Pedro Recio is the doctor who keeps Sancho Panza from enjoying life as governor of the Island of Barataria.

91 BOURGET Paul Bourget (1852–1935), famous for his *Essais de psychologie contemporaine* (1885), developed his ideas in four novels, *Le Disciple*, *Cruel enigma*, *Crime d'amour*, and *Mensonges* written between 1886 and 1888 portraying the states of mind of people caught in psychological crises. Clarín read installments of his work published in *La Revue des Deux Mondes*.

Cold And The Pope

95 CECILIA METELA Wife of the triumvir Crasus the Younger, daughter of Meticlus Creticus, Cecilia Metela became famous because of her tomb built in the Appian Way in Rome during the reign of Caesar Augustus.

Leon Benavides

99 *LA PRUDENCIA EN LA MUJER* Tirso de Molina's play is set against a background of civil strife, the reign of Fernando IV (1295–1312).

99 CARRERA DE SAN JERONIMO The central avenue of Madrid connects the Puerta del Sol and the Prado.

100 LEGIO An early archeological discovery of a Roman inscription beneath the city of Leon reads "Leg. VII Gem. P. F." and thus has been interpreted as Legio Septima Gemina Pia Felix, which confirms the popular etymology.

100 THE CID Clarín refers to the "Third Cantar," lines 2278–2310, of the *Poema del Mío Cid*.

100 BENAVIDES "Nobleza y calidades/ en el reino de Leon/ los Benavides abonan/ y nuestro valor pregonan/ los que honran nuestro blasón": "The Benavides increase the nobility and quality of the kingdom of Leon and those who honor our shield declare our valor." Tirso de Molina, *La prudencia en la mujer* I: 421–5.

Keen

103 EGGER Emile Egger (1813–1885) was professor of Greek and Latin in Paris and author of more than twenty works in comparative grammar, ancient history, philosophy and literature.

100 STENDHAL Marie Henri Beyle (1793–1842) wrote *Le Rouge et le Noir* (183?) and *La Chartreuse de Parme* (1839).

100 CLAY Edmund R. Clay (pseudonym) was the author of only one work, *Alternative Contributions to Psychology* (London: 1882) which was published with a translation into French by August Burdeau. He believed asceticism and abnegation are essential for human perfection, that suffering and denial are the *via crucis* to salvation.

100 BRADDON Mary Elizabeth Braddon (1837–1897), wrote more than fifty novels describing the English aristocracy between 1869 and 1914.

100 OLIPHANT Margaret Oliphant (1828–1897) contributed several hundred articles to the popular *Blackwood's Magazine*.

104 PUJO Maurice Pujo (1872–ca. 1947) wrote philosophical and moral treatises: *L'idéalisme integral* (1894), *Le règne de la grâce* (1894), and *Essais de critique générale: la crise morale* (1898).

106 THERSITES In Shakespeare's *Troilus and Cressida* (1601–1602), Thersites, "the railer" mocks Ajax and thereby informs him of Hector's challenge to single combat with any Greek willing to meet him on the field.

106 PASCAL Clarín refers to "Diseur de bons mots, mauvais charactère," *Pensées*, ed. Louis Lafuma (Luxembourg: Editions du Luxembourg, 1952) I:391.

111 MORETO Augustn de Moreto (1618–1669) is a Golden Age Spanish dramatist whose most famous work is *El desdén con el desdén*.

112 ARIADNE The daughter of Minos, King of Crete, Ariadne fell in love with Theseus and gave him the clue of thread to lead him through the labyrinth to slay the Minotaur.

Satanmas Eve

117 SALIC LAWS From the code of the Salians who invaded France in the fifth century and established the French monarchy, the Salic Laws were invoked in Spain by the Carlist faction seeking to deny the throne to Isabel II.

118 BE NOT AFRAID Luke 2:8; 2:14.

118 MURILLO Bartolome Esteban Murillo (1617–1782) used models from Seville for his madonnas and established a Spanish national style for religious painting.

119 I.N.R.I. Mark 14:7.

121 EUROPA Jupiter assumed the form of a bull to abduct Europa, the daughter of Agenor of Phoenicia, who bore him a son, Minos, in Crete. Jupiter assumed the form of a swan to seduce Leda, who bore him Polux and Helen. To win ALCMENE, who bore him his son Hercules, Jupiter assumed the appearance of her husband, Amphitryon.

Trap

130 REAL A *real* is a silver coin worth thirty–four *maravedíes*, one quarter of one peseta.

331 NINON DE LENCLOS Ninon de Lenclos (1620–1705) was the patron of Boileau, La Fontaine, Racine, Molière, Mme. de La Fayette and Voltaire.

132 QUEL GIORNO PIU NO VI LEGEMMO AVANTE. "That day we read no more." Dante, *Inferno*, Canto V, 1. 138.

133 ARISTOPHANES An Athenian comic poet (448–380 B.C.), Aristophanes satirized Socrates, the sophists, warfare, women, and politics.

Don Patricio or the Grand Prize in Melilla

137 MELILLA Rif tribesmen in North Africa occupied Spanish territory surrounding the military outpost of Ceuta in 1843 and attacked the city of Melilla in 1844.

139 RECAREDO Crowned king of the Visigoths in Toledo in 586 A.D., Recaredo suppressed popular uprisings in Toledo and Evora and defended Spain against the invasion of Gontron, king of Orleans.

139 CATACHINCHI V A parody of Charles V (1500–1558).

The Substitute

141 OTUMBA On July 7, 1520, in Otumba, Mexico, Cortez was surrounded by 40,000 Aztecs. When a Spanish soldier killed the Aztec warrior who had taken the Spanish flag, the Indians abandoned the field. This reversal occurred eight days after the *noche triste*, June 30, 1520, when Cortez and his army had been routed.

141 PAVIA During the battle of Pavia in 1525, Charles V took François I captive.

141 TYRTAEUS A Greek poet of the seventh century B.C., Tyrtaeus was famous for encouraging the Spartans to victory over the Messenians.

141 PINDAR Pindar was a major Greek lyric poet (ca. 518–438 B.C.).

141 QUINTANA During the Spanish Wars of Independence Manuel José Quintana (1772–1857) wrote patriotic verse and biographies of Spanish heroes.

144 DON QUIJOTE *Don Quijote* I, xxvi.

146 *ILIAD* Homer's epic poem sings the Greek hero Achilles's feats during the Trojan War; the *RAMAYANA* of the fifth century B.C. recounts Rama's battles to rescue his wife Sita; Virgil's *AENEID* (30–19 B.C.) presents Aeneas as founder of Rome; Camões's *OS LUSIADAS* (1572) follows Vasco da Gama's voyage to India; Ercilla's *ARAUCANIA* (1569) paints Hurtado de Mendoza's unsuccessful attempts to subdue the Indians of Chile; the *BERNARDO* (1624) is Bernardo de Balbuena's twenty–four volume epic describing the battle of Roncesvalles.

Snob

152 MOSCO Mosco of Syracuse, a student of Theocritus, wrote an epitaph for Bion of Smirna.

152 BION Bion of Smirna studied with Theocritus and wrote "Epythalamion of Aquilles and Deidanus" in which he presents Achilles disguised as a woman hiding among Lycomedes's daughters.

152 TABOADA Luis Taboada (1848–1906) was a Spanish humorist.

152 FELIPE PEREZ Felipe Pérez y González (1854–1910) wrote the famous *zarzuela, La Gran Vía*.

154 LOHENGRIN The Knight of the Swan, a knight of the Holy Grail, is the hero of a thirteenth–century anonymous epic written as a continuation of Wolfram von Eschenbach's *Parzival*.

Knight of the Round Table

160 LULL Raymond Lull (1235–1316) was a nobleman, poet, linguist and mystic in the court of James II of Majorca.

168 BUFFON Georges Louis Leclerc de Buffon (1707–1788) was a French naturalist, renowned for his fondness for luxury, who coined the phrase, "Le style c'est l'homme même."

171 DON QUIJOTE *Don Quijote*, I, i.

Queen Margaret

178 ARISTARCHUS Aristarchus of Samothrace (ca. 160–85 B.C.) included the entire texts of Homer's *Iliad* and *Odyssey* in his *Escolios*, with notes which have clarified many textual questions about the poems.

179 A CERTAIN CLASSICAL COMPOSITION Clarín refers to Giacomo Meyerbeer's *Les Huguenots* (1836).

181 GOUNOD Charles Gounod's *Faust* (1860) brought French opera to the attention of European audiences enamored of Italian and German composers.

182 CONSUMMATUM EST John 19:30.

184 PALENCIA Palencia is one of the least populated of Spain's forty–nine provinces.

184 GRIJOTA In Palencia, this town had a population in 1910 of 1,229 inhabitants, two flour mills and two bodegas.

185 MARITORNES In *Don Quijote* I, xv, Maritornes is the serving girl whom Don Quijote mistakes for a princess.

185 SINFOROSA Sinforosa is the younger daughter of King Policarpio in Cervantes's novel *Persiles y Segismunda* (1615).

185 THE ILLUSTRIOUS KITCHEN MAID Constanza is the illustrious kitchen maid in Cervantes's story *La ilustre fregona* (1605).